The LADY of BOLTON HILL

The
LADY *of*
BOLTON
HILL

A NOVEL

ELIZABETH CAMDEN

BETHANY HOUSE PUBLISHERS

Minneapolis, Minnesota

Published by Bethany House Publishers
11400 Hampshire Avenue South
Bloomington, Minnesota 55438

Bethany House Publishers is a division of
Baker Publishing Group, Grand Rapids, Michigan.

Printed in the United States of America

Library of Congress Cataloging-in-Publication Data

Camden, Elizabeth, 1948–
    The lady of Bolton Hill / Elizabeth Camden.
      p. cm.
    ISBN 978-0-7642-0894-2 (pbk.)
    1. Women journalists—Fiction. 2. Bolton Hill (Baltimore, Md.)—Fiction. I. Title.
    PS3553.A429L33   2011
    813'.54—dc22

                                     2011008205

For my husband, Bill.
Since the day we married,
you have propped me up, cheered me on,
and run the extra mile alongside me. Thank you.
A thousand times, thank you.

PROLOGUE

Baltimore, Maryland, 1867

C ome on, boy. Your dad needs you."

Daniel looked up from his exam in disbelief, certain his father would never pull him out of this test. But a grim-faced Joe Manzetti stood in the doorway of the classroom, trails of perspiration streaking through the soot on his face. Being summoned to fix the aging equipment at the steel mill was a regular occurrence for Daniel, but it wasn't going to happen today.

"I'll be there in an hour," Daniel said as he glanced around the classroom, noting the glares of resentment among the other students competing for the same scholarship. They all had the advantage of decent schools and private tutors, while Daniel's only knowledge of engineering came from tinkering with the equipment in the steel mills of Baltimore's east end.

"There's been an accident and your dad is trapped," Manzetti said. "You need to come right away." The blood drained from Daniel's face. Everyone at the steel mill knew what this test meant to him and would not have summoned him for anything short of a life-and-death catastrophe. He threw his pencil down and shot up from his seat, not even glancing at the proctor as he bolted from the room.

"It was a boiler explosion," Manzetti told him as they left the school and ran across Currior Street. "They've put out the fire, but your dad was trapped by the tank that got blown off its base. He's still pinned beneath it."

Daniel broke out into a sweat. There would have been tons of steam if the boiler tank had been blown out of its brick encasement, and his father's entire body would have been scalded. "How badly was he burned?"

"It's not good, boy. We can't get the canister off him until the fire tubes are disabled. The boiler was mangled in the blast, so we need to do some quick work before the pressure makes it blow again."

And that was why they'd summoned Daniel. Anyone could operate those boilers under normal circumstances, but when the equipment broke down they relied on Daniel to figure out what was to be done. He was only nineteen years old, but he'd always had a knack for tinkering with machines to make them work better or do something different.

His legs were trembling after sprinting the two miles to the mill, a stitch clawed at his side, and his lungs were barely able to fill, but the workers parted as he and Manzetti entered the boiler room. Clouds of steam and soot still hung in the air, bricks were strewn everywhere, and on the concrete floor, crumpled beneath a massive copper boiler, Daniel's father lay sprawled like a broken doll.

"Dad?"

His father's eyelids flickered. "Fire tubes still attached," the words rasped from his father's throat. "Be careful, lad."

Daniel glanced at the twisted fire tubes and the ruined boiler. Soldering the tubes closed would work, but it would take hours. He had to think of another way to disengage the tubes before they could lift the boiler from his father, or there would be another explosion.

"I need a sledgehammer and a steel pin," Daniel said. "Get a couple of valve clamps and some leather gloves," he added, his gaze fixed on the white-hot fire tubes. A wave of murmurs passed through the workers who circled the site of the accident, but a few of them ran to get the tools. There was no time to explain the unconventional solution that was taking shape in his head. He wasn't even sure it would work, but trying to disable those fire tubes directly would be suicide. "And I'll need a lot of water . . . just in case." Stupid to worry about it, since he and his father would both be killed instantly if this didn't work.

The men brought the equipment to him, and the assembled workers began pulling back to a safe distance. A tremor ran through his father. "You know what you're doing, laddie?"

Daniel didn't meet his father's eyes, just placed the steel pin against the first of the mangled fire tubes, the heat so fierce it penetrated his thick leather gloves. "Yup," he said with more confidence than he felt. "Just like pricking the crust on one of Mom's pies to let the steam out," he said as he positioned the sledgehammer atop the pin. The first whack did nothing other than send a shrill *ping* through the air. Neither did the second, but the third blow pierced the pipe, and the escaping steam sent out a high-pitched whistle. Daniel reared away from the burning steam. "Clamp down the safety valve," he yelled over the noise. Two workers moved in, arm muscles bulging as they wrenched the equipment into place. It took a minute, but the pipe lost pressure, and the whistle lowered in pitch and then fell silent. The fire tube was disabled.

A smattering of applause came from behind him, but Daniel didn't tear his gaze from the ruined mass of the boiler. There was still one more pipe to disable. Sweat rolled into his eyes and he brushed it away with a grimy forearm before he set the next pin into place.

"Want you to know . . . proud of you, boy," his father said.

Daniel kept his eyes fastened on the fire tube. He wished his father wouldn't talk like that, like this might be the end. "Yeah, okay," he said, keeping his gaze steady on the task before him. He struck the first blow at the remaining fire tube. It was a good, solid blow, as was the second. On the third blow the high-pitched whine began.

An instant later the pressure burst in the tube and shot the pin free and straight into Daniel's face. He was hurled backward and crashed to the ground, blood pouring from a cut across his brow. The roars of approval from the men signaled he had succeeded in disabling the fire tube.

Daniel grinned as he pushed into a sitting position, barely able to see through the sting of blood in his eyes. A dozen men were pushing bricks out of the way, lifting the copper boiler up a few feet. He couldn't see his dad because of the cluster of workers surrounding him.

Then a worker with a soot-stained face walked over and squatted down to look directly at Daniel. A hand clamped him on the shoulder. "I'm sorry, boy. Your dad is dead."

This is probably the prettiest place I've ever seen, Daniel thought as his gaze drifted past the cemetery walls to roam over the tree-shaded lawn and a church that looked like a medieval castle. Clara's father was the minister of this church, which was the only reason Daniel's father could be buried in a nice neighborhood like Bolton Hill. Daniel didn't know how much it cost to bury a person, but he gathered it was expensive, and he should be grateful that Reverend Endicott was letting his father be put to rest in such a fancy place for free.

Daniel turned his head so he could see Clara from his one good eye. She was standing on the other side of his father's grave, and her heart-shaped face winced every time she looked at him. Daniel cursed the patch covering his bad eye. He might end up being blind in that eye, but the swelling was still so bad the doctor had not been able to get a good look at it yet. Anyway, he knew his face looked horrible and it bothered Clara. She was only sixteen, and this sort of thing really ripped her up.

As they lowered his father's casket into the freshly dug hole, Daniel tightened his arm around his mother's narrow shoulders and wished her weeping would stop. He and his mother shared the same black hair and gray eyes, but that was where the resemblance ended. For three days his mother had done nothing but alternate between despondent stares and gut-wrenching sobs, whereas Daniel had been too busy taking care of the girls to let grief catch up to him. At least he could sometimes cheer up his sisters, but he had been a complete failure at trying to ease his mother's hollow-eyed pain. He would have to figure out what to do about that, although all he could concentrate on now was how badly he wanted to see Clara. Guilt tore at his insides for even thinking such a thing, but just for a blessed few hours he needed to be with Clara.

When the ceremony came to an end, people began to wander away from the grave site. If he didn't catch Clara, she would go back to her father's house and he wouldn't see her again for another week. Clara was his best friend, but running off to see her when his family needed him was shameful.

And the real reason he wanted to see her was even worse.

The day before the accident, Clara sent him a message saying she was learning a piece by Frederic Chopin, the Polish composer they both idolized. If it weren't for their mutual love of Chopin, Daniel would never have met a person like Clara Endicott. He lived in Baltimore's grubby east side, while she came from the privileged world of Bolton Hill, an enclave of manicured lawns, clean air, and old money. They came from entirely different worlds, but they bought music at the same shop in Merchant's Square. Every Tuesday a shipment of sheet music arrived from Paris, and he always raced to the store after his shift to see if there was anything by Chopin he didn't already have. Five years ago, just after his fourteenth birthday, he had arrived at the shop to learn that an entire batch of newly delivered Chopin scores had been sold to a young lady. He finagled Clara's name out of the clerk and paid a call to her house that very evening.

It didn't seem odd to him, seeking out a fellow enthusiast of the great Chopin. What could be more natural than wanting to meet someone else who shared his immense passion for the composer? It wasn't until he saw Clara's house, an imposing mansion set back an acre from the street, that he realized he was stepping into a very different world. Nevertheless, he straightened his shoulders, knocked on the door, and asked to see Miss Clara Endicott. He was surprised to see that Clara was merely a girl, not even twelve years old. She was a skinny little thing with hair like spun gold and wearing a frilly dress so white it made his eyes hurt just to look at it. Still, she adored Chopin, so that meant there must be something worthwhile underneath all those ridiculous hair ribbons.

"Hello, my name is Daniel Tremain. I hear you like Frederic Chopin, and I think we should meet."

"You like Chopin, too?" The joy that lit her face was as though Santa Claus had stepped onto her front porch.

From that day on, they had been inseparable. Over the next five years Daniel spent every moment he was not at the steel mill beside Clara as they worked through the various Chopin ballades, études, and sonatas. Before meeting Clara, the only piano Daniel had access to was the out-of-tune upright in the public school. He was entirely self-taught, but Clara had the benefit of private lessons and had helped him improve his technique. Even better, Clara had access to the instruments in the Music Conservatory across the street from her father's church, and Daniel became proficient on the cello, as well.

He looked across the stretch of cemetery to see Clara being pulled by her brother, Clyde, toward a waiting carriage. Daniel gritted his teeth in frustration. He *needed* to see Clara, and her brother could be so irritating. Ever since he became friends with Clara, Daniel had been hearing about Clyde's accomplishments. Clyde went to Harvard, Clyde won an award from the Smithsonian . . . on and on it went. Clyde had the best education money could buy, while Daniel was stuck shoveling coal into a furnace.

Daniel sprinted across the lawn toward Clara, reaching her just before she stepped up into the carriage. "Clara, wait!"

She whirled around. Her face was a mask of concern and her lower lip was trembling. "Daniel, I'm so sorry about your father," she said as she laid a hand on his arm.

"Never mind that. I need to speak with you."

And he didn't need an audience. He tugged Clara a few feet away, but like a watchdog, Clyde's eyes narrowed and he raised his chin. "Not too far, Tremain," he warned.

Daniel threw an annoyed glare at Clara's brother. It should not be a surprise that Clara's family was starting to become suspicious of him. For years he had been hanging around their house so much they had practically accepted him into their family, but Clara was starting to come of age. He pulled her a few feet away from the carriage.

"Do you have sheet music for the nocturne?" he asked in a low voice. He ought to be roasted alive for even thinking about music at a time like this, but for the life of him, he just wanted to get his hands on that Chopin nocturne so he could forget about steel mills and funerals and his mother's shattered face. Music could do that, create a magical oasis where nothing else mattered except hearing the next line of the score.

Clara looked hesitant. "I've got it, but my father is hosting a political conference all week. They will be using the Music Conservatory for meeting rooms, so we won't be able to play."

Being shut away from music for another week was unacceptable. This had been the worst few days of his life and he *needed* to escape. Daniel glanced over his shoulder. His mother was waiting for him with that desperate look of anxiety. In another moment she was going to break down again.

"Meet me at the Music Conservatory tonight," he whispered to Clara. "I'll figure out a way to get us in and we can play there."

Clara looked as though he'd asked her to set a house on fire. "We can't break into the Conservatory. It's against the law!" But the way she bit her lip and clasped her hands let him know that she *wanted* to do it, even if she couldn't muster the courage.

"Don't be such a rule follower," he said. "Meet me at midnight outside the Conservatory. And don't forget the sheet music."

Without a backward glance, he dashed back to his mother, knowing Clara would not let him down. His mother's thin frame stood before him, and along with her came years of responsibilities. Even if he was lucky enough to someday have another shot at a college scholarship, there was no way he could leave his family without income. He'd have to figure out how to pay the crushing weight of bills that would accumulate quickly now that his father was dead, and do his best to support what was left of his family. For a while he had dreamed of a chance for college and a better future, but that was over. Now his life was going to be lived inside the stark brick walls of a steel mill.

But for a few hours tonight, he would escape into a magical world of music, and that was enough to keep him going for now.

❧

Clara clutched the sheet music to her chest, her eyes fastened on the ground before her feet as she scurried toward the Music Conservatory at the top of the hill. The glow from the moon made it easy to see as she cut through the backyards of her neighborhood. She hated to admit it, but she was still a tiny bit afraid of the dark. Sneaking around like this was simply awful, but it would be worse to abandon her best friend when he needed her.

Clara reached the end of the street and could see the Conservatory plainly in the moonlight. The Music Conservatory, a rambling gothic monstrosity of a building with a few practice rooms and an oversized auditorium for performances, belonged to the city. She and Daniel used the practice rooms every chance they got, and her fondest memories were here while they played Beethoven and Chopin and sometimes even their own fledgling compositions. Normally the Conservatory was a haven for her, but tonight it loomed like a ghostly fortress in the moonlight. She had no idea how they would get into the locked Conservatory but knew Daniel would find a way. He could do anything.

She dashed across the street, her heart pounding and her palms sweaty. She would feel better once Daniel got here and told her to quit being such a sissy.

She heard a low chuckle behind her. "The way you're hunched over that sheet music, you'd think an army of Pinkerton's agents were hot on your trail." She whirled around to see Daniel step from behind the sycamore trees, radiating that supreme sense of confidence he seemed to effortlessly possess. A smile broke across her face. Only seconds ago she had been scared to pieces, but Daniel could always ease her pathetic worries.

"I already popped the lock on the back door," Daniel said. "Let's go."

He must have been here for a while, because Daniel had already set up the cello beside the piano. "Do you want to play Chopin or try composing something?" Clara asked. For the past few months they had been writing their own music, Daniel on the cello and Clara on the piano.

"Let's play Chopin. I don't want to have to think too much tonight."

She was afraid he was going to say that. "Well, there's a problem with the cello part," she said. "It's written in a different key than the piano."

Daniel took the cello score from her and made quick work scanning the lines. "Not to worry. I can transpose it to the higher key as we play."

She'd been taking music classes for years but could never transpose on the spot like that. Pale moonlight filtered through the French doors, providing enough illumination for Clara to see the music, but Daniel was holding it close to his face, his head cocked at an odd angle as he scanned the lines from his one good eye.

"Is there enough light for you to see?" she asked. "We can go in the back room if we need to light a lantern."

"I can see well enough. I can certainly see that hideous bonnet on your head. It looks like a potato sack."

Clara pulled off the offending bonnet. "I didn't want my hair to show in the moonlight. I know it's ugly. I've been told it looks like I pulled it out of the garbage."

"Oh? Who said such a thing? Give me the name and I'll thrash him for you."

"Clyde said it. And no thrashing . . . you weren't any nicer about my poor bonnet."

"I'm allowed to say rude things to you. No one else can."

"That's true enough." Daniel did tease her mercilessly, but she never minded because she knew he didn't mean a word of it. Daniel would slay dragons for her if she asked him. Clyde said rude things to her all the time, but she didn't want to discuss her frustrating, brilliant older brother. She knew Daniel envied her brother the opportunity to attend the best schools in the country. Now, after Daniel had to walk away from the test that would have awarded him a scholarship to Yale, he would probably never get the chance.

"How is your mother doing? And your sisters . . . do they even understand what has happened?"

Daniel sagged a little bit. "Please, Clara, not tonight. Anything but that." He straightened. "Tell me about Edmond Dantès. Last I heard he was about to convince Villefort's wife to poison him."

For the past month, Clara had been telling Daniel the story of *The Count of Monte Cristo* as she read each chapter. Daniel didn't have time for books, but he loved listening to her summarize whatever she was reading. They liked adventure stories best, and Clara had already read most of the works by Victor Hugo and Daniel Defoe.

"I would give anything if I could write like Victor Hugo," Clara said. "Did I tell you that my aunt Helen met him when she was in Paris?" Aunt Helen's poetry had brought her notice in both Europe and America, and Clara thought her father's sister was an extraordinary person.

"So when is she going to come home? Ever since I've known you, she has been traipsing around Europe like a vagabond."

Clara shrugged. She dreaded telling Daniel that she was on the verge of being sent to live with Aunt Helen in London. Daniel had once told her that their friendship was the only ray of light in his world of coal-fired boilers and dingy tenements, but her father was determined that Clara should go to London. He wanted the Endicott family to be a force of change in the world, and had been grooming both Clara and her brother for that very purpose from the time they were old enough to walk.

"My father says Aunt Helen should keep working her way among the power circles of Europe," she finally said. "Everywhere she goes she helps advance his cause of free education for the poor.

And next month Clyde is heading off to South America to give smallpox vaccinations to the natives. Of course, I'm the howling disappointment of the family. My entire family is brilliant, and I'm like a firecracker that fizzles when lit. I can't even transpose music as I play."

"Clara, you are sixteen years old. You aren't supposed to be successful yet . . . it would go to your head."

"*You're* successful at everything you do."

Daniel winked at her. "That's how I know."

She elbowed him in the ribs, but could not help noticing that Daniel was very fine looking when he grinned at her like that. With his tousled dark hair and that eye patch, he was as dashing as any pirate from an adventure story. The girls at her school, Miss Carlton's Academy, would fall over themselves for a boy like Daniel, but Clara forbade herself to develop a crush on him because it would ruin everything. Daniel had a lot of girlfriends, and she wasn't about to stand in line with the rest of them. It was much better to be his best friend.

She took a seat at the piano bench and positioned the music so the moonlight illuminated the page without her shadow interfering. Daniel sat on the corner of the bench and propped his music on a stand. She pecked out a few notes to get her fingers accustomed to the keyboard, and Daniel leaned his head toward her. "Ready?" She nodded. "On three, then."

Daniel counted out loud . . . then Chopin's nocturne filled the air as her fingers lifted the music from the piano. A moment later the warm tones of the cello joined the melody, dancing and weaving in between her notes. It was a lyrical piece, beautifully capturing the forlorn mood of Chopin's work.

It was enchanting, to be alone in this darkened room with moonlight streaming through the windows. They felt like the only two people in the world as the lift and fall of the haunting melody filled the empty chamber. It was always like this when they played music together.

Which was why she was so startled when Daniel hit a clumsy note. The music from the cello went off-key, then skidded to a stop altogether. Daniel dropped his bow and buried his face in the crook of his elbow.

He was sobbing.

Clara flew off the bench to kneel before him, but Daniel turned farther away from her. He held up a hand to shield his face. "Clara, don't. Don't look at me."

He curled over the seat and now the sobs were coming from deep within his chest, raw sounds he could not hold back. Even his shoulders were shaking from the strength of his weeping. Clara pressed herself against his back and wrapped her arms around him. "Please don't cry," she said uselessly. Daniel was the strongest, smartest person in the universe, and seeing him like this made Clara cry, too. Her tears spilled over and wet the back of his shirt as she clung to him, wishing she could ease the burden of his grief.

"Everything is falling apart and I don't know what to do," he said between his sobs. "My mother is a wreck and the girls keep crying, too. I don't know what to do." A shudder racked his tall frame as another round of weeping overtook him. Raw, painful sounds came wrenched from deep in his chest. "I keep seeing my father crumpled on the ground," he choked out. "I can't get the sight out of my head. Blisters were already coming up through the burns on his face."

She winced at the images his words conjured. "Daniel, your father is in heaven now. He'll never know pain or suffering again."

As quickly as it began, Daniel swallowed back the tears, although his breathing was still ragged as he wiped his face with his sleeve. He kept his face averted from her, and his voice was so soft she could barely hear it. "I'm not sure I believe in heaven."

Clara swallowed, uncertain how to respond. Her belief in God and an afterlife was absolute and she never questioned such things. She wished her father were here; he always knew the right thing to say.

"Well, I *do* believe in heaven," she said softly. "And your father did, too, and we both know that he was smarter than a whole stack of encyclopedias, so he couldn't be wrong." Daniel gave a gulp of laughter and squeezed her hand. "You can trust us on this, Daniel. Your father is in heaven and his suffering is over."

Daniel heaved a ragged sigh, then nodded his head. "Okay, thanks for that." He said it in that casual, offhanded manner of his, and Clara figured he was probably just humoring her. He brushed back the straight black hair that had fallen down across his forehead. "Try again?" he asked as he picked up the bow of the cello.

When she hesitated, he turned to look at her, his one good eye still reddened with tears. "Please, Clara, I really need this tonight." His voice wobbled as he said the words.

There wasn't anything on earth she wouldn't do for Daniel, but Clara felt like a traitor. She would be leaving him soon, and now was the worst possible time for him to be alone.

She turned back to the piano and straightened her sheet music. "On the count of three, then." Moments after she began playing the piano, Daniel's cello joined her, this time solid and confident. The gentle, surging melody filled the chamber, and the melancholy nocturne mirrored the longing in Clara's heart. She knew that in a perfect world Daniel would be free to pursue music and go to college, while she would pen great works of literature that would let her express the passion in her soul.

Clara was not precisely sure what the future held for them, but of one thing she was certain: Daniel Tremain was the best friend she had ever had, and no distance or class or circumstance would ever tear them apart.

CHAPTER 1

London, England, 1879
Twelve years later

Clara was startled by the metallic clank as the lock on her cell door turned. The other two women in the jail cell also stirred, as a visitor at this time of day was odd. Clara sprang to her feet, while the others remained sprawled on their cots. After all, Nellie and Rosina had already been sentenced and were serving their terms, while Clara's case was still wending its way through the British legal system. For weeks she had been expecting her verdict to be handed down at any moment, making it impossible to do anything other than wait and hope and pray.

Not that she expected good news. After all, she could not prove she was innocent of the libel she had been charged with, since the evidence she had compiled while spying on the mine owners and operations in the coal mines had been destroyed. The door of the prison cell opened to reveal the hulking shape of Mr. Loomis, the prison warden. He pointed at Clara.

"You are to come with me," he growled. "Get your belongings. You ain't coming back."

Clara felt the blood drain from her face. As horrible as this cell was, the thought of being transferred was even more frightening. Would they send her out of London? At least here she had supporters who knew and cared about her cause. If she was deported to one of the island prisons, she would be utterly isolated from the rest of the world. Her gaze darted around the small cell, the faces of Nellie and Rosina the only source of comfort in the downward spiral of her life. She reached out to clasp Nellie's hand, and Rosina came to put an arm around her shoulders. Clara's pulse raced so hard she could hear the beating of her heart.

"Where am I going, then?" she asked Mr. Loomis.

"The judge just handed down your verdict. You're guilty. Time to pay the piper."

The last glimmering bit of hope Clara had been nurturing for the past month was extinguished. There would be no miraculous change of heart from the prosecutor, or further proof to be found that would mitigate her case. How strange that she felt no urge to cry or temptation to run. All she felt was a wall of grief that settled over her like a weight driving her to her knees. This must be what it felt like to lose all hope.

Nellie squeezed her hand. "Don't worry, Clara," she said. "Maybe they'll go easy on you since you are an American."

"Don't bet on it," Mr. Loomis said. "Being a foreigner makes what you did even worse." And Clara knew Mr. Loomis was right. The articles she had published in *The Times* would have ignited a wave of indignation no matter who had written them, but she had been especially reviled because she was an outsider.

Nellie leaned in. "Don't believe him, Clara. You'll be out in no time; don't you fear."

She didn't believe Nellie, but she did her best to muster a smile. "I'll be fine. I'll be okay," she said, although she could not bring herself to look either woman in the eye when she said it. Clara straightened her shoulders and raised her chin. "Well, let's get on with it. I suppose it would be poor form to be late for my own sentencing."

"Don't forget your pillow," Rosina said, handing her the rolled-up jacket Clara had been wearing on the horrible evening she had been arrested. Rosina was a girl who ought to be in school, not turning tricks as a prostitute, and yet she had a sweet demeanor that Clara could not help but like.

"Thanks, Rosina," Clara said as she pulled on the jacket with shaking hands. For a month this poor jacket had been balled up to serve as a pillow, a footrest, even a makeshift weapon to shoo away the mice, but still the jacket held its smartly tailored shape.

"Bye, luv," Rosina said as she gave Clara a little hug. "It was fun having you for a cell mate. Even if you were real afraid of those mice. Never seen a girl so scared of tiny little rodents."

Clara returned the hug, trying to fight back the sense of desperation that was threatening her thinly held composure. How strange that leaving this windowless cell was suddenly proving so difficult. "Promise me you'll go back to school when you get out of here," she whispered in Rosina's ear. "You are a fine, bright girl and deserve much better than what you've asked from the world." She pushed Rosina back so she could look the girl directly in the eyes. "There is *nothing* you can't do when you leave here. There is no taint that can't be overcome. You are a child of God, and that means that there is great, shining beauty within you."

Rosina flushed and dipped her head. "When a fine lady like you says that, I can almost believe it."

Clara smiled, and this time her smile was real. "I've believed in you all along, Rosina."

Clara turned to Nellie, a pickpocket who had almost completed her two-year term. "Thank you for showing me the ropes when I first got here, Nellie. I don't know how I would have survived without you."

Nellie gave her a gap-toothed grin. "You'd have learned everything sooner or later, but I figured I owed it to you. My own two boys worked down in them same coal mines you wrote about, so I don't hold no grudge against you for what you did."

Clara reached out for another desperate hug. A pickpocket and a prostitute. In her old world of concert halls and titled aristocracy, she would never have come into contact with such women; now here she was clinging to Nellie for dear life. Perhaps there was at least one good thing that had come from this horrible ordeal. Clara had learned to see the humanity beneath the soul-destroying poverty that drove otherwise decent women into vice.

"Ain't got all day, lady." Mr. Loomis's words caused another rush of anxiety, but prolonging this mess would not make it any easier.

"I'll try to write to the both of you whenever I get to where I'm going."

"Sure, Clara," Nellie said. But they both knew they were empty words. Nellie would be released into the underworld of London soon, and Rosina did not even know how to read. Still, the words seemed to make this moment a little less stark. Less final.

Clara walked out of the cell without looking back. She couldn't bear to see the pity in the eyes of her two cell mates. At least they were to serve their terms here in London, but heaven only knew where Clara was destined to be sent.

"Might I have a moment to pull myself together?" Clara asked as she paused in the grim hallway outside her cell. Her jacket was hopelessly wrinkled, but at least it covered the grubbiness of her shirt. Her work had been rejected, her carefully prepared research confiscated and destroyed, and now she was facing a new life as a convicted felon. Still, she was an Endicott, and Endicotts did not go about shabbily dressed, no matter how dire the circumstances.

She pulled the sides of her jacket in a vain attempt to remove the wrinkles, smoothed a few strands of blond hair back into her bun, and tried to smile. "Well, then. 'It is a far, far better thing that I do, than I have ever done.' "

Mr. Loomis looked at her blankly.

"It is from *A Tale of Two Cities*," Clara said. "The prison scene, just as Sydney Carton is led away to his execution."

"They ain't going to execute you, lady. Ten years of hard labor is what the oddsmakers in London are betting."

Clara swallowed hard. Ten years. That meant she would be thirty-eight when she got out of prison, and that wouldn't be so bad, would it? She remembered the swaggering self-confidence of the boy she had loved when she was only sixteen years old. She could almost hear Daniel's voice telling her to buck up and stop being such a sissy.

She tried to smile. "Did you place a bet?"

He shrugged. "I'm not a betting man. Could be ten years, could be twenty. I've seen the judges do too many crazy things to waste my hard-earned coin on guessing what they will do."

Clara nodded, but was at a loss for anything to say. Surely they would not sentence her to twenty years in prison, would they? Not when she had risked her life to reveal the tortured conditions children endured when they were shoved beneath the surface of the earth to mine coal. Anyone who saw what such labor did to the spinal column of a young child could not possibly sentence her to such a fate.

And due to the brilliance of her attorney, Robert Townsend, such evidence had been presented to the court on her behalf. Clara thanked God she had the most skilled attorney in all of London defending her. He normally commanded an astronomical fee for his services, but his bills were being paid by an anonymous supporter who had heard of her case and offered to lend assistance. Such was not unusual. There were thousands of forward-thinking people who wished to advance the cause of social justice. Clara was grateful for it. Her modest salary as a journalist could never have footed Mr. Townsend's bill, and she hadn't wanted to ask her father.

Clara blinked when they stepped outside into the light of the morning. A month of imprisonment with no natural light had dimmed her senses, and it took a moment for her eyes to adjust. When she was finally able to open her eyes and look about her, she almost wept at the beauty of the simple prison courtyard. Ivy grew in a splendor of vibrant green shades on the stone walls of the prison, and the scent of newly cut grass in the breeze was exhilarating. And the sky . . . *the sky*. How had she lived for twenty-eight years and never noticed the stunning shade of blue that was directly over her head? If she had understood how wonderful a gift it was, she would have looked up and given thanks to God every day for its blessing. She paused as she soaked in the sight. She tried to memorize the precise image of the wisps of clouds against the sky, to store it away so she could recall it in the coming years of darkness and isolation.

A carriage rolled to a halt before the prison, and her attorney, Mr. Townsend, sprang out of the passenger door and vaulted across the short space between them. He grabbed her arm. "Come along," he said as he hustled her into the waiting carriage. "We need to get you out of here immediately."

Clara looked across the yard to the courthouse, where all the official business was conducted. "I thought I was going to hear my sentence," she stammered.

But Mr. Townsend did not stop in propelling her toward the carriage. "No need. Parliament has granted my petition for amnesty on the condition I get you out of the country by sundown. Hurry."

When she whirled around to Mr. Loomis for confirmation, she could see that he was smirking. He had *known* she was being set free. "See?" he gloated. "Good thing I wasn't a betting man, or I'd be out five quid."

And then Clara got the second shock of the day when another man descended from the carriage. The unmistakable sight of the buckskins, the long braid of hair, the nine-inch knife strapped to his leg. What on earth was her *brother* doing here!

"Clyde?" she gasped in disbelief.

Before she could get out another word, Clyde had swept her from her feet and whirled her in the air. "Hello, mouse. I came to see how a puny girl like you could cause such a ruckus. But let's get you out of here before the folks in Parliament change their minds."

Clyde released her only to shove her up and into the carriage. Clara landed on the carriage seat in an ungainly lurch, and both men quickly followed her inside.

The moment was so pure, so desperately hoped for, that Clara dared not even draw a breath lest the moment vanish. She refused to let elation get the better of her and she turned to Mr. Townsend as he landed in the seat opposite her. "Is this a dream?" She asked the question calmly, rationally. No histrionics would be permitted, even in a dream.

Clyde pulled the carriage door shut and rapped on the window to signal the driver to get moving. "You are not dreaming. We are on our way back to America."

Clara looked at Mr. Townsend sitting opposite her. "So, it appears you really are worth your infamously high fees," she said with a grateful smile. "You could probably buy a small estate for what all this must have cost."

Mr. Townsend straightened his starched collar. "Nonsense. It ought to buy me a medium-sized castle." He leaned over to lower the window casement and a wave of cool spring air flowed into the carriage. Clara became distinctly embarrassed about how putrid she must smell.

"It is a pity Parliament could not get a whiff of me," Clara said. "They would have declared me an undesirable alien and tossed me out of the country weeks ago."

A gentle smile curved her attorney's mouth. "Miss Endicott, this country would be a far better place if all of our 'undesirable aliens' sported such trophies of their compassion."

The back of Clara's throat began to ache and her vision blurred at the kind words. He had proven to be a lion defending her. She had been branded a liar, a spy, and a rabble-rouser. Even as her attorney's office had been vandalized and excoriating letters demanded he drop her case, Mr. Townsend had not wavered in his support of her.

Clara had not intended to create a scandal when she began her work—she had simply been trying to make one small corner of the world a safer place for children. She was not a famous preacher like her father or a missionary physician like her brother Clyde, but she could use her pen to help educate the world about the injustice she saw. A major piece of legislation reforming child labor had been passed in England years ago, but the abuse had not come to an end. For two years Clara had made a careful study of the ages of the workers being used in the coal mines, convinced that children as young as twelve were being used to cart wagons of coal through passages too narrow for a fully grown man to crawl in. When Clara began publishing her findings in *The Times*, she set off a firestorm of controversy.

Not that she ever had any such intentions of journalistic fame when she arrived in England as a confused and lonely sixteen-year-old girl. No one here knew the real reason Clara's father had sent her to England, and it was certainly not the kind of story she cared to circulate.

"I've already arranged for your things to be delivered to the Portsmouth dock," Mr. Townsend said. "Your clothing and personal belongings should all be there. I don't think it would be safe for you to return to your lodgings."

"Are they serious about my need to leave the country by sundown?"

"Do you really want to test their patience?" Mr. Townsend asked.

A nervous laugh escaped her lips. "I suppose not."

So this would prove to be her last carriage ride in England. Her gaze strayed out the window to look at the country she had come to love. She was twenty-eight years old and had spent almost half of her life in London. She had become a woman here, finally learning to stand up to her father. It was here that her broken heart had mended and her dream of becoming a writer had been fulfilled. And for a few short years she had been given the opportunity to be a foot soldier for the Lord through her work in the press. Her articles had gained her acclaim as well as a fair share of enemies, but throughout it all, she had the satisfaction of knowing she was doing good work.

And yet, she was still a failure. The notes documenting her discoveries in the coal mines had been confiscated and destroyed. Without that proof, all of her work amounted to nothing more than a load of sound and fury. No children had been rescued; no mine owner had been punished. It was as if she had never come to London. She had failed.

"What will you do once you return to America?" Mr. Townsend asked.

Did she even have any choice? Clara looked him in the eyes. "I've had a taste of what it means to make a difference in the world, and I can't stop now. I will write for my father's newspaper in Baltimore." Reverend Lloyd Endicott was a well-known minister, and his weekly newspaper, *The Christian Crusade,* had a loyal readership even beyond the city of Baltimore. It only seemed natural she would write for her father's publication. If the Lord wanted to silence her, she would be sitting in jail for a ten-year sentence.

The seed of resolve had taken root and was nourishing her with a new sense of buoyancy. Clara had been conquered, convicted, and was still wearing stained clothes, but she had been blessed with the gift of freedom, and she would not let that go to waste.

❦

"Have there always been that many stars in the sky, or have I merely failed to notice?" Clara asked.

Clyde leaned against the side of the ship, looking at her rather than at the night sky. "The same number as always. Aren't you ready to go below yet? It is freezing out here."

But Clara merely leaned into the wind, savoring the feel of the crisp ocean air against her face, the roar of the ship slicing through the waves below. Tiny droplets of cold seawater dotted her face and evaporated in the brisk wind. The thought of returning to her enclosed cabin was unthinkable when the sky, spattered with a thousand blazing stars, stretched out above her. The dark radiance was enthralling. "I can't go down below just yet," she said. "I'm still afraid that I am dreaming and that when I awake I will be back in that cell. I want to savor as much of this night as possible."

Clyde turned to look out into the ocean. "Fair enough." From inside his coat he pulled a pocketknife and a small block of wood, which he began whittling. One of Clyde's many talents. "So," he said casually. "Have you kept in touch with Daniel Tremain?"

The name was a cherished echo of the past. Once it was impossible to believe she could live a life without Daniel in it. Of course, those days were more than a decade old. "Did Father put you up to asking that?"

"Nope," Clyde said. "I'm simply dying of curiosity to know whatever happened to the princess and the pauper."

Anxious to appear as if his question did not rattle her, she tried to make her voice sound casual. "I've followed him in the newspapers, of course," she said.

It was hard to believe that a boy who started out shoveling coal into furnaces would grow up to become one of the most powerful industrialists in America, but Clara had never doubted that Daniel was destined for something great. She could still remember the day she had seen a tiny mention in the business section of *The Times*, announcing a patent filed by a young inventor in America for a new alloy of steel that would improve the strength of railway lines. That single invention had been the basis for a technological empire, and Daniel Tremain was at its helm. She had nothing to do with Daniel's success, but that did not stop her from being immensely proud of him. The pressure in her heart swelled when she thought of all he had accomplished.

"I wrote a few letters to him after I got to London," Clara confessed. "I never heard back from him."

But it had been more than just a few letters. She and Daniel had begun composing music together before she left Baltimore, and he had begged her to keep sending him her piano compositions so he could write the accompanying music for the cello. Of course, that was before his mother had died. Clyde had written her a few letters that let her know of Mrs. Tremain's death, and that Daniel had taken up additional jobs to support his sisters. How could he have had time for something as frivolous as composing music?

"I had assumed that since Tremain is now rolling in riches, he would have figured out some way to come see you in England," Clyde said.

She turned to face him. "Why is it you never liked Daniel?"

"Have I ever said such a thing?"

"You don't have to. You can barely say his name without wincing."

Clyde continued to whittle, and Clara waited patiently, the sound of the rushing waves swirling below filling the silence of the night. "I've always thought him a bit too hotheaded," Clyde finally admitted. "There is no doubt he is brilliant, but he was always so arrogant about it. Pushy, I suppose."

Clara bit back her uncharitable thoughts. Clyde had come halfway around the world to rescue her, and she wouldn't chastise him for not understanding her adolescent fascination with Daniel Tremain.

"Perhaps it was Daniel's brashness that Father objected to, as well," she conceded. "We all know I was not sent to London simply to broaden my education."

Clara always suspected her father's ambition for her musical career was why he initially encouraged her unlikely friendship with Daniel Tremain. Daniel encouraged her to compose, nourished her love of Chopin and Beethoven, and helped her reach new creative impulses as she played on the piano and he accompanied her on the cello. But what Clara truly wished to do was write, like Margaret Fuller or many of the other women who were just beginning to be allowed to write for newspapers. And when Daniel encouraged her to follow her own dreams of writing rather than music, her father saw it as a threat and sent her to London.

Clara watched the chips of wood drift into the swirling waters below. "I wonder if Father will object to Daniel, now that he is rich as sin."

"The short answer is a resounding *yes*," Clyde said without hesitation. "Tremain is still a nutcase over that whole business with Forsythe Industries. Any man who can keep a grudge stoked for twelve years is a little off-kilter, Clara."

She turned to face him. "If you believed Alfred Forsythe had murdered your father, I think you might hold a grudge, too," she pointed out.

"It wasn't murder, Clara; it was an accident."

"That was what the court said, too." Which did not mean it was the truth. Alfred Forsythe had a cadre of lawyers to cover up the facts surrounding the explosion of that boiler, and Daniel had been a nineteen-year-old boy with no money and three little sisters to support. What chance did he have of proving his case in court?

Clyde's blade continued to make progress on his carving. "From what I hear, Tremain has made it his life mission to grind Alfred Forsythe and his company beneath the heel of his boot. That company employs more than seven thousand people, and they are all pawns in this private vendetta Tremain is waging." Clyde folded the pocketknife and slipped it back into his coat. "You are a grown woman and free to make your own choices," he said. "But I don't want you getting in over your head with that man. You are too sweet-natured to handle a dynamo like Tremain."

Maybe Clyde was right. There was a time when she and Daniel could finish each other's sentences, read each other's minds. If ever there were two kindred spirits, it was she and Daniel.

But twelve years had passed since she had seen him, and now he was a man in control of a vast fortune and on a crusade for vengeance. It was hard to believe he could have changed so drastically, but then again, Clara would never have believed he would have failed to write to her once she was in London.

Did Daniel even remember her? He had been such a huge force

in her life, an earthquake after which nothing was ever the same. Had she had that same importance to him?

Clara drew a deep breath. It really did not matter. She had found her calling and her banishment was over. It was time to rebuild a new life in America.

CHAPTER 2

If looks could kill, Daniel would be a dead man.

Lou Hammond, the company's lead attorney, was having difficulty maintaining a calm voice as he stood in the gilded interior of the company's private railcar as it rolled through the Pennsylvania countryside. "Mr. Tremain, your insistence on this bizarre licensing arrangement will cost too much money in sheer profit," he said.

Daniel quirked a brow. "We are not on our way to the poorhouse, are we?"

A glance around the impressive private railcar was proof that Carr & Tremain Polytechnic was doing just fine. Some of the country's finest craftsmen had provided the brass fittings and highly varnished teakwood moldings that lined the car's interior. Velvet draperies framed the view of the rolling landscape of western

Pennsylvania as they sped home from New York. It would have been quicker to travel on the stretch of railroad that linked Philadelphia and Baltimore, but it was well known that Daniel would never ride on a railroad controlled by Alfred Forsythe. He would return to Baltimore by donkey cart before paying a single dime into that man's coffers.

After this week's round of meetings with bankers, lawyers, and judges, their company was on the verge of becoming a publicly traded corporation on the New York Stock Exchange. As soon as this deal closed, Daniel and his partner Ian Carr would be among the wealthiest men in the country.

But only if Daniel permitted the deal to go through. "As long as I am in charge of this company," Daniel said, "I will never permit any of my patents to be licensed to Alfred Forsythe. This is nonnegotiable. Everyone in this railcar knew that before we went to New York."

"But the company won't be *yours* after it goes public," his attorney said. "The company will belong to the shareholders. And any sort of decision that affects the value of the company will need to be disclosed to the public."

Daniel shrugged. "Then take out an advertisement in *The New York Times* and tell it to the world. It is no secret that I despise Alfred Forsythe and won't do business with him. I would rather scuttle the deal than let Forsythe use my technology."

"Are you sure about that, lad?" Ian Carr's lilting Scottish accent was gentle, and Daniel felt a twinge of remorse. Ian was more than just his partner; Ian was the person who gave Daniel his first leg up in the world by hiring the penniless nineteen-year-old to work the timing devices on his fledgling railroad. Within six months, Daniel had figured out a way to alter a standard timing device into one which could operate without human intervention, making the timer not only cheaper to operate but safer by removing the danger of human error. The thousands of dollars that poured into their company from licensing that invention had allowed for more innovations that helped to revolutionize the railroad industry.

The reason their company worked was because Ian let Daniel run the technical side of development without interference, and Daniel deferred to Ian's natural business acumen to license, market, and promote their inventions. Together they controlled the railroad industry's best timing devices, rails, and routing systems.

Daniel met his partner's eyes. "Ian, I'll defer every business decision in the company to you, except for this. I can't license those patents to Forsythe. Even if it scraps the Wall Street deal, I won't do it."

Mr. Hammond cleared his throat. "Now, Daniel, it is no secret that you are a brilliant innovator—"

"Stop, you will make me cry," Daniel said dryly.

His attorney held up his hand. "The reputation of Carr & Tremain will suffer if we use the company to carry out a personal vendetta. Negative financial consequences will result."

"We've been paying negative financial consequences for almost a decade," Daniel said, "but it doesn't amount to a fraction of what Forsythe has lost. He has to replace his rails twice as often as the companies who use my technology. Every time he has to commission another set, he thinks of my father and regrets what he did. That's exactly how I want it." By all that was holy, it felt good to have Alfred Forsythe by the throat, and never, *never* would he relax that grip.

Jamie Carr, his partner's son, shifted in his chair. "That accident was more than ten years ago," Jamie said. "Can't you just accept the man's apology and be done with it?"

A silence fell over the group and tension rippled through the men assembled in the railcar. Nervous glances flew among the men, all of whom knew of Daniel's temper when it came to Forsythe. Daniel stiffened, but he wouldn't rebuke the boy. After all, Jamie was only nineteen years old and knew nothing of the stench of burned skin or the agony of being scalded to death. He had never witnessed the eyes of a widow turn hollow until suicide was the only way out of her despair.

Daniel forced his voice to remain calm. "But, Jamie, Mr. Forsythe has failed to offer any sort of apology, and I am convinced he never will."

Alfred Forsythe planned on running for governor of Maryland next year, and filling his resume with charitable works and publicly funded hospitals was the sort of thing he excelled at. Taking responsibility for the careless death of his workers would not fit into the public image he had created for himself.

Daniel turned his attention back to Ian. "I am aware that my issue with Forsythe has cost you, as well, and I'm sorry for that. Do whatever you need to structure this deal, so long as it stops short of licensing to Forsythe." Daniel knew Ian was utterly trustworthy to protect the business affairs of their company, and he would find a way to honor Daniel's request.

❧

Kerosene lanterns were lit as the sun dropped below the horizon. The business meeting was long over, and a few men played cards at one table, while the gentle rocking of the railcar had prompted others to nod off to sleep in the plush, overstuffed chairs. It would be at least three more hours before they arrived in Baltimore.

Daniel sat with his assistant, Joe Manzetti, and his personal attorney going over his affairs. Who would have thought back when he worked a second shift shoveling coal into a furnace that someday he would have a corporate attorney, an estate attorney, a patent attorney, and a personal attorney? But they were all necessary. A man did not rise to the heights he had without relying on attorneys to look after his various endeavors. Along with his attorneys, Daniel had Manzetti, who served as his bodyguard, business assistant, and an extra set of eyes. Daniel had never regained sight in the eye that had been blinded in the boiler explosion, and the dim light cast by the lanterns made it a strain to read once the sun had set.

"The bills for your sister's wedding have been paid in full, but the balance has yet to be paid on the house you purchased for Miss Lorna as a bridal gift," his attorney said. "Did you wish to pay that outright, or shall I prepare installments?"

Daniel hated being indebted to anyone, but most of his fortune was locked up in the company. It was the reason everyone was so anxious to sell shares to the public. Ready cash had not been available when he purchased a house for his sister last summer, but it would be as soon as Ian could list their company on the New York Stock Exchange and begin selling shares. "I want it paid outright, but we'll have to wait until the funds from the public offering become available. Hopefully in September."

"Very well."

Certainly the biggest fringe benefit of taking his company public in the autumn would be the ability to ensure he could always provide for his sisters.

"And Miss Kate has requested that you renew your membership at the Colchester Sporting Club. Either that, or she suggests that perhaps you would consider constructing a tennis court on your own property."

"She thinks I'm going to build her a tennis court?"

"She has hopes," Manzetti said. "She doesn't know you as well as I do." Daniel and Manzetti had worked together back when they were both employed by Forsythe Industries. It had been Manzetti who had run to get him out of the scholarship exam after the boiler explosion. Although Manzetti had profited nicely from working alongside Daniel, neither one of them would ever forget the squalor and anxiety that accompanied a life of relentless poverty.

"Renew the club membership," Daniel said. "I'm not going to spoil Kate any more than I already have." If Kate had her way, his backyard would be consumed by a private golf course, a croquet green, and tennis courts. Spoiling his sisters was one of the few pleasures he afforded himself. For the past ten years, his life had been consumed by a voracious need to grind forward in developing his inventions. That left little time for raising his sisters, and he assuaged his guilt by bestowing little luxuries on them. He still remembered the time he had hoarded enough money to purchase the girls their first little beaded reticules. Those minor luxuries were soon followed by private schools, music lessons, trips to Washington. It was as though showering them with such opportunities somehow compensated for the death of their parents, and, essentially, the loss of their brother, as well, since he was generally closeted with business associates and attorneys most nights.

"Miss Kate assumed that would be your response," Manzetti said. "She would therefore like access to the carriage to take her to the club to practice her tennis on days you are at the office."

Daniel rubbed his forehead. "Truly, Manzetti, I can run my company, or I can control Kate. I can't do both. Tell her she can't use the carriage when I'm not there. She'll bicker, but that's what sixteen-year-old girls do. What's next?"

His lawyer removed a file from the stack. "The bill for Miss Endicott's defense last month. Shockingly high, but the attorney came highly recommended."

At the mention of Clara's name, Daniel jerked to attention and his gaze darted to the stack of newspaper clippings on the table. He scanned them quickly. He'd already heard of her deportation, of course. That had made the newspapers here in Baltimore. When she had proven herself as a writer in London, Reverend Endicott began publishing his daughter's articles about the horror of child labor in *The Christian Crusade*. Now Clara was another glittering ornament on the Endicott family tree, just as her father had wished.

Naturally, Daniel had followed Clara's career. He never learned why she failed to write to him after arriving in London, but he could not blame her. Or not too much, anyway. She had been surrounded by the best musicians and writers in Europe. It was unrealistic to think that a girl with those opportunities would remember the poor kid she had once let use her piano.

Still, he was proud of her. Clara had the wealth and connections to live an idle life if she had chosen. She could have taken up tennis and golf like Kate and never worried about what being stooped over in a mineshaft did to a child's spinal column.

"So what precisely did these legal fees buy Clara? A deportation ticket?"

"It bought her a suspended jail term. Without Mr. Townsend's intervention, it is likely she would have been required to serve a number of years in prison."

The thought of Clara, with her bright blue eyes and sparkling humor, locked in a stark jail cell made his blood run cold. "Money well spent, then."

As he skimmed one of the articles, he imagined her standing in a courtroom as charges were read against her. She could not have looked so bright and sparkly then.

He tossed the newspaper down. "Find out if she intends to return to Baltimore, or if she is headed elsewhere," Daniel said.

It had suddenly become very important to discover what precisely had become of the girl who had once vowed she would be his best friend even if she lived on the moon.

CHAPTER 3

Finally back in Baltimore after two weeks at sea, Clara braced herself for an evening in which she was, lamentably, the main attraction. The mayor of Baltimore lived in an imposing mansion built from blocks of rough-hewn granite that looked as if they had been carted off from an ancient castle. Torchlight flickered along the walk leading up to the house, and the interior was illuminated with massive chandeliers. The reason for this evening's soiree was ostensibly to welcome her back home, but Clara knew the real reason the glittering circle of high society would be here tonight. The Reverend Lloyd Endicott was still one of the most influential religious leaders in the country, and currying his favor by attending a party in his daughter's honor was essential for the politicians, socialites, and captains of industry in Maryland. Florence Wagner, the mayor's wife, would have offered up her firstborn child in exchange for hosting the festivities. People were always eager to court her father's favor, and as the most colossal social climber on the east coast, Florence Wagner was thrilled down to her pearl-encrusted satin pumps to host the party in Clara's honor.

"Don't look so nervous," her father said from the carriage seat opposite her. "I know you are looking forward to this as much as having a tooth extracted, but all the right people will be in attendance tonight. If you wish to relaunch your writing career, these people will be excellent connections."

Clara adjusted the pleats of silk that flared from the wasp waist of her evening gown. The overskirt was a simple turquoise brocade, but as it gathered back to a carefully draped bustle, a splendid underskirt of embroidered silk charmeuse was revealed in the front. With her hands encased in white kid gloves up to her elbows and the fine boning of her corset keeping her rigidly erect, Clara was oddly grateful for the added bit of confidence the structure of her ensemble provided.

The carriage drew to the front of the mayor's house, and Clara tried to force a smile to her face. "I know you are right," she said. "It has been so long since I've been home and I won't really know any-one here." She felt like a stranger in Baltimore, with little memory of anyone outside of her immediate family. And Daniel, of course.

Of all the people in Baltimore, Daniel Tremain was the one she was most curious to see again. Even though Daniel had become a powerful industrialist, her father said Daniel rarely attended society functions. "That man just doesn't fit in," Lloyd had said, and Clara could easily believe him. Daniel had always been too brash and opinionated to blend in with the Byzantine manners of high society.

"I wish Clyde could be here tonight," Clara said. "It would be nice to know at least one other person." As a man who had spent the last decade working as a missionary doctor among Indians on the reservations of the American West, Clyde tended to look askance at all the "social nonsense of Baltimore" and had remained at home.

"It is not so important for Clyde to be here," her father said. "After his visit here he will be heading straight back to the Navajo reservation in Arizona Territory; that is where Clyde will make his mark in this world, not among the blue bloods. And even though you may not relish taking part in tonight's sort of entertaining, a journalist can't afford to pass up these opportunities. You've made me very proud with your work in London, and with the right connections, I know you can do equally splendid work here in America."

And that was what she wanted more than drawing her next breath of air. Some might think it strange for a woman to be so driven to succeed, but her father had planted the seeds of ambition in her before she had even stopped sucking her thumb. God had put her on this earth for a purpose, yet in the weeks since she had been banished from England, she had done nothing but nurse her battered soul and wallow in regrets. She needed to find a new way to make a life-affirming contribution to the world, and since her father was one of the few men in the entire country who was willing to publish the writings of a woman, Clara knew she had to get back to her writing.

The disaster in London was no excuse for this self-indulgent malaise that had been plaguing her. If she ever hoped to regain any level of pride in her work, she was going to have to walk through those imposing front doors and try to pretend that she was not an utter failure. Clara squared her shoulders and forced her chin up a notch. Self-confidence could be feigned, even though she felt as charismatic as an oyster.

Florence Wagner swept into the foyer the moment Clara set foot inside the mansion. Poured into a slim-fitting sheath of sapphire Dupioni silk, Florence's petite little body was topped by a mass of tightly curled red hair with jeweled combs strategically placed like a crown around the top of her head. "Clara, darling," the woman drawled as she rushed forward with outstretched hands. One would have thought they were long-lost friends, although Clara had been a girl of only sixteen when last she set foot in Baltimore. "Welcome back home, my dear." She turned outward to face the crowd of assembled people. "Everyone . . . here is dearest Clara Endicott, just back from London."

Heads swiveled and gentlemen raised monocles to inspect her. Everywhere Clara looked she saw stunningly attired women, appearing like glorious butterflies draped in watered silk and satin gowns while diamonds winked from throats and fans wafted in the jasmine-scented air. The elegant notes of a string quartet played in the distance. Clara was overwhelmed with an odd sort of dissonance. Was it only a month ago when she was trapped in a dank stone prison? It did not seem possible for such splendor to exist on the same planet as the cell where she had lived with Rosina and Nellie.

Florence took Clara's arm and led her forward into the group.

"Come along, my dear. Simply *everyone* in Baltimore has turned out to welcome you home. Let me introduce Senator Bronson to you."

Clara murmured a few pleasantries to the senator, but her gaze was sweeping the room. Was it possible that Daniel Tremain might be among the "everyone" who had come this evening? Even though her father had said Daniel rarely indulged in such events, perhaps he would have come in order to see her again? She wasn't even sure she would recognize Daniel today—the boy who was the center of her childhood crush was always dressed simply in trousers and a plain shirt, whereas all the gentlemen in this room were wearing black cutaway jackets with starched white collars riding high on their necks. No longer a gangly teenager, Daniel would be a full-grown man. There had to be more than one hundred people in the room, but none of them resembled Daniel. Her shoulders drooped just a fraction. His absence was to be expected, of course, but still . . .

Florence kept Clara moving around the perimeter of the foyer, introducing her to dozens of people whose names she had little hope of remembering. "Clara, may I present Mr. Joshua McAllister," Florence said as they approached a young man who dared to buck fashion by wearing a scarlet silk vest amid the sea of black frock coats. "Mr. McAllister runs two of the cotton mills down in the southern part of the city. He is quite the up-and-coming young man."

Mr. McAllister bowed over Clara's hand. "Enchanted, Miss Endicott. I've read about your work in London and was most impressed with your accomplishments. Those poor children . . .

terrible, terrible. What a relief it must be to have all that nonsense behind you and be back in the bosom of your family."

Clara was not quite sure how to respond. "I'm most pleased to have a chance to visit with my father once again, yes."

"Quite impressive work for a woman," Mr. McAllister continued. "Of course, one would expect nothing less from one of Lloyd Endicott's children. I expect now you will want to settle down and get married, yes?"

Actually, marriage was the last thing Clara wanted. While in London she had suffered a disastrous broken engagement. Another romance would not be welcome, but she could hardly say as much into the eager face of Joshua McAllister. Throwing herself into her work as a journalist had been what salvaged her battered pride when Nicholas Spencer had broken off their engagement in London. Clara had agreed to marry Nicholas for all the wrong reasons—she knew that now—but at the time he abandoned her it had been a crushing blow. "I still have hopes of resurrecting my journalistic career," Clara said. "I'm hoping to write for my father's publication, *The Christian Crusade.*"

Mr. McAllister appeared to be pleasantly surprised. "Quite right. Quite admirable. In fact, I myself would welcome the opportunity to get to know your father a little better. What a gift to the country that man is." As Mr. McAllister continued to sing praises about Reverend Endicott, Clara was not quite sure if he was trying to court her or her father. Not that it really mattered. She was here only to meet as many people as possible in order to begin forming the necessary connections for her work.

They continued speaking for a few more minutes until their hostess came to retrieve Clara. "Well, that seemed to go quite well," she gushed. At Clara's quizzical expression, Florence continued, "Mr. McAllister stands to inherit quite a fortune in a few years. And he is a divine wit, and from the best of families." Florence leaned closer and lowered her voice. "And he is quite the most *eligible* bachelor in the city. You don't mind if I play at a tiny bit of matchmaking, do you?"

Clara's eyes widened. Obviously, gossip of her broken engagement had not reached Baltimore, or people would not be hurling eligible gentlemen in her path. Whenever a woman was unceremoniously dumped by her fiancé, people looked askance at the jilted woman, no matter who was to blame for the demise of the engagement. "I've just returned to town," Clara hedged. "I'm hoping to get settled and spend some time with my brother before participating in any sort of romantic entanglement."

Florence perked up at the mention of Clara's brother. "Is Dr. Endicott back in Baltimore?" she asked, looking as stunned as if Queen Victoria herself was about to descend upon the town.

Clara shook her head. "He is here, though not yet ready to be making social calls."

"My goodness," Florence breathed. "Your brother was in town three years ago when he came to testify before a congressional panel in Washington . . . something about the plight of the poor Indians. He garnered quite a bit of attention from our young ladies. Is there any hope he could be persuaded to stay a bit longer in Baltimore?

After all, he need not sacrifice his entire life for the heathens. Perhaps it is time he settle down amongst civilized people."

Clara was embarrassed to confess she knew very little about Clyde's intentions these days, but she certainly knew he had a much better opinion of the people he lived among than to consider them heathens. "I think you will have to put that question to Clyde when you see him," Clara said.

It was surprising, but the very mention of her brother's name caused a group of young ladies to cluster about Clara and Florence like honeybees drawn to a particularly delicious flower. "Dr. Endicott? Coming back to town?" The voice belonged to a gorgeous woman with piles of blond hair amassed atop her head. She looked beautiful enough to be a Greek goddess.

"Clyde Endicott?" another woman demanded. "I don't believe it! Where is he?"

A third young lady pushed her way forward to stand directly before Clara. "Is it true? Your brother will be coming back to town?"

Clara looked at the faces of the half dozen young ladies, all breathless in anticipation of her answer, and wondered how Clyde had convinced them he was anything but the most annoying human being to ever walk on the face of the earth. "Yes, Clyde is back in town, but only for a very short visit." Clara was beginning to understand Clyde's instructions to his father that his visit was to remain strictly a family affair. If he inspired this frenzy of delight among his admirers, no wonder he hoped to get in and out of town without notice. Clara was already beginning to feel claustrophobic with the crush of young women breathless for news of Dr. Clyde Endicott.

"I knew he could not stay away," the Greek goddess said. "Miss Endicott, you simply *must* host a tea party to welcome your brother back to town. That poor man cannot be permitted to return to the wilds without a chance to meet some ladies of his own class."

Another lady began waving her fan over her heated face. "I declare, it is impossible to look at that man and not want to be the woman who finally tames him. He is the most delicious male specimen . . . or at least he will be when someone finally civilizes him. He must not be allowed to escape again."

Now it was Clara's turn to blush. Her older brother was many things, but *delicious* was never a word she would have used to describe him. And yet, the mere mention of Clyde's name was apparently enough to fuel a lengthy discussion of the various eligible young men in Baltimore. The girls clustered around Clara as they contrasted Clyde's ruggedness with the safety of Joshua McAllister's comfortable life as owner of a cotton mill. A number of other men's names were tossed into the mix as the ladies debated the merits of each. Baltimore appeared to possess an endless supply of eligible bachelors who caused rounds of gushing, cooing, and fervent speculation.

And then the Greek goddess brought a stunned halt to the conversation. "What about Daniel Tremain?" she asked. "More than any other man I've ever seen, I daresay he is the mystery I would most like to unravel. Piece by mesmerizing piece."

Apparently, even the mention of Daniel's name was enough to stop all conversation. After a moment, Florence Wagner regained her breath. "Elizabeth Ginallette, you know that man is not suitable company. It is easy to see how young, foolish girls may find him attractive, but there is a reason he never attends social functions such as these. That man is as dangerous as a rattlesnake."

Miss Ginallette persisted. "I heard he donated a fortune to build the new Opera House. A man who funds such things can't be all bad, can he?"

"He may throw his money around, but that doesn't make him a gentleman," Mrs. Wagner warned. The stiffness in the woman's voice rubbed Clara the wrong way. Was it merely that Daniel had come from poverty, while these esteemed young ladies came from generations of blood bluer than a summer sky? Daniel had worked harder than any man she ever knew, including Clyde and her father, and it was not right that a woman of privilege would cast aspersions on him because he was not born in the right part of town.

"I knew Daniel Tremain before I left for London," Clara said. "He was a brilliant young man and never the least bit ungentlemanly." All the women swiveled their heads to stare at her.

"You've actually *spoken* with him?" Miss Ginallette asked. The awe in her voice sounded as though Clara had made contact with a deity.

"Yes, of course," Clara said, "I considered him a friend." It seemed such a paltry word—Daniel had cried in her arms the night his father was buried.

"I saw him at his sister's wedding last year," one of the ladies said, "but no one I know actually worked up the nerve to speak with him. He was wickedly attractive but seemed so frighteningly remote."

Mr. Wagner, the mayor of Baltimore, joined in the conversation. In contrast to his tiny wife, Mayor Wagner was a huge man whose wide belly was decorated with a thick gold watch chain. "That's because his entire life has been spent in a laboratory scheming ways to make a fortune and ruin Forsythe Industries," he said. "Tremain never comes out of his fortress unless he can lob a bomb at someone, preferably Alfred Forsythe. Then he disappears back into his lair to plot some other form of world domination."

"World domination?" Clara could not hide the skepticism in her voice. "That seems a little high-flying for this corner of Baltimore."

The mayor's eyes turned flinty. "You must understand, Miss Endicott, our way of life is now entirely dependent upon the smooth operation of the railroads. Tremain doesn't own many railroads yet, but he's in the process of acquiring them. And those he does not own, he already controls by granting or withholding access to the technology that makes railway transportation affordable. He is a robber baron with a stranglehold on the industry and is perfectly willing to use it to punish competitors he dislikes."

Clara's gaze darted around the lavish interior of the mayor's home, filled to capacity with the town's leading entrepreneurs and trendsetters. Everyone she had met in this room had been born into a world of silken sheets and had breakfast trays delivered at the dawn of each day. What would people like this understand of abject poverty? "Perhaps if Daniel Tremain were welcomed into gatherings such as these, he might not seem so intimidating," Clara said.

Mrs. Wagner raised her chin but lowered her voice. "It has been many years since you left Baltimore, so you may not be familiar with what has transpired since you've been gone. Daniel Tremain is as warm and compassionate as a spider. Gold-leaf invitations could be hand-delivered to the man, and he'd toss them into the trash bin."

"Not true," the Greek goddess said. "Every time I've gone to a performance at the new Opera House, I have seen him in attendance. He always sits in the very back row."

"Yes, and he arrives and leaves alone," Mrs. Wagner said dispassionately. "Heaven forbid he should stay five minutes after a performance and actually *speak* to someone."

Clara stood a little straighter. "I don't believe a lack of social graces automatically correlates to evil-minded intentions."

"Of course not," the mayor agreed. "But if you lived in this city last year, you would have had a front-row seat to watch Tremain's spitefulness in action. Alfred Forsythe spent a fortune building a college for this town. He bought the land, paid for the construction of classrooms and dormitories. It was to be called Forsythe College and would have been a fine addition to this city. Just before they began hiring a faculty for the college, Tremain stepped in to scuttle the whole project. He found some old title that said the land had been ceded to an Indian tribe back in the 1790s. That tribe had long since disappeared from the area, but Tremain hired a lawyer and argued the case in court. The judge ruled that until the descendants of the original title holders could be found, nothing could happen to that land. No college, no sale, nothing. Those buildings sit empty today because Daniel Tremain will stop at nothing to ruin Alfred Forsythe."

A quick glance at the faces of the other women confirmed what the mayor had said, and Clara fought the urge to wilt. Daniel's very name seemed to inspire hostility, but Clara no longer knew Daniel well enough to defend him. The aloof stranger they described bore no resemblance to the young man she had once idolized.

In the years since those days, Clara had met famous composers, known literary success as a journalist, and traveled the world. And yet, those stolen hours with Daniel remained her most cherished memories of sheer, unmitigated happiness.

CHAPTER 4

As Clara wandered the hill outside the new Opera House, she had to admit, everything about Baltimore's new music facility was vastly superior to the old Music Conservatory in Bolton Hill. She'd suffered a terrible wave of nostalgia when she heard that the beloved old building had been shuttered and had fallen into disrepair. "It was a firetrap and should have been torn down years ago," her father had told her. The new Opera House had room for a proper performance auditorium, complete with space for a backstage and a modern lighting system. The auditorium had more than tripled in size and was filled with comfortable seating. The outdoor amphitheatre was used not only for music but for plays and political gatherings, as well.

Today, the amphitheatre was the site of a Fourth of July

celebration. The morning was already warm, but at least her bonnet shaded her from the worst of the direct summer sun. She stood near the back of the crowd and listened to a quartet perform until the nearby church bells tolled the noon hour. The crowd began filing inside the Opera House, where the main feature, a performance of patriotic music supplied by the U.S. Marine Band, would soon commence.

Once inside the auditorium, Clara took a seat in the center section. She could not prevent her gaze from straying to the back row, where Daniel Tremain supposedly haunted the music hall for each performance. She scanned the silhouettes seated near the back of the audience, but none of the people filling the seats looked remotely familiar. He wasn't here—she would have recognized him instantly. Even though twelve years had passed, Daniel's image was still emblazoned on her memory.

Clara shifted to arrange the folds of her skirt as the familiar sounds of musicians tuning and warming up their instruments began to punctuate the air. When the conductor entered the hall and the sounds of tuning tapered to a close, Clara swiveled around one final time to peek at the back row of the auditorium.

Daniel! Her breath caught in her throat at the sight of him. How foolish she had been, thinking he would look the same. She'd thought he might be a little taller and a little broader across the shoulders. That he might look a tad older, but he would still be essentially the same person she had known before.

She was wrong on all counts.

Daniel Tremain was simply staggering. He leaned negligently

against the back wall of the auditorium, and the masculine confidence in his stance gave the impression of barely leashed power. Yes, he was tall and his shoulders had broadened to match his impressive height, but it was the intensity carved onto every plane of that severe face that arrested her attention. His hair was jet-black, and dark brows slanted over his eyes as he watched the band, his arms folded across his chest. She immediately understood how Daniel could have caused such commotion among the young ladies of Baltimore. In a room full of tame house cats, he was a panther.

Clara jerked her head around and stared at the band. Daniel's physical transformation was astounding, so shocking as to make her wonder if what Florence Wagner had said about the changes in Daniel's character could possibly be true.

A smattering of applause sounded as the conductor stepped to the podium. Before beginning the first tune, he bid the audience to stand while he recited a short prayer for the nation's president and for the fallen heroes who had given their lives for this country. Clara bowed her head as the words washed over her. Although her expulsion from England had been painful and humiliating, she was glad to be back in her home country, where she was free to celebrate this simple, most American of holidays.

A rasping sound of fabric came from the row behind her as someone leaned forward to whisper directly in her ear. "I certainly hope someone sends up a prayer on behalf of that pitiful bonnet. It really is terrible, Clara."

She would know that voice anywhere. It had the melting quality of warm caramel and it brought back every sensation of the sheer, uninhibited delight of being in Daniel Tremain's presence. By the time she whirled around, Daniel had already shifted his weight back to stand at respectful attention while the prayer continued, his face the epitome of pious concentration as he watched the conductor at the front of the stage.

"Daniel, what are you doing here?" she asked in an urgent whisper. She had never seen him dressed so finely before. A custom-tailored navy frock coat fit his broad shoulders perfectly, and the silk tie and vest made him look as polished as any aristocrat she had seen in the mansions of London. Daniel's face was recklessly handsome, with high cheekbones and a long blade of a nose that gave him a fierce, hawkish look. A slight scar split an eyebrow, and the lid on one eye hung a little lower than the other, but that was the only sign of his blindness in that eye.

Daniel's face was completely impassive as he continued to watch the band, but he leaned forward and whispered in her ear, "Came to see if you found any sense of fashion over in London." His gaze flicked back to her bonnet. "Tragic, Clara."

The laugh bubbled up so quickly that when she tried to stop it, an ungainly snort emerged. The people in the seats surrounding her cast disapproving glances her way, and Clara felt a flush creep up her cheeks. When the prayer was over, the audience resumed their seats while the director tapped his baton and proceeded with the first song, a traditional fanfare of trumpets mixed with a dash of percussion. Clara knew the piece would last at least five minutes, but she could not endure another *five seconds* without speaking to Daniel.

She whirled back around and caught a glimmer of the old roguish humor in Daniel's eye. "Come on, let's get out of here," he said.

❧

She followed Daniel out of the Opera House. She'd always
been on the petite side, but now Daniel towered above her and
the top of her head barely reached his shoulder. Sunlight streamed
through the old sycamore trees that sheltered the top of the outdoor
amphitheatre, now empty of visitors. Daniel's hand guided her to
the low stone wall that divided the amphitheatre from the gardens
outside of the Opera House. How wonderfully strange this felt. Was
Daniel the big, bad wolf described by the matrons of Baltimore?
Or beneath the fine frock coat of the fully grown man, was he still
her oldest, most cherished friend?

"I must congratulate you on the splendid Opera House," Clara
said. "I heard you had a lot to do with getting it built, and it is quite
an improvement over the old Music Conservatory." Clara sank onto
the low wall while Daniel remained standing beside her, resting his
booted foot on the wall as he leaned over her.

"It is certainly more modern than that ramshackle old firetrap,"
Daniel said. "Besides, I wanted my sisters to have an appreciation
for music, and Katie was terrified of the Conservatory. She was
convinced ghosts were living up in the turret on the north side."

"And how is Katie?"

"She's competing in a cycling race as we speak. Last summer
I was foolish enough to purchase one of the newfangled bicycles
from Paris for her, thinking it might keep her amused within our

own neighborhood. Now she's off most weekends with the Baltimore Cycling Club and who knows where else. She'll be lucky to see her seventeenth birthday if she keeps trying her hand at every sport known to mankind."

"And Rachel and Lorna?"

"Both safely married and no longer my responsibility. Thank heaven. I keep hoping some naive young man who can be bribed to take Kate off my hands will stumble into my life."

She smiled up at him. "What a liar you are. You try to sound so fierce, but your face positively radiates when you speak about your sisters."

"Nonsense. That's the look of howling anxiety from raising girls. No one should be foolish enough to embark on such an endeavor."

"Foolish or not, you are to be commended for the way you raised your sisters," she said. Her gaze flicked to the fine silk of his vest and the heavy gold watch chain hanging at his waist. "What a shame you had such spotty luck in business, though."

"Clara, the only real tragedy is that awful scrap of fabric on your head."

She threw up her hands in exasperation. "Daniel Tremain! Never once, in all the years we have known each other, have you ever said a single nice thing about any bonnet I have worn."

"That's because they've all been atrocious." With his serious face and bland delivery, it was easy to see how people would think Daniel cold and blunt . . . but Clara had endured too many years of Daniel's teasing to mistake the humor lurking in those pale gray eyes.

She untied the ribbon beneath her head, lifted off the offending garment, and then smoothed her hair into place. "Is it all bonnets you dislike? Or just mine?"

"All bonnets, because a woman's hair is one of her best features and should not be hidden. *Your* bonnets are especially loathsome because you have particularly beautiful hair."

Clara looked up in surprise. It was true that she was shamefully proud of her hair, but Daniel had never, *never* complimented her on her looks before. And it was more than his words, it was the way he was looking at her, with admiration and almost a hint of tenderness. He swiveled and took a seat beside her on the stone wall. "So tell me, Miss Endicott, what caused a promising young writer to become diverted into the world of muckraking journalism?"

"If you think I'm going to take offense at the word *muckraker,* you are destined for disappointment."

"No. I'm simply dying of curiosity to know how the timid girl who left Baltimore ended up a convicted felon in London." Humor danced behind his eyes. "That really takes some doing, Clara."

She flashed him a grin. "What good adventure story doesn't have a stint in prison?" How odd that only this morning she had still been mourning the demise of her career in London, but somehow when she was sitting with Daniel Tremain, it no longer seemed so tragic.

"No sidestepping. Tell me how it happened," Daniel prodded.

She traced her fingernail along the moss that grew on the wall while she struggled to find the words. "When I went to London, I thought I might publish poems or essays, like Margaret Fuller or Henry David Thoreau. But everything I was writing seemed so pale and vapid. Then I met a doctor who was treating children who had been injured in the coal mines." Daniel listened intently as she recounted the next few years, how she had to earn the coal workers' trust, watch the children entering and leaving the mines. "I never intended to write those sorts of explosive articles, but once I knew what was happening, I could not keep silent. As soon as I became a journalist I felt as though the pieces had clicked into place. I was good at it, and I believed I was making use of the talents God intended for me to use. Of course that didn't stop me from making a complete and total disaster of everything."

Daniel lifted an eyebrow and slanted her one of those curious half-grinning, half-reproving looks. "Clara, I hope you aren't going to subject me to one of your blistering rounds of insecurity. After all these years, has nothing changed?"

"Not really," she confessed. And there under the shade of the sycamore tree, Clara poured out all the anxieties and regrets of her final year in London. To whom other than Daniel could she speak so freely? During her years in London she had fabricated an image of sophisticated self-confidence that fooled most people, but Daniel had known her when she was a raw, awkward teenager without artifice. Twelve years had passed, and by all rights he should be a stranger to her, yet he was a familiar stranger with whom she felt absolutely safe sharing her terrible failings as a journalist. Pouring out her shortcomings was like ridding herself of a pestilence that had been weighing her down for months.

Through it all, Daniel listened to her without comment or condemnation. He merely watched her with that speculative, captivating gaze that made her feel she was the object of his complete and total attention. After she had finally cataloged her every fault, Daniel posed the oddest of questions.

"Clara, give me the name of one other woman in the English-speaking world who has done more than you to end the scourge of child labor."

The question took her aback. She was but one small foot soldier among thousands who had been working toward this cause. "Well, there is Thomas Gilbert, for one. And Henry Mayhew has done extraordinary—"

Daniel interrupted her. "I said name one *woman*. Your gender puts you at a distinct disadvantage, and I don't enjoy watching you pummel yourself into despondency over your perceived inadequacies. You are a woman of extraordinary accomplishment, and I hope you intend to continue your publishing here in America."

How odd, the way Daniel's words seemed to inject a surge of confidence straight into her bloodstream. Whenever she was with him she always felt as if she could dream bigger, see farther. A smile broke across her face. "I hope so," she said. "Learning about the world around me and publishing my work has been the most fulfilling thing I've ever done. I still like to play the piano—I still *love* playing the piano—but I don't compose anymore."

"Is that why you never sent me drafts of the duet we were working on?" Daniel asked.

The phrase hung in the air, and Clara had to process it several times to be sure she heard him correctly, but there was no mistaking the look on his face: curiosity blended with the hint of an old wound. He masked it quickly, but she caught sight of it in the instant before he flicked his gaze away from her. Her jaw tightened, and terrible suspicions began to form in the back of her mind. "I sent you dozens of compositions," she said.

That seemed to surprise him, if the lift of his brows and quickly indrawn breath were any measure. "I never received anything. I waited for months but nothing ever came. Did you get what I sent to you?"

She stood and turned to face him. There was no deception on his face, no trace of teasing or misguided humor. She felt the blood drain from her face as a growing realization of what had happened began to penetrate her stunned senses. "You sent me music?" she asked. "I just assumed you were far too busy with everything to be bothered with music."

"Too busy to be bothered with Chopin?" She could tell he was trying to sound lighthearted, but she heard the anger simmering behind the words. "I sent the music to your aunt Helen's house in London. I sent letters, too. And none of this got to you?"

"None of it," she said weakly. Her father had done this to her. Her father and Aunt Helen had conspired together to pry the most meaningful person in her life away from her. The sense of betrayal was enormous, but even worse was the knowledge that Daniel must have believed she had abandoned him. During the most gut-wrenching few months of his life, she must have appeared to be the most frivolous girl on the planet, darting off to Europe and not even bothering to return the letters he had taken precious time from his day to write to her. There were no words she could say to apologize for what her father had orchestrated.

Daniel braced his elbows on his knee and yanked a blade of grass, rolling it between his fingers. Finally, he let out a harsh laugh. "Well, I'm a prize idiot."

"How do you mean?"

"I noticed the way your father looked at us, toward the end. I certainly was not the kind of man the esteemed Reverend Endicott wanted for his only daughter. Your aunt Helen obviously prevented any letters you sent to me from leaving her house. And she made sure none of mine got to you."

"I can't believe they would have stooped to this," she said. But she knew they had. When she was growing up she thought the sun rose and set with Daniel Tremain's smile, and that was simply too much of a threat for her father to handle. She felt awful as she dragged her gaze to Daniel. "I'm so sorry. My father had no right to cast you out of my life just because you were poor."

The wistful, damaged look on Daniel's face lingered for just an instant; then his mouth twisted into a bitter smile. "Don't be naive. Your father spotted trouble before either one of us knew it was on the horizon." He lowered his voice and leaned forward. "And we *were* trouble, Clara." His voice roughened when he said the words, and the way he gazed at her with that gleam in his eye made her breath freeze in her throat.

When he picked up her hand and pressed a kiss to it, she nearly jumped out of her skin, but Daniel kept a firm grip on her hand. "Big, breathtaking, unrelenting trouble." He touched his lips to her hand again. She shouldn't have let it affect her so, as the gentle kiss was as proper as could be. He could have kissed the queen of England like that and no one would have thought anything of it, but the thrill that raced up her arm from that tiny touch of his lips was splendid.

At last he released her hand, and Clara knew that everything he said was precisely correct. What girl of sixteen had the ability to manage the torrents of infatuation she experienced when Daniel was the center of her universe? Even now she was intensely conscious of the magnetic pull that hummed between them. It was awkward and exhilarating at the same time, so Clara took the safe route and changed the topic.

"So was it any good? The music you sent me?"

Daniel rolled his eyes. "Adolescent dreck. Pure self-indulgent grandiosity. Do you want to come by my house and listen to it?"

"You've still got it?"

"Naturally. I wrote it for you."

"Then I must hear it." She took the seat again beside him on the stone wall. "So tell me about this grand company of yours. I should probably treat you with a little more deference, now that you are some exalted corporate titan."

"Yes, you certainly should," Daniel agreed. But he did tell her about his corporation, and the house he had built for his family on the north side of town, of which he seemed particularly proud.

The years fell away, and once again, they were like two enraptured youths. As Daniel talked, he leaned forward and a lock of his hair tumbled onto his forehead, just as it had when they were kids.

It was so familiar, but now Clara had to clasp her hands together to prevent herself from smoothing the lock of hair back from his forehead. The skin around his eyes had tiny fan lines that deepened when he smiled, and he still had that eager, roguish look when he grinned. Her best friend had returned to her, but he had grown into a man. And for the life of her, Clara did not know if it would be possible to stay friends with Daniel Tremain anymore. How could she maintain an even keel when she was so utterly enthralled by him? Daniel's magnetism had the strength of an incoming tide that grew stronger by the minute, and Clara had little desire to resist it.

All of a sudden, the sun was low in the sky, with shadows lengthening across the lawn. Clara tried to ignore the lateness of the hour, as this had been one of the most magical afternoons of her life and she wanted to cling to every moment. The concert had let out hours ago, and her father was liable to send out men to search for her if she did not return soon.

"It's getting late. . . ." she said finally but hesitantly.

"I'll let you go if you agree to meet me again." The immediacy of Daniel's request made Clara bite back a smile.

"When?"

"Tomorrow."

Clara hesitated. "I can't," she said. "I promised Clyde I would accompany him to Washington, D.C., for a few days. He is meeting with a committee about the Navajo reservation, and I would like the chance to get acquainted with some members of Congress. I can't pass up an opportunity like this."

"I have a copy of *Two Rhapsodies* by Brahms. A new work, opus 79," Daniel said. "It arrived by special delivery last week."

Clara's breath caught in her throat. "You're joking!" She adored Brahms, and judging by the wicked gleam in his eye, Daniel knew his lure was a mighty temptation.

"We can meet at the Music Conservatory for old times' sake," Daniel said. "It has fallen into disrepair, but it's still there."

Clara rose and shook the grass from her skirts, hearing her father's warning voice in her mind. *"You must not let Daniel derail you from your life's goals."* How many times had she heard that refrain when she was growing up? She pursed her lips, angered that her father's words made so much sense at this particular moment. The sting of his betrayal in intercepting her letters to Daniel was still fresh, but on one level her father was correct. Daniel had always had the power to utterly dazzle her, and she had only a few weeks left with Clyde before he returned to Arizona Territory. Daniel was already proving to be a dangerous temptation, and she could not turn her back on Clyde for the sake of hearing a Brahms rhapsody.

"I'll be back in Baltimore in three days' time," she said. She would not let him budge her from her resolve. A good sister would go to Washington with Clyde as she had promised, and not suffer the least bit of temptation from Daniel. She ought to feel guilty for even contemplating it.

"Near the end of the B minor rhapsody, the fingering is so wild and intense, I doubt even your hands could keep up with it."

She glanced over at him and could not help but wonder what

Mr. Brahms had come up with this time. She bit her lip, aching to get her hands on that score. "That complex?"

"Want to give it a try? We can meet up tomorrow."

She elbowed him in the side, then gave a gasp of surprise when he elbowed her back. When she was a teenager, she would have succumbed to temptation, but she would like to pretend she had learned a few things since then. She sent a flirtatious glance over her shoulder as she walked away. "Meet me in three days' time at the old Music Conservatory," she said. "And don't you dare forget that score."

CHAPTER 5

Deep in the Vermont woods, isolated by endless miles of hardwood forests and far away from any road that appeared on a map, a granite mansion was hidden from the eyes of the world. Surrounded by guardhouses, a series of wrought-iron fences, and a cadre of bull mastiff dogs, the mansion was an impregnable fortress. And in a remote room in the northern wing, a young man with the face of an angel studied in an opulent library. With blond hair and cool blue eyes, he looked even younger than his seventeen years.

Alexander Banebridge, or Bane as he was generally known, had been steadily devouring the contents of Professor Van Bracken's library whenever he had the chance. Spread before him were books covering every detail of the Ming Dynasty, including the structure of the government, the trade routes, and the strategy of the army.

Bane had never been to school a day in his life, but he needed knowledge of the world if he was going to wield the kind of power he craved. He had already mastered geography—he could identify the caliphates of Arabia and the provinces of China as easily as the states in his own country. He knew the location of every navigable river in the United States and had a comprehensive understanding of tidal currents. He had mastered economics and political science with similar ease, but Bane needed to learn history if he was to have the same air of refinement that made Professor Van Bracken so successful. Never would Bane allow himself to be seen like the ham-fisted thugs the Professor often used to carry out his operations. Knowledge and cunning were much more effective than brute force.

Bane was in the process of memorizing Chinese military philosophy when the door of the library opened. The matronly figured Letty Garfield entered the room, wiping her hands on an apron and looking at him with expectation.

"Alex?" she asked as she approached him. She was the only person who called him by his first name, as if she refused to reduce herself to the crudeness of the rest of the people living here. "I've just taken a fresh apple pie from the oven. Would you like me to bring you a slice?"

Bane straightened in his chair and feigned a look of disappointment. "Apple? When I heard you were baking, I had so hoped it would be a peach pie."

He studied Mrs. Garfield as her forehead wrinkled in distress. "Oh, heavens . . . if I had known . . ."

"I've been craving peach pie all day. The kind with pecans in the crust."

Mrs. Garfield patted him on the shoulder. "Then you shall have one," she said kindly. "I'll begin at once, so it will only be a couple of hours, and then you shall have your pie, dear boy."

Bane smiled, although it was so easy to manipulate Mrs. Garfield, he really should not take so much pleasure in it. "You're the best, Mrs. Garfield."

Bane watched the door close behind the cook, feeling not the slightest twinge of guilt for manipulating her into making a pie he did not even want. After all, this was the woman who slipped him a steady stream of opium to compel his submission when he was only six years old. Those weeks after he had first been kidnapped were a haze of temper tantrums and opium-laced tea before Bane learned how to survive in this shadowy world. He still remembered the sight of Mrs. Garfield stirring spoonfuls of the sickeningly sweet opium into his tea before she served it to him with a smile.

Two hours later, just after Bane had begun studying the import regulations in Canadian shipping ports, Mrs. Garfield returned with a slice of steaming peach pie. "Here you are, Alex." She set down the plate as well as a glass of milk. "Peach pie, just as you requested. And the Professor asked me to give you this file that arrived in today's mail. He said you would understand its importance."

Tucked beneath Mrs. Garfield's arm had been a fat envelope she now extended to him. "Excellent!" Bane said, with no need to feign enthusiasm this time. For weeks he had been anxiously awaiting this delivery from Baltimore. He pushed the books to the far side of the table and tore open the envelope.

"Is there anything else you need?" Mrs. Garfield asked. When Bane shook his head, she nodded and backed out of the library. "Very good," she said just before leaving. "I'm going to change the linen in the tower room. I'll be up there preparing the room, if you need anything else."

Bane merely nodded, completely engrossed in the pages of information he pulled from the envelope. A grainy photograph of Daniel Tremain accompanied a newspaper article documenting the recent developments in Carr & Tremain Polytechnic. The Professor had a scheme up his sleeve to get the better of Tremain and was trusting Bane to lead the mission. He was young to be taking on this level of responsibility, but the prize the Professor dangled was too tempting for Bane to resist. If Bane could succeed in knocking Tremain out of business, the reward would be huge.

Canada.

The Professor had offered control of the Canadian opium trade to Bane.

At last, Bane could move thousands of miles away from the Professor to oversee their smuggling operations in Canada. Vancouver was as far as Bane could conceivably distance himself from the Professor yet still partake in the criminal empire that had made them all rich. Not that Bane cared much about money. It was power he craved. The ability to control his own destiny had been stripped from him when he was a six-year-old child, and nothing was more tantalizing than being able to take back control of his own life.

For months he had been studying everything there was to know about his future home. It had been a joy to devour every book he could find about Canadian history and culture. On his bedroom wall, he tacked a series of postcards that depicted the burgeoning town of Vancouver, and every night he stared at those pictures as he drifted off to sleep. A newly constructed townhouse overlooking the bay of Barkley Sound was where he would live. It was within walking distance of a library and had easy access to the ports for business purposes. He would still have to answer to the Professor, but with thousands of miles between them, he would have room to breathe for the first time in his life.

But only if he passed the Professor's test. Bane studied the article about Daniel Tremain, and after a few minutes, a slow smile curved his mouth.

It was as he suspected. Daniel Tremain was a brilliant innovator, but he was also reckless and hotheaded. A man ruled by a volatile temper was easy to manipulate. Bane had learned how to suppress those inconvenient emotions and rely on cool, clearheaded logic to control a situation. How interesting it would be to match wits with Daniel Tremain. Bane pushed the article aside and looked at the next page, a short biographical summary of Tremain's life. It said the man obtained his first patent when he was only twenty-one years old and had filed a steady stream of them ever since.

Bane studied the photograph. It was hard not to admire a man who had risen so quickly without the benefit of fancy schools or family connections. Would he really be able to best the man? In a battle of logic versus passion, who would win?

Then, suddenly, a thought that had been niggling at the back of his mind came to the forefront. Why was Mrs. Garfield preparing the tower room? Bane stood so quickly the chair behind him upended onto the floor, the clatter breaking the cold silence of the mansion.

He left the library and vaulted up two flights of stairs until he found her. She was making up the bed when he pushed open the door. "What is going on here?" he asked.

"Why, the Professor is going to have another visitor, I expect," she said as she tucked a sheet beneath the mattress.

Visitor. Hostage was more like it.

"There hasn't been a *visitor* since young Kenny O'Hanlon was here," Bane said calmly.

Shame suffused Mrs. Garfield's face. Her gaze darted around the room and the corners of her mouth turned down, but she reached for another blanket and began laying it atop the mattress. "Such a tragedy," she finally said. "Poor Kenny."

Bane scanned the room. It had everything a young boy could want: toys, drawing supplies, books of all kinds. And outside there was even a pony in the stable. If the next captive was lucky, his father would concede to whatever business arrangements the Professor demanded.

Bane's jaw tightened. There was very little compassion left in his body, but nothing brought it flickering to life faster than the abuse of a child.

"No opium," he said bluntly.

Mrs. Garfield looked up from the sheets. "What was that?"

"Don't feed him any opium. If he proves difficult, come get me and I'll show him how to behave so he won't anger the Professor. There will be no need for drugs." Mrs. Garfield had the decency to look ashamed as she nodded.

Perhaps someday Bane would be clever enough to outwit the Professor and take control over this entire criminal enterprise, but until then there was very little he could do to help the child. Bane knew better than anyone in the world that if the boy was very clever and very patient, it was possible to survive here.

The next victim in the Professor's game could not be Bane's concern. He needed to carry out the Professor's test and knock Tremain out of business. Only then would the Professor trust Bane to head up the Canadian branch of his empire. Only then could Bane put thousands of miles between him and this gothic horror house.

In the meantime, he needed to start planning the optimal way to outwit Daniel Tremain.

CHAPTER 6

At the knock on his front door, Daniel bounded down the curved staircase in the double-story foyer of his home. Manzetti always drove him to his downtown office each morning, but today Daniel had something he needed to discuss before the bustle of the workday.

Morning sun streamed into the house as soon as he flung open the front door. "How much will it cost to buy up all the coke on the East Coast?" Daniel asked in an impatient voice.

Manzetti took the cap from the top of his head and stepped inside. "And good morning to you, too, Daniel."

Daniel tossed the cap impatiently on the front hall table. "Come back to the library. I've got a new plan I need to discuss." Why Manzetti wanted to bother with pleasantries when they had business to strategize was a mystery, although he supposed these little social graces needed to be tended to. In the middle of the night, Daniel had snapped awake, the beginnings of an entirely new tactic in his war against Forsythe waking him from a deep sleep. Coke was a byproduct of coal that was essential to the smelting of iron ore. No steel could be made without a healthy supply of coke, and if Daniel bought all the coke available on the market, it would be months before manufacturers could produce more for Forsythe Industries.

Once inside the study, he crossed to his desk, pulled out his chair, and sat. "I want you to buy up all the coke in the Philadelphia markets and send someone to hit the Chicago mercantile exchange, as well. If Forsythe wants a pound of coke, he is going to have to go begging for it from his competitors."

Manzetti plopped onto a sofa, dragging a ham-sized hand through his dark hair. "You don't even have the money to finish paying for Miss Lorna's house, and now you want to buy up all the excess coke in the country?"

"It's not like it will go to waste. We will use it sooner or later."

The silence was broken only by the ticking of an ormolu clock on the mantelpiece. Manzetti shifted his weight, rubbing his hands along the rough twill of his pants as he mulled over the idea. Manzetti's instincts were good, and Daniel knew there was something about the scheme that didn't sit well with the man.

"Spit it out," Daniel said. "Whatever is bothering you, just say it."

Manzetti straightened. "If we choke off the supply of coke to

Forsythe Industries, his steel mills will go dark for weeks. Maybe even longer."

"Precisely."

Manzetti's brows lowered. "And what about their workers? Forsythe won't pay their wages if they aren't making steel. I haven't forgotten what it feels like to be hungry. Have you?"

The only time Daniel had been hungry in his life was in the weeks following his father's death. Five days after the explosion that killed his father, Daniel learned that the safety valves on the boilers were defective. Forsythe knew about the defective parts, but he was too cheap to replace them. It was only a matter of time before one of them blew, and it was Daniel's father who was tending the boilers when it happened. Alfred Forsythe might as well have pulled the trigger. Daniel quit his job within minutes of discovering what had happened. It was a reckless, impulsive thing to have done, but all Daniel could see was a haze of red as he stormed out of the mill. In the following weeks, Daniel had known the grinding fear of being unable to support his family. He had quietly pawned whatever he could from the home and went without meals so his sisters could eat. A few weeks later he joined forces with Ian Carr, who needed a jack-of-all-trades to keep the equipment of his small railroad company in order, but hunger was not something a man ever forgot.

"I am not unmindful to the trouble this will cause," Daniel said slowly. "But in the long run, it will be better for his workers and this city if Forsythe is driven out of business. Let those mills be owned by someone who operates a safe shop and pays his men a decent wage."

Manzetti rested his elbows on his thighs as he stared at a spot on the carpet near his feet. If anyone on the planet could understand Daniel's slow-burning rage, it was Joe Manzetti. He had been with Daniel on the day of the explosion. He had smelled the scent of burning skin and witnessed Daniel's helplessness as he clutched his father's broken body to his chest. And Manzetti had been beside Daniel for every step as they slogged their way out of poverty and into the cool relief of prosperity.

"You know I would follow you over the side of a cliff," Manzetti finally said. "But I won't do something that will starve Forsythe's workers. You'll have to find another man for the job."

Daniel did not let his astonishment show, but Manzetti's blunt refusal was a rude shock. He locked gazes with Manzetti as he mentally rattled through his options to get Manzetti on board. "I'll find jobs for any Forsythe worker who wants to cross over to Carr & Tremain."

Manzetti rolled his eyes. "There are close to a thousand Forsythe workers in Baltimore alone. You can't afford to hire them all without going under yourself."

That was true. The company had embarked on a number of expansion plans in anticipation of selling shares on the stock exchange. Now that the deal was in jeopardy because of Daniel's intransigence over licensing to Forsythe, they would have to fund the acquisition of railroad lines from their own coffers.

"Buying up all the coke will probably only slow Forsythe for a week or two," Daniel said. "Three at the most. No one will starve."

Manzetti's voice was calm but emphatic. "You'll have to find another man, Daniel."

The breath left Daniel's lungs in a rush. Manzetti was the closest thing to a friend he had. Well, Clara seemed to have waltzed back into his life, but it was Manzetti who was with him through those gritty, hard-bitten years as he fought for every patent, opened each new office. In the past, Manzetti had always supported Daniel's crusade against Forsythe, but apparently there were limits as to how low Manzetti would stoop.

Not Daniel. He knew Forsythe would not go down without a fight and Daniel was prepared to lead the campaign down to the bitter end. "You know I can easily find someone else who will do my bidding."

"Probably. You can fire me if you want, but I need to be able to sleep at night."

Daniel made an impatient gesture with his hand. He would no more fire Manzetti than he would hack off his own right arm. Besides, he had another task he needed help with. Clara would be returning to Baltimore tomorrow, and he needed to find those old pieces of music he had written for her. He shoved talk of business to the back of his mind and rose to his feet.

"Come up to the attic with me. I've got some musical scores that are buried beneath some of the old equipment, and I'll need your help getting them out."

Clara's sudden return to Baltimore could not have come at a worse time. He had just destroyed Forsythe's attempt to build a college, and if he succeeded in causing a blackout in Forsythe's steel mills, it would arouse another round of bad publicity. Not that he was ashamed of his actions, but he did not want Clara to be a witness to them. She was everything that was pure and unsullied in his life, a shining memory he wanted to protect from the ugliness in his soul.

Despite the early hour, the summer heat was palpable in the attic as he stepped into its dusty confines. The attic of his house had become the official graveyard of his company, where Daniel stored old versions of his original timing devices, routing equipment, even a couple of old railway ties. In the dim light eking through the dormer windows, the hulking silhouettes of his inventions loomed like ghostly sentinels of his past.

"Remind me what we are looking for?" Manzetti asked as his footsteps thudded on the bare plank floors of the attic.

"A couple of musical scores I want to give to Clara Endicott. I think they are in a filing cabinet underneath that old lever frame box."

"Is this the Clara Endicott you used to moan about when you were in your cups?"

Daniel had forgotten he used to do that, but Manzetti was right. In the early days, cheap beer at O'Reilly's Tavern was the only recreation he, Manzetti, and his partner Ian Carr could afford, and Daniel inevitably started rambling about Clara after he had a few.

"This is the Clara Endicott who worked for *The Times of London*," he said brusquely. He reached beneath the framing of the lever box and waited for Manzetti to join him on the other side. The box weighed around two hundred pounds, and hoisting it off the cabinet was a good excuse to drop the topic of Clara Endicott. In the years since she had left, he had been able to keep his emotions about her safely stored away as neatly as the scores in this cabinet. Now she was here stirring everything up again.

With a mighty heave, he and Manzetti lifted the lever box off the filing cabinet and set it down with a thud. Relieved of the pressure, the drawers of the cabinet slid open with a rasping creak. As Daniel lifted the pages out, the distinctive scent of musical score paper brought back a rush of memories. It had been ten years since he had held these scores. Ten years since he had given up on Clara and packed these compositions into storage. If Manzetti weren't standing three feet away, he would have pressed the pages to his face and breathed deeply of the scent of wood pulp and old memories.

Manzetti wiped the sweat from his brow. "She must be some reporter, to have put that look of pure, stupid joy on your face."

Whatever expression had been on his face, Daniel shook it off and closed the filing drawers. Clara was not someone he wanted to talk about. These raw, unwieldy emotions were too volatile for him to discuss in a cogent manner.

"Let's get to work," he said as he tromped out of the attic. "We need to do a new round of tests on the heating element for the smelting process." He continued to pour out instructions for the day, but only half his mind could concentrate on them, because in his hands he held a stack of musical scores that once meant more to him than all the inventions in the world.

Standing next to Daniel, Clara's heart sagged when she saw the old Conservatory again. She needed to lift the skirt of her delicately embroidered eyelet walking dress well over her ankles in order to step over the tall weeds and around the broken roof tiles that littered the ground where they had slid from the top of the Conservatory. Paint curled away from the walls like scrolls of old parchment, and a gutter hung at a haphazard angle, just waiting for a good stiff wind to blow it off.

It was going to be impossible to play music today, as the instruments from the Conservatory were long gone and the building was in such bad shape it wasn't even safe to go inside. Daniel proceeded to tell her the city was on the verge of condemning it as a public nuisance, but he did not seem upset.

"I've found the old scores, and you can come to my house, where we will play them. Don't look so tragic."

Clara shot Daniel an amused glance as she pulled a vine of English ivy from an old stone bench. She used a handkerchief in a futile attempt to swipe away the husk of an old beetle from the bench.

Daniel spared her from further misery when he brushed the rest of the debris from the bench and tossed his jacket over it so she could sit without getting moss stains on her pale yellow dress. It was a shame she would not be able to play music with Daniel this afternoon, but that wasn't so bad. The scent of the wild mulberry shrubs that were growing rampant along the crumbling stone walls was enchanting, and she loved just being in the shadow of this beloved old building once again. Her gaze tracked along the gabled roof and the gothic arches of the windows, most of which were now broken and boarded over. It was silly, but Clara felt that if she stayed here long enough, she would be able to hear the echoes of the music and laughter that had once filled this building.

Still staring at the old gothic arches, she could not resist asking the question, "Did it mean as much to you as it did to me?"

A little wind rustled the mulberry leaves, and the drone of a dragonfly came from far away. Now that Daniel had gone on to become a great success, perhaps those stolen hours were only a trivial part of his youth, and she held her breath while she waited for his answer.

"Back then we were too young to know that some dreams are impossible," he said with a note of aching wistfulness in his voice. "So we dreamed them anyway, and it made those years feel glorious. It was probably the finest time in my life."

She caught her breath. It was true that neither one of them had gone on to become the next Chopin, but did that mean their dreams were for nothing? "But, Daniel, you *did* go on to greatness. More so than anyone could have imagined!"

"That wasn't the sort of thing I was dreaming about." He glanced back toward the Conservatory, and she knew he was remembering the music they had played, how they both allowed it to carry them away to a world of staggering beauty. Even after all these years, it was impossible for her to hear the swelling of a Beethoven symphony or the quiet grace of a Chopin prelude without remembering how it had touched her in her youth. The memories caused a surge of longing so intense Clara did not trust herself to delve any further. It was easier to take the safe route and change the subject.

"So have you read *Twenty Thousand Leagues Under the Sea* yet?" she asked, which provoked an entire discussion about Jules Verne's thoughts on space travel and undersea exploration. Clara thought space travel was pure nonsense, but Daniel was not so sure. They loitered for hours in the grassy lawn outside the old Music Conservatory while they debated Jules Verne, the absurdity of cricket versus baseball, and the artistic merit of impressionistic painting. Shadows were lengthening in the late afternoon sun when a man on horseback came galloping down the road toward them. The man tossed the reins over a fence, leapt over the stone wall, and headed directly toward them.

Daniel rose to his feet. "That looks like my assistant, Manzetti."

The man called Manzetti was winded when he reached them. He dragged a handkerchief across his grimy forehead and replaced his cap. "It's Miss Kate," he said breathlessly. "She never returned from the cycling competition this afternoon. The contest was over by noon."

Daniel consulted his pocket watch. "It's four o'clock. Did you check with any others who competed in the race? Perhaps they went out for a celebration. She's liable to run off without telling us these things." Clara could see the annoyance on Daniel's face, but it was mingled with concern.

"Everyone left after the race was over. There is trouble with strikers brewing down at the docks—"

"I know. I told her to stay away from that end."

Manzetti shook his head. "It has spread. The streets are blocked all the way to the Camden Yards and workers are rioting. All the freight and passenger traffic has been blocked off. No one is getting in or out of there—I've already tried."

Daniel's face went white and a sheen of perspiration broke out on his skin. "I've got to get her out of there," he snapped. "I don't care what it takes. I want Kate out of there."

Clara was well acquainted with the rioting that often accompanied labor unrest, having covered plenty of labor protests while working in London. Riots always frightened her to bits, but she had never been harmed in one. "She'll be okay," Clara said. "These things look like a lot of chaos to outsiders, but it is controlled chaos. Workers have no interest in assaulting well-bred young ladies." She knew that from experience.

"Doesn't matter," Daniel bit out. "I want Kate out of there."

"I told you, the roads are all blocked off. . . ." Manzetti said.

"What about cutting through buildings to get around the barricades?" Clara suggested. The buildings in the commercial district of London where rioting occurred had large footprints, often taking up an entire city block. It was almost always possible to enter a building through one door and weave through the building to leave on the opposite side, skirting a barricade entirely. "I did it plenty of times when I covered labor stories in London," Clara said. "I know the buildings down by the Camden Yards are large enough to do the same thing. I'll show you how."

"Manzetti, we're taking your horse," Daniel said. He vaulted onto the horse and held a hand down to Clara.

Clara gulped. There were plenty of things on this planet that she feared, but horses were near the top of the list.

"Don't tell me you are still afraid of horses," Daniel said.

It didn't help that this horse was particularly big, and she instinctively flinched away from the thirteen hundred pounds of sweaty, twitching horseflesh that was looming before her. "I think 'cowering terror' would be a more accurate description," she said as the horse shifted and stamped.

Daniel refused to let her succumb. "Come on, Clara. You'll be safe with me." She swallowed hard and looked up into his stern, confident face. Just a few inches away his hand was waiting for her, and Clara intuitively trusted him. She placed her hand inside his, set her slippered foot on top of his boot, and closed her eyes as he hauled her up behind him. A moment later she was riding behind Daniel, her arms wrapped around his waist and clinging for dear life as the horse cantered down the street.

***

They left the horse tied up in a stable just outside of Wilshire Park. As Clara suspected, the buildings in this part of town were large and could be used to circumvent the barricades. It was Saturday and most buildings were closed, but she suspected that would not cause Daniel much difficulty. The cigar factory looked like their best bet for skirting the barricade that blocked McNeill Street.

Daniel used his pocketknife to work a bolt open but had more difficulty on the door lock. "Hand over your hairpins," he said. Clara removed the pins that anchored the heavy coil of hair to the crown of her head. Daniel didn't even glance at her as he took the pins. He twisted the wires straight, then angled them into the lock, a look of fierce concentration on his face. With the care of a surgeon he twirled and lifted the two pins until at last Clara heard the lock slide open.

"We're in," Daniel said triumphantly. The pungent odor of tobacco filled the darkened interior. After navigating a maze of hallways and storage rooms, they made their way into a huge interior room where the cigar rolling took place. Daniel pulled her along as they raced to the far side and found an exit on the south end, where getting out of the building proved much easier than entering.

Immediately upon leaving the building she could see the chaos in the street was worse than she had expected. The stench of burning oil assaulted her nose, and Clara saw a wagon had been overturned and soaked with petroleum. It was now burning uncontrollably as bystanders backed away from the scorching heat. Broken windows and overturned street signs littered the roadway. A few brave policemen mounted on horseback picked their way along the street, dodging flying rocks and keeping the worst of the rioters at bay.

"The sporting club is on the south end of this street," Daniel said. "If Katie has any sense, she'll be holed up inside."

Daniel put his arm around Clara's shoulders as they hustled down the street, the sound of glass crunching beneath each of her steps. A group of men were prying cobblestones up from the street, piling them up for use as missiles against the descending police force. As she and Daniel approached the entrance of the post office there was a knot of rioters trying to shove through a chain-link barricade guarding the post office doors.

"Why are they rioting in front of the post office?" Clara asked.

"The postal union refuses to support the steel workers. It's payback," Daniel said. She flinched at the sound of a rifle blast, and Daniel tugged her back. "Let's take the alley behind us. Too dangerous here."

Clara didn't argue with him. The random yelling from the crowd was turning into organized chanting, a sign that momentum was taking hold among the crowd. It was quieter along the back alley, which was mostly deserted except for anxious travelers trying to find their way home. They made quick progress toward the Colchester Sporting Club, where Clara prayed they would find Katie.

The club was nestled beside a public park, which was entirely engulfed by mob action. On closer inspection, Clara noticed they were mostly young boys, throwing rocks and clumps of mud. Not hardened strikers.

"Let's dash through as quickly as possible," Daniel said. "We'll take shelter in the club."

Clara was breathless by the time they reached the small brick building. "That's Katie's bicycle," Daniel said with relief. The bike lay in the dirt at the front of the building. He banged on the front door, but was not surprised when no one answered. He dug out his pocketknife and Clara's hairpins, making quick work of the lock.

"Katie?" Daniel's voice roared as soon as they were inside. "Katie Tremain? Get down here so I can tan your backside!" Daniel stalked through the first floor, flinging open doors and checking closets. The front hall was empty, and there was no sign of anyone in the back rooms.

"Daniel? Is it really you?" A thin voice came from upstairs, followed by Katie herself as she peeked around the corner. Clara saw a perfectly lovely young woman with Daniel's dark hair and a slim, athletic build. Daniel said nothing; he just opened his arms wide and Katie came flying down the staircase straight into them. His arms had barely closed around her before she burst into tears.

"I knew you would come," she sobbed. "I knew it, I knew it." Clara was surprised she could even understand Kate through all the tears.

Daniel clutched his little sister in an enormous bear hug. "Don't you ever scare me like that again, Kate," he said. Did she imagine it, or was there a tremor in Daniel's voice?

"I didn't know what to do," Kate said. "The other bicyclists had all gone home, but I had a flat tire. I was trying to fix it when I heard the shouting. I'm so sorry, Daniel. I didn't know what to do, but I knew you would come."

Daniel said nothing, merely kept her clenched in that tight embrace while he rocked her from side to side. At last he raised his eyes. "Clara, this is my baby sister, Katie."

Kate peeled herself away from Daniel's chest. "Hello, Clara," she said through a ragged voice. "I've heard an awful lot about you over the years."

"You have?" Clara had thought about Daniel throughout her time in London, but had always assumed he had long since forgotten about her. She never dreamed his sisters would know the first thing about her.

"Oh, heavens, yes." Kate swiped at the tears in her eyes with the back of her hand and managed a watery smile. "Whenever we neglected our studies, Daniel was quick to point out how we should work hard so we could become successful like his old friend Clara." Daniel pressed a handkerchief into Kate's hand and she wiped her eyes. "It didn't matter if it was music or languages or writing," she continued, "you were always the model he wanted us to aspire to."

Surely Kate must be pulling her leg, but when she looked at Daniel she saw the flush on his face and knew Kate spoke the truth. As a woman who had always been in the shadow of her family, never had she been paid so high a compliment.

"I hope I didn't prove too much of a burden for you. My father waved Joan of Arc in my face as a role model—which was always a bit overwhelming."

Daniel looked about the vacant rooms of the sporting club. "We may be here awhile," he said. "And I don't like the look of all these windows."

"There aren't many windows in the kitchen," Katie said. "That's where I had been hiding, but I ran upstairs when I heard someone trying to break in."

Once they were settled in the kitchen, Clara saw a bowl of fruit, and a ferocious sense of hunger came over her. It was past dinnertime and she had eaten nothing since breakfast. Suddenly she was convinced if she didn't eat, her stomach would begin to consume itself. She glanced at Daniel as she felt a guilty flush heat her cheeks. "Do you think it would be all right?"

"Of course it would be all right," he said. "I'll leave a few coins on the table if you feel guilty."

It was all the permission she needed. Clara ripped the peel off an orange and devoured a section as soon as she had it liberated from the peel. Daniel did likewise. How curiously familiar it felt, to be sitting on the floor of a kitchen while they tore through a quick meal. Clara's life had always been filled with the utmost propriety, except where Daniel Tremain had been concerned. With him she had always been free to be exactly herself.

As soon as their hunger was satisfied, Daniel turned to Kate. "Now I'd like to hear how you found yourself in this mess, and what you plan to do to make sure it never happens again."

It was a reasonable question, and Clara thought Kate ought to have noticed the serious tone that lay just beneath the surface of Daniel's calmly worded question.

"It wasn't my fault," Kate proclaimed. "As though I have any control over a riot. Truly, you have more influence over rioters than me."

Daniel raised his eyebrows. "And what is your reasoning for that comment?"

"Well, you're one of the robber barons everyone is complaining about. If people like you paid their workers better, we wouldn't have this sort of thing."

Daniel fixed Kate with a stare that would have made lesser mortals wither, but with the overconfidence that came with extreme youth, Kate held her ground. "I'd complain, too, if I had to live on the wages the railroad pays. Little better than dirt, so what other recourse do they have?"

"And here I had been bragging to Clara about what a bright

young lady you have grown up to become," Daniel said. "My apologies, Clara. I was premature in my assessment."

Kate straightened, bristled, and her gray-eyed gaze locked with Daniel's dark glower. The air practically crackled with electricity. Finally, Kate backed down. "Just because you are smart doesn't mean you are *wise*, Daniel!" The exasperation in her tone made Clara certain this was a common phrase Kate rolled out when attempting to compete with her older brother's unquestionable dominance. Kate flounced into the corner of the kitchen and wadded her jacket into a makeshift pillow. "I'm exhausted and am not going to listen to your lectures, Daniel. I'm getting some sleep," she said as she turned her back to them.

❧

Darkness had fallen, but the rioters had not dispersed. Bonfires flickered in the park as young hoodlums lit piles of garbage on fire and threw eggs against the sides of buildings. Her father would be out of his mind with worry, but there was nothing Clara could do to assuage his fears. It would be far more dangerous to venture out into the street, where fires set by the rioters were now consuming at least two buildings she could spot from the upper window of the sporting club. Manzetti had been instructed to tell Reverend Endicott about her plans, so surely he knew that Daniel would look out for her. The three of them would be here until morning, and Kate had already fallen asleep, leaning against the corner of the kitchen wall.

The temperature dropped as the moon rose, and Clara wrapped

her arms a little tighter around her body. The moment he noticed Clara's movement, Daniel shrugged out of his jacket and dropped it around her shoulders. "You should have told me you were chilly."

The silk-lined wool coat still carried Daniel's scent, and Clara sank into the luxurious warmth. She wasn't so cold that she needed his coat, but the gesture carried a whiff of gallantry that was oddly touching. The weight and quality of the coat's fabric were a tangible sign of Daniel's success, and she smiled a little as she turned her head toward him.

"Is there any truth to what Kate says?"

Daniel and Clara were sitting on the floor of the darkened kitchen, legs stretched out before them, eating a bowl of cherries. Clara whispered the question so as not to awaken the sleeping Kate.

"That I'm a robber baron who doesn't pay my workers a fair wage? Not much."

"What part of it is true?"

Daniel sighed. "Ian Carr and I are both self-made men, and most of every dollar we earn gets plowed directly back into the company to fund our expansion. We don't live like Vanderbilt or Carnegie. We don't have gold fixtures in our bathrooms or summer homes in the country. And I don't have a lot of money to splash around on employees. I pay a fair wage."

"You needn't be so defensive. I'm not attacking you."

"It felt like it." At her pointed look, he continued. "I have read your articles, Clara. I have a subscription to *The Times*, and I've read everything you ever wrote. I know what side you are likely to come down on here."

She gestured to the door leading to the street. "You think I approve of that? Rioting in the street and destroying the work of small business owners?"

"Do you?"

"Of course not." Although he was right that she generally sided with the workers over the owners. She nibbled on a cherry while choosing her next words very carefully. "I've heard things about you, though. That you won't do business with Alfred Forsythe or any of his companies."

"That's right."

"Doesn't that hurt your own business? Wouldn't your profit margins soar if you stopped locking yourself out of thirty percent of the railroad market?"

Daniel pushed himself away from the wall and leaned closer to her. "Unlike some businessmen, there are things I care more about than money."

"And hurting your own workers is one of those things you care about?"

He looked as though she had blindsided him. "What's that supposed to mean?" he snapped.

"I mean that if you licensed your inventions to Forsythe Industries, the revenue you earn will be pure profit. With that much extra income, you could afford to pay your workers a better wage." She was on very thin ice. Never had she seen a look of such antipathy simmering on Daniel's face directed at her, and she shrank back a few inches.

"If my employees don't like their wages, they are free to go work for someone else," he said in a low voice vibrating with anger. "I want revenge, Clara. My mother committed *suicide,* did you know that? Lorna found her hanging in the kitchen and came running to me at the station, sobbing her eyes out. Katie was there and saw everything when I cut my mother down. Do you think I'm going to forget that?"

Clara felt herself blanch at the horrible image. It hurt to look Daniel in the face, and when she did she saw his mouth twisted with bitterness, the expression in his eyes making him unrecognizable. It was the face of vengeance, and it was heartbreaking to see a man as fine as Daniel succumbing to it.

"You've held on to this anger for twelve years," she said gently. "If you wish to nurture this rage in private, it hurts no one but yourself. But the kind of vengeance you are carrying out causes innocent people to suffer. Proverbs says that you should not repay evil, but wait for the Lord, and He will deliver you."

The look he sent her was withering. "Do *not* quote Scripture to me about this."

The words sliced through her, but he was entitled to his resentment. She couldn't begin to imagine what he had endured in those first few years after the accident.

"I'm sorry, Daniel. It isn't for me to judge you, and I shouldn't have tried."

And just like that, the ice thawed in Daniel's eyes and a sad smile appeared. He sighed and met her eyes. "Do you know what I'm sorry about?"

"What?"

"I'm sorry that the first evening we've spent together in over a decade has us stuck on the floor of a horrible old building with me snapping at you."

The apology was unexpected and it made her want to leap into his arms, stroke the dark hair that curled on his forehead, and assure him that she'd forgive him anything. Instead she held up the bowl of fruit resting in her lap. "At least the cherries are good."

Daniel snagged one. "I promise to do better next time. Give me another chance?"

She smiled. "As if you even need to ask."

Chapter 7

Lloyd Endicott was sitting at his desk, penning his sermon for next Sunday, when Clara confronted him. Each step weighed more heavily as she approached, knowing that this would be one of the most painful conversations she would ever have with her father. He looked up when he heard her, welcome twinkling in his blue eyes. How many times over the years had she come to him at this very spot, to be greeted by those welcoming eyes? Clara's mother had died when she was only ten years old, and from that day forward, Lloyd Endicott had made sure Clara had everything she could possibly want. No matter how weary he was, her father had always been willing to set aside his labors and make time for her.

She pulled a Windsor chair close to his desk. Her legs felt a little weak as she sank into the chair and set the stack of musical scores on the corner of his desk.

"What are these?" he asked as he laid a hand over the stack of compositions. "Music you've written after all this time?" The hopeful tone in his voice was unmistakable.

"No," Clara said softly. "These are copies of something I wrote years ago. I sent the originals to Daniel Tremain, but he says he never received them. And I can think of only one reason for Aunt Helen to have intercepted our mail."

Her father's gaze dropped to the floor. "I see," he said in a voice that sounded as though he had aged ten years in the space of a few seconds. Whatever tiny glimmer of hope Clara had harbored that her father was not responsible for what had happened was extinguished.

"But I *don't* see," Clara said. "Daniel was the only friend I had in the world. Did you have to cut him out of my life so completely?"

"Clara, you were beginning to feel far more than mere friendship toward Daniel."

It was pointless for her to deny that, but it did not mitigate the sense of betrayal. "Didn't you think the space of an ocean was enough to ensure I would be safe from whatever adolescent foolishness I might have been tempted to commit?"

Her father still would not look at her; instead he stared at the musical scores resting on the corner of his desk, the yellowed paper beginning to curl with age. He placed the palm of his hand over the delicate pages, his fingers barely touching them. "It was more than a mere adolescent crush I was concerned about," he said.

"Clara, I believed you were destined to become a person of great influence. At the time, I thought that music would be your avenue for changing the world. Daniel was an adolescent distraction who interfered with that."

Clara was astonished, but her father continued. "I remember the transformation you went through during those years. You were a bright, curious girl who morphed into someone whose every sentence began with 'Daniel says' or 'Daniel thinks.' It was far more important for me to know what *you* said or what *you* thought."

"And you believed that sending me thousands of miles away was the best way to learn what I said or thought?"

"It was certainly the best way to make sure you would continue on your rightful path without becoming diverted by a young man who did not belong in your orbit."

Clara hadn't been sure how her father would react, but the last thing she expected was for him to defend his actions. This man was not a father; he was a drillmaster seeking to sculpt her into a magnificent creation that would further illuminate the Endicott name. She picked up the scores and clutched them to her chest.

"Can't you at least say you are sorry?" she asked in a broken voice.

Her father's eyes crinkled in sympathy. "No, Clara. I am not sorry I saved you from certain derailment."

Clara felt a lump swell in her throat. She could never accuse her father of not loving her. From the moment she had been born he had showered her with affection and opportunities, but the price he asked of her was so odd. It wasn't love he wanted in return; it was accomplishment.

Clara rose to her feet. "I'm all grown up now, Papa. I think I understand my calling in life and I've been working toward it as though my soul depends on it." The gleam that lit her father's eyes at those words was maddening. Would she ever be anything to him other than another fabulous ornament on the Endicott family tree? "But if I should ever go astray again, can I expect you to be meddling behind my back? I need to know if I can ever trust you again."

"Clara, you can always trust me to act in your best interest."

Clara scrutinized her father, but there was no guilt, no embarrassment for what he had done. Even the tiniest bit of regret would have helped smooth the ragged edges of her wound. Clara's gaze wandered around the spacious study, the comforting sanctuary where she had spent so much of her childhood. She had simply assumed she would go on living here, but her sense of betrayal was too intense to allow her to continue living under the same roof.

"Father, I think I'd better start looking for a different place to stay."

"Clara! You can't. . . . You are an unmarried woman. It would be unheard of!"

As though bucking trends was ever something that had discouraged her father in the past. She had some money in her bank account from her work in London, which gave her the freedom to live independently, at least for a little while. "Clyde will help me find a place."

Her father pushed away from his desk. "This is utter nonsense.

All this business happened twelve years ago, and you can't waltz out of here over something that was done with your best interest at heart."

Clara met her father's gaze squarely. "Watch me."

◆◆◆

Walking down a city street in Baltimore's middle-class shopping district beside her brother Clyde was an experience of epic proportions. The rather pretty young man Clyde had once been was gone, replaced by a grown man who wore buckskins and carried a knife strapped to his leg. His skin had become bronzed beneath the relentless sun of the Southwest, and he wore his light brown hair in a braid. The respectable matrons at her father's church had nearly fainted when Clyde first swaggered into the chapel. Despite his startling appearance, Clara could not be prouder of her brother. He had spent more than a decade living in some of the wildest corners of the world.

Now Clara was trying to convince the landladies and rental agents that she and her brother were a perfectly respectable pair seeking temporary lodging. Their names were well known among Baltimore society, but until someone saw Dr. Clyde Endicott in person, Clara could never be quite sure how he would be received.

"What about this one," Clyde said as he gestured to a row house sitting well back from the busy city street. They had spent the better part of two days searching for furnished lodgings that could accommodate the two of them for the duration of Clyde's visit. "It has the best location of any of the rentals we have seen all day," he said.

But it was tiny inside. "It doesn't have any room for a study," Clara said. Clara needed a full-sized table when she wrote, and a study was especially important now that she had learned Clyde was writing a book about his life on a Navajo reservation.

Clyde shrugged. "It has two bedrooms, which is all I care about. I'm planning on using Lloyd's library for my research. I suggest you do the same." Clyde had always enjoyed the affectation of calling their father by his first name, and Clara's current frosty relationship with her father made her inclined to do the same.

"I think running back home every day to use his library would rather defeat the purpose of my moving out, don't you?"

"And tell me, sister dearest, where exactly are you planning on getting access to research materials? This isn't London, with a plethora of magnificent libraries on every corner. You are not likely to find a better library in Baltimore than Lloyd's. Besides, aren't you still planning to publish your writing in his newspaper?"

"Of course." Clara was too pragmatic to cut off her nose to spite her face. Lloyd Endicott was one of the few editors in the entire country who would publish the writings of a female journalist, so she had few options if she wished to salvage her battered pride and begin writing again.

"Then consider making use of Lloyd's library a professional obligation. Besides, not having to worry about study space would let us rent this townhouse until you are over your snit. I like the view here."

Clara had to admit that the covered front porch provided an excellent vantage point from which to watch the bustle surrounding the local shopping markets. But her favorite feature of this row house was in the backyard—an actual garden. It had been long neglected, but Clara relished the chance to sink her hands into the soil and try to coax some life into the overgrown vines and shrubbery.

"All right, you win," Clara said. "Of all people, you ought to be entitled to bask in the luxury of Father's house for a few weeks, so I am in your debt for chaperoning me."

Clyde merely shrugged his shoulders. "Consider it a small token of penance for all the years of torture I inflicted on you growing up. Not that I intend to let you run amok with the robber baron. Daniel Tremain has always been a little arrogant for my taste."

Clara let her gaze wander across to Clyde lounging on the front porch with a knife longer than her forearm strapped to his leg. "Oh, Clyde, coming from you, charging someone with the sin of arrogance is just rich," she said with a smile. "Besides, you need not worry about Daniel, as I intend to look into this rivalry between him and Alfred Forsythe for my next article. I don't think he'll thank me for the attention, but it is an important issue, especially if it has been fueling some of the discontent among the working class."

Even as she spoke, Clara felt uneasy. Daniel had never been shy about flaunting his hatred of Alfred Forsythe, but that didn't mean he would relish Clara's involvement. Every instinct in Clara's body was screaming that this was a story that needed to be told, but she knew Daniel would resent any attempt on her part to foster a reconciliation between him and Forsythe. Daniel's reputation for stoking the fires of enmity among his business rivals was well known. She could only hope it would not fan out to burn her, as well.

CHAPTER 8

The offices of Alfred Forsythe Industries were nothing short of decadent. The walls were adorned with red velvet wallpaper and densely covered with artwork from the Renaissance masters mounted in gold-leaf frames. When Clara's eyes continued to travel up, she saw gilded crown moldings and a painted ceiling filled with cherubs dropping flower petals from a cerulean blue sky.

The railroad magnate had agreed to meet with her to discuss the simmering tensions within the labor unions. At least, that was what she had told this man of business. What she really needed was to get a sense of who Alfred Forsythe was, and if there was any prayer of brokering a truce between him and Daniel Tremain.

Alfred Forsythe had been a Union general during the Civil War, and he still had the ramrod-straight bearing of a man accustomed to being in command, but his eyes were kind as he welcomed her into his office. His face was creased with the lines of age, and he sported an immaculately trimmed Van Dyke beard.

He offered her tea and a chair at the small table in his stately office. "I appreciate your willingness to speak directly to me about your concerns," he began as they settled at the table. "I fear that it is easy to believe the worst of us capitalists, because we simply don't command as much attention as stories of burning barricades and families starving for want of decent wages."

"Do you believe there is any truth to such stories?" Clara asked.

To her astonishment, he did. "Hunger is a scourge on our society and the shame of our generation. With the productivity of American industry there is no cause for any child to go hungry in this country. But rioting and sabotage will hardly result in more jobs. These actions taken by the labor unions result only in greater tension, not progress toward a more just society."

The ease with which Mr. Forsythe delivered these lines made Clara suspicious. Forsythe was planning to run for the governor's office next term, and filling a journalist's ears with such careful wordplay was to be expected from a man on the verge of a political career. They spoke for almost an hour before Clara began steering the interview in her ultimate direction.

"And what about tension among the leading capitalists? Does the competition play any role in the wages paid to workers?"

Mr. Forsythe straightened in his chair. "I presume you are alluding to Daniel Tremain?"

"Yes."

He paused as he chose his words. "Mr. Tremain is to be admired for the manner in which he rose from the working classes into a man of considerable means. I gather he had a difficult life as a youngster, and still carries some scars from that."

No journalist worth her salt would settle for such a glib response. "I am acquainted with Daniel Tremain, and I think we both know his grievances relate to a very specific incident."

"So I have been informed."

"Would you care to comment on the incident?"

Mr. Forsythe leaned forward. "How well acquainted are you with Mr. Tremain and his history?"

There was no point in denying anything. "Daniel Tremain has been a close friend of my family for many years. But I've only heard his side of the story. I'd like to hear yours."

"I see." Forsythe rose to his feet and walked to the window overlooking the commerce square. "I have over seven thousand people who work in my company, ranging from Wall Street lawyers down to boys who shovel coal in the foundries. Producing steel and laying track is a tough, dirty job, and my workers are well compensated for that. But it's a dangerous job, too. People get hurt, and sometimes people die."

He turned to look her in the face. "I have six steel mills, and each one of those mills is filled with boilers and forges and furnaces. And each piece of equipment has hundreds of mechanical parts. I hire people to keep the equipment in good working order. Miss Endicott, I can't be held responsible if a valve is incorrectly installed on one of those machines."

"Mr. Tremain believes the safety valves were defective. That this was known before the accident, but the policy was not to replace defective parts unless they failed."

"An investigation at the time of the accident exonerated my company from wrongdoing. The accident happened twelve years ago. There isn't a prayer of gathering better information at this point."

Mr. Forsythe pulled a chair close to her and sat down, losing a little of the starch that kept him so meticulously formal. "Miss Endicott, if there is any insight you can provide to help me bring this vendetta to an end, I'd be grateful to hear it. That accident has cost both of our companies and has served no purpose. What is it that this man *wants*?" Forsythe's voice was tense with frustration as he looked to her in appeal.

"I think he wants an apology."

The steel returned to Mr. Forsythe's spine. "That is not going to happen."

"It is your best shot at bringing this feud to an end."

"I haven't done anything wrong," he ground out. "I refuse to apologize for something that happened more than a decade ago, on a piece of equipment I never touched. I refuse." His voice cracked like a whip and Clara almost flinched at the ferocity. It was spoken with the same intransigent tone that Daniel had used when he referred to Forsythe, and Clara knew there was very little hope for a compromise.

Daniel's house was a sleek and modern structure, with a portico stretching the length of the front facade. Inside were dark slate floors and ivory paneling. Light streamed in through the oversized windows that graced each of the rooms, which were comfortably furnished in masculine leather furniture.

Daniel seemed oddly hesitant as he showed Clara through the rooms, all of which smelled of lemon polish and were entirely devoid of the bric-a-brac that decorated most houses of the elite. He watched her as she strolled through the rooms, noting where her gaze landed and what objects snagged her attention. That he was immensely proud of his home was apparent, but he also seemed determined to seek her approval as she toured the house. "This is what I bought with the royalties from my last patent," he said as he gestured to the painting above the fireplace in the parlor.

It was an awe-inspiring image, filled with vivid splashes of amber and saffron exploding across the canvas. Clara stared at it for several moments. "Is it . . . is it a sunset?" she asked.

Daniel studied the painting. "I think so. Sometimes I think it looks like a fire burst. Or perhaps the inside of a flower. It can be whatever you want it to be."

Clara had never seen a painting in which the artist made no attempt to be realistic, but the radiance of the work was powerful and oddly mesmerizing. "It seems so surreal," Clara said. "The colors are lovely, but I'm not quite sure what to think of it."

"It's modern," Daniel said. "I like things that are new and forward-looking."

"I can see that," Clara said as she looked about his house. If

Daniel wanted to escape memories of his crumbling old tenement house, he accomplished it in this home.

"And this is my favorite room," he said as he guided her into a library that was lined with books from floor to ceiling. It was a two-story room, with a wraparound balcony spanning the interior of the library. A splendid skylight crowned the room and provided a view straight up into the clouds. The library doubled as a music room, and of course it had a grand piano in one corner. A cello was propped against the wall, and stacks of musical scores surrounded a brass music stand. A massive library table dominated the center of the room, on which sat an odd assortment of equipment, mechanical instruments, and drafting tools.

Daniel strolled to the chair beside the piano and pulled his cello into place. "Are you ready to hear the great masterpiece I penned on your behalf?"

She took a seat on the piano bench. "I've been waiting for years."

"I warn you . . . I was in the throes of adolescent torment when I wrote this. I'm sure it still shows." And yet, when Daniel pulled the bow across the strings, releasing the low, mournful tune of the cello, the lovely notes were infinitely soothing to Clara. She closed her eyes and remembered the fleeting twilight hours of her youth when Daniel used to play for her in the Music Conservatory. Time slipped away as she let the tones wash over her.

The music tapered to an end, and she waited for her heart to stop pounding before she opened her eyes and looked at Daniel. There were no words; all she could do was smile.

"When I never heard back from you, I wrote the piano accompaniment, as well," Daniel said. "Want to have a look at it?"

The lump was still in her throat, so she merely nodded. Daniel placed the score on the piano before her, and Clara studied the lines while her fingers subconsciously pressed out the notes in the air. Daniel sat shockingly close on the bench beside her. "Give it a try," he whispered in her ear.

She placed her hands on the cool ivory keys. The introductory passages were simple, something she could peck out with one hand. She casually played the notes, and then, before she was fully aware of what he was doing, Daniel's hand covered hers. His hand was so much bigger, the skin darker and rougher than hers, but infinitely gentle as he played the notes along with her, gently manipulating her fingers along the keyboard. His palm was warm and she could feel his soft breath against her cheek.

She kept her face directed squarely at the score, but turned her eyes in Daniel's direction. All she could see was the side of his jaw and the corner of his mouth, tilted up in the slightest of smiles. He was so close the scent of his soap teased her nose, and she could see a faint shadow of stubble along his jaw. She didn't know the music at all, but let him guide her fingers across the keys, gently coaxing out the melody.

When the music became more complicated, his other arm encircled her waist and he began working the keys with both hands. There was no point in even pretending she was playing the piano; she simply surrendered to the manipulation of his hands as the melody filled the room.

Then the music was over, and his fingers tipped her chin toward him. An electrical current flared to life between them, tempting her closer to Daniel's enigmatic gray eyes as they beamed down at her. This moment seemed inevitable, but she knew that if she let him kiss her, it would alter the course of their relationship forever. And that was something she simply could not put at risk just yet.

She turned her head and nodded to his cello. "Are we going to try to put this thing together?" He did not move, just traced his thumb along the side of her jaw as he gazed down into her face. Her skin tingled beneath the gentle sweep of his thumb. It was difficult to breathe and so tempting to lean into him and throw caution to the winds.

Daniel rose. "I suppose we'd better." His tone was perfectly casual, as though nothing had just happened. He moved to the chair and pulled his cello into place, waiting for her to get in position on the piano, just as they had done a thousand times in the past. He nodded for her to begin.

They quickly perfected Daniel's duet, and then spent an hour delving through Daniel's treasure trove of newly imported music from Europe, including the scandalously difficult Brahms rhapsody. She was careful to stay at least three feet away from him—any closer and it was too tempting to get pulled in to the magnetism that radiated from him with each breath he took. When they were finished, Clara could not resist exploring his eccentric library, filled with mechanical trinkets and blueprints of works in progress. Although the other rooms in Daniel's house were decorated with tasteful artwork on the walls, this room was different. The one wall of this room not lined with books was covered with odd scraps of papers and blueprints carefully framed and displayed.

Clara moved closer to examine them. One document looked like a menu from a pub, the margins of which were filled with simple line drawings and a few mathematical equations penciled along the bottom.

"That was a sketch Ian Carr and I did while having a beer at O'Reilly's Tavern," Daniel said. "It's a rough outline of an idea I had for a timing switch. Eventually it became the first thing I ever patented." Clara looked over the assorted documents on the wall, most of them patent certificates, but a few of them were drawings that captured the initial spurt of inspiration for one of Daniel's ideas. "I'd still be shoveling coal into furnaces today if it weren't for those scraps of paper," he said.

Clara shook her head. "I doubt that, Daniel. Somehow I think you were always meant for something beyond a steel mill. I wish your parents could see how far you have come in the world. They would be so proud of you . . . I know that I am."

Daniel pulled the top desk drawer open and retrieved a small photograph. Clara recognized both of Daniel's parents smiling out from the frame. His mother's face was beaming with joy and she wore a crown of daisies on her head.

"This is the only photograph I have of my parents," Daniel said. "They had it taken on the day they learned my mother was expecting Lorna. They had gone so long without conceiving another child, they thought there would be no more children. I remember how my mother made that crown of daisies in celebration of the new baby. She danced all around our apartment wearing that silly crown, but that was the kind of thing she used to do when she was happy. All day long she couldn't stop smiling, and finally my dad took her out to have her photograph made."

Daniel's thumb traced the rim of the picture. "I try to remember her when she was happy like that, but it is hard, Clara. The dark memories always crowd in. I wish she could have lived long enough for me to take care of her. *Really* take care of her." Daniel's voice became very soft. "She never had a wedding ring. Did you know that? She loved my father so much, and I think she always wanted one, but there was never money for things like that." He tossed the photograph on the desk and sank into the chair. "Now I could buy her an entire jewelry store, but it just doesn't matter anymore."

There was a hollow look in his eyes that tore at her heart. She knelt at the base of the chair and took his hands between her own. "You're right, Daniel. It doesn't matter anymore. More than anything I wish your mother had lived to see the fine things you have accomplished. But she isn't here, and she would not have wanted you to grow hard and bitter on her behalf."

He stared out the window and nodded slowly. "You are probably right." When he shifted his attention back to her, there was humor lurking behind his eyes. "There are a few more things she would have wanted me to accomplish that are still a work in progress."

"What are those?"

"I've got to get Kate decently married. She's playing at a tennis match this weekend, where I have hopes some fine, upstanding man will see her and be inspired to carry her off. Would you like to attend the match with me?"

Clara eagerly agreed, as she'd never seen a tennis match.

Satisfied, Daniel continued, "Next, my mother would have liked to see *me* decently married, and on that front I've never bothered to make the least bit of effort. I'm thinking about changing that sad state of affairs, so I ought to put you on notice about that."

Her heart skipped a beat. It would be utterly presumptuous to assume that she would be first on his list of potential marriage partners. For all she knew, there was already some woman he had been squiring around for years. She raised her brows and pretended a nonchalant air. "Notice for what?"

"Miss Endicott, your powers of observation are a little less than razor sharp," he said as he strolled to a cabinet on the far side of the library. "And you call yourself a journalist." He was using that cool, remote voice that used to frustrate her when she was a girl, but now she knew he was toying with her. And she was enjoying every moment of it.

CHAPTER 9

C lara fed a little more kerosene to the wick of the lamp, then twisted and rubbed the base of her spine. She'd been curled over these documents for the better part of two days, and it made for difficult, dreary reading.

But it had to be done. Curled up in her father's study, she pored over several years of newspaper accounts documenting the rising hostility in the railroad industry. The entire East Coast had been engulfed in massive riots in 1877, and now, only two years later, tensions were simmering again. It was only a matter of time before the riot she had been swept up in last week became a sustained campaign of rage. And Daniel Tremain was part of it all. His workers, along with most laborers in the railroad industry, were threatening to strike should wages and conditions not improve.

And when the railroads struck, commerce throughout the country ground to a halt.

"Look here, Clara," her brother, Clyde, said. "It says that the Baltimore police used bayonets to disperse the crowd back in the labor riots of 1877. Can you believe that?" She and Clyde had been working in her father's study every day that week. Clyde pushed the newspaper article toward her, and she was amazed that such barbarity was still in practice.

"Things aren't that bad yet," Clara said, "but I worry they are headed that way if something isn't done soon." She was convinced that the labor question should be addressed in her father's newspaper. *The Christian Crusade* was a weekly publication, but it was sent to almost a million subscribers throughout the United States. Roughly half the articles dealt with religious topics, but the paper also tackled social issues. At first she had worried that Baltimore's labor trouble was too provincial a topic for a national newspaper, but as Clyde had reminded her, *"Anything that puts the railroad in danger is a national topic."*

The more time she spent with Clyde, the more impressed she became. Far from the boastful, aggravating older brother of her childhood, Clyde now had a remarkably rational way of looking at the world. She pushed back from the table, and broached the topic that had been plaguing her for days.

"Clyde, do you think it's possible to be a truly good man without being a Christian?"

Clyde looked stunned. "Given where I have chosen to live and spend the majority of my life, you ought to know my position on such a basic thing."

"I do. The questions are about to get a lot harder."

Clyde rubbed his hands together in delight, loving nothing better than a good academic debate. "Fire when ready."

"When a man rises to a position of great power and influence, he is charged with protecting the innocents, correct?"

"Yes, I believe Jesus taught we have a responsibility to protect those who are weaker."

Clara wandered to the window, where she looked out at the perfectly manicured and vibrant lawn. How far this was from the world of grinding poverty where laborers were scalded to death due to lack of basic safety of equipment. "But what if those innocents have been sinned against?" she asked. "Who shall seek justice on their behalf if not a man of great power?"

"I imagine this is Daniel Tremain you are referring to," Clyde said. Her brother's knowing gaze pierced straight through the calm intellectualism she was trying to maintain.

She threw a wadded-up piece of paper at him that bounced harmlessly off his forehead. "Yes, it is Daniel I'm talking about," she admitted.

"Has Daniel been seeking justice or has he been seeking vengeance?" Clyde asked. "There is an important difference, Clara."

She remembered the night of the riot when they had sat and talked in the kitchen. Daniel's face was tight with anger and he proclaimed that he wanted revenge. That was exactly the word he had used, *revenge*. "Explain it to me."

Clyde hesitated. "Well . . . let me go fetch Father." Before Clara could stop him, Clyde had bounded from the room in search of Lloyd, and Clara rolled her eyes in frustration. It was so obvious what Clyde was doing. "*I have every hope of smoothing this little rift out before I head back to the Navajo,*" he had told her a few days ago. Leave it to the doctor to think he could magically heal a wound that ran more than a decade deep. Each day she came to use her father's study, Lloyd gave her a wide berth. They were like polite strangers, while Clyde played matchmaker, but any hope she had of forgiving Lloyd was completely useless until her father at least pretended to be sorry.

Clyde returned with one of those maddening gloats on his face, pulling Lloyd along behind him. "So Clara has a question about the difference between justice and vengeance," Clyde said. "I thought you could shed light on that."

Lloyd eased himself into a chair, casting a polite smile Clara's way. "Well, I'm glad you've given me the opportunity to talk about it," he said cautiously. Lloyd was no idiot, and he knew precisely who was responsible for inviting him into this conversation. He continued, "Justice is intended to restore order. When a crime has occurred, it must be stopped and then made good in some way. We can't restore things to the perfect order they were before the sin, but justice provides us with a system of laws and procedures for the restoration of order. Justice is administered by society, but revenge is something totally different, Clara. Revenge is not administered by society, but carried out by an individual. And the intention is purely to punish, not restore order."

"And if it is impossible to restore order?" Clara asked. "What if the victim is dead or there is no longer any proof to convict the wrongdoer? What then, Father?"

Her father's eyes crinkled in sympathy. "That is one of the harder lessons we must struggle with. If justice cannot be administered by man, we must wait and allow the Lord to balance the scales. He always will, but we may not be there to see it. We must surrender our will to the Lord, and know that He will do what is right."

"It sounds like Tremain has Forsythe pinned right down the barrel of his gun," Clyde said. "I don't think he's the type to ease up just because Jesus says he should."

Funny how older brothers could still be annoying even after everyone was all grown-up. She wished Clyde had not brought Daniel's name into this, as Daniel's weaknesses were the *last* thing she wanted to discuss in front of her father. Undoubtedly, that was why Clyde had done it.

Lloyd smiled in sympathy. "Clara, the craving for revenge is a very basic instinct. It can be profoundly difficult to surrender the desire for vengeance. Not everyone who has been sinned against can learn to do it, but if they fail in this task, the rancor will grow and corrupt the entire spirit. You need to understand this about Daniel."

The words were gently spoken, but his meaning rang through with the force of a clarion trumpet. No matter how strong their friendship, how great her respect for Daniel, she could not go through her life alongside a man with the stain of vengeance corroding his soul.

"Have you got the workroom cleaned up yet?"

Manzetti stood in the doorway of Daniel's office, frustration on his face. "It would take a lot of work to even make a dent in cleaning that place up."

Daniel vaulted from his chair. "Well, get a move on it, then. Clara will be here in less than an hour, and I don't want this place looking like a hovel." He glanced at his private office to be sure everything was in order. The furniture was freshly polished, the tables cleared of stray papers. Everything here looked like the office of a respectable man of business.

The workroom was another story. Carr & Tremain Polytechnic occupied the entire top floor of the downtown building, and they'd knocked out most of the interior walls to construct an oversized workroom that doubled as a laboratory. The worktables groaned under the weight of drafting tools, surveying equipment, measuring rods, and scales. The walls were covered with well-used blackboards, and much of the floor space was dominated by pieces of a hydraulic lift Daniel had designed. To an uneducated observer this room would appear to be a chaotic pile of junk, and that was not how Daniel wanted Clara to see him.

"Can't you stash that hydraulic lift somewhere? It looks terrible."

A half dozen employees stared at him as if some germ of insanity had taken root in his brain. Tidiness was not a prized trait among engineers, and the office looked exactly as it always did. Daniel had never fussed over his employees' workspace like a meddlesome housekeeper before today. Then again, he'd never brought Clara Endicott to see his office.

"The central body of that lift was disassembled last week," Manzetti said. "That thing isn't going anywhere."

Daniel shoved a pile of stray drafting equipment into a filing drawer and wiped away the dust stain. "Well, at least put on your suit coat and quit looking like a gypsy. That goes for the rest of you dawdlers, too." The look of amusement that skittered among his employees didn't escape his notice, but he hardly cared about their opinions. Clara was another story.

That she had requested to meet him in his office was good. Surprising, but good. She had taken up writing again and intended to use her father's newspaper as her venue. If writing was what she needed to feel successful, he would do everything possible to make it happen for her, including granting her an interview about his business. Exposing himself to the glare of the public spotlight was abhorrent, but if it helped Clara, he would do it.

Carr & Tremain had always avoided publicity. There were only a handful of railroad conglomerates who could afford to license his technology, and they were all very well acquainted with his company. Any other attention only meant trouble. Trouble with the labor unions, with competitors, even trouble with regulators should their company ever go public.

Which appeared increasingly unlikely. Last week Daniel had insisted they withdraw their attempt to become a public company when he learned that the newly appointed Board of Directors was going to lift the ban on selling their technology to Alfred Forsythe.

The entire purpose of the Board of Directors was to act in the best interest of the shareholders, and Daniel's refusal to do business with Forsythe was precisely the sort of thing boards loved to overturn. Ian had been fiercely disappointed with Daniel's decision to withdraw from the sale, but he was forced to concede. Their company's fortune was built entirely on Daniel's innovations, and Ian knew it. If Daniel left and took his patents with him, Carr & Tremain would be gutted.

Daniel cast another critical eye over the workroom. Not much more could be done to bring order to the wild tangle of equipment, but at least he could get rid of the bit of dust clinging to the upper panes of the windows. "Jasper, grab a broom and knock down whatever filth is on those windows." He shrugged into his suit coat and straightened his collar. No coal-shovel boy here, he ran a respectable operation now.

He need not have worried about Clara's reaction to the workroom. Rather than disapproving of the chaos, her eyes widened in delight as she saw the array of equipment. "You *must* explain everything to me!" she said.

He allowed his engineers to do that. As he walked her from station to station, he prompted each man to explain the project he was working on. Daniel observed their reactions to Clara. Her tiny frame was encased in a mauve dress that accentuated her delicate, feminine features. It was an obviously feminine dress, with velvet piping in her snug jacket and a modest bustle behind her hips, but the starched collar and smart little tie mimicked a man's business suit. The effect was charming. That Clara was pretty was obvious to any man with a pulse, but how many women could ask such intelligent questions about these mechanical devices? How many women had that natural graciousness that made each man feel that he was brilliant and engaged in fascinating work? But that was the effect Clara had.

Now that she had come back into his life, it was increasingly clear he should keep her here. Her humor and optimism were simply enchanting. For over a decade, Daniel had devoted his days to his relentless compulsion to create, invent, and earn. Now he wanted a woman by his side, and no one else but Clara would do.

After her tour of the workroom, they returned to the privacy of his office, where she set her notepad on his worktable and he took the chair opposite her. She flipped open her notepad and asked a series of brisk, intelligent questions with ease.

They were straightforward questions, about the nature of his inventions and how they advanced railroad operations. He explained how five years ago they had begun buying railroad lines, investing a fortune to diversify their company so as to ensure their long-term viability. "Railroads are expensive," Daniel said. "Most of my available capital has been plowed directly back into the company, but we've got to have them. Unless we have railroads, our company could be wiped out tomorrow should someone else patent an invention that is better than ours."

It wasn't until half an hour into the conversation that Clara started poking around the sensitive areas.

"And as you sink more capital into railroad lines, surely you encounter more difficulty with your laborers?"

He gave a slight nod of his head. "Naturally."

"Have your railroad workers formed a union?"

"They tried during the strikes of 1877," he said. "It was not successful."

"Why wouldn't you permit them to unionize?"

He didn't want to discuss this with her. Clara was the person who had always helped him escape the troubles of the world. He wasn't about to allow their afternoon to be spoiled by a labor uprising over which he had no responsibility.

"I had nothing to do with what happened back in 1877," he said. "The strike covered the entire eastern half of the country and didn't end until federal troops went in city by city to crush it. You can't blame it on me, Clara."

"No one would have stopped you if you permitted your own workers to form a union."

Daniel folded his arms across his chest and wished she would drop the topic. "That's a business question. My partner, Ian Carr, handles business operations and employment."

"And yet the decision not to license your technology to Forsythe was your doing."

"The sole exception."

"How does Ian feel about this?"

That wasn't exactly a secret. "He doesn't like it. Ian knows it would be easy money to let Forsythe use our technology, but he respects my reasons for refusing. We would not be business partners were it otherwise."

The scratching of Clara's pencil as she took notes was the only sound in the room. Ever since she began this interview she had displayed the utmost professional competence, asking probing questions in that flawlessly polite, precise way of hers. He was fiercely proud of her, but that didn't make being the subject of this interview any easier to tolerate. Daniel felt like a specimen under a microscope and wondered how much longer this would last.

"When Carr & Tremain becomes a publicly owned company, will you be able to continue denying your technology to Forsythe?" she asked.

"We are not going public. I won't relent on my position regarding Forsythe, so the deal is over."

Clara set her pencil down, her eyes troubled. "I see," she said quietly. She took a deep breath and leaned her head back, studying the ceiling of his office as though some terrific secret was hidden up there.

He reached across the table to close her notebook. "What's bothering you? It's not labor union troubles."

She smiled a bit. "You always could read me."

That's because you're the other half of my soul. "I'm not doing such a good job now. What's troubling you?"

She met his gaze frankly. "Will you go to church with me on Sunday?"

It was the last thing he expected to hear, but he could see by the anticipation on her face how important this was to her. Clara was a believer, and it had always bothered her that he did not share the same level of commitment.

He would have to handle this carefully. "Why is it important that I should attend services with you?"

She pushed away from the table and strolled to the window, looking down into the streets of Baltimore four stories below. "Because you are one of the finest men I know, but there's a deep, wide hole inside of you, and I want to help you fix it."

He clenched his fist, but kept his face expressionless. If it was *anyone* but Clara who dared to lecture him, he would have shut them down as quickly as snuffing out a candle. Instead he forced himself to look her in the eye and try to help her understand. "If you're referring to my quirk about doing business with Forsythe, this isn't a shortcoming that you can fix. It is a deeply held principle that means something to me. I'm honoring the memory of my mother and father, and I hardly consider that to be a hole that needs mending."

When she turned to face him there was hope shining in her eyes. "I wish you would become a Christian," she said. "If you could learn about and accept the principles of Jesus, so many things would change for you."

"And you believe these magic principles of Jesus are going to cause me to forgive Forsythe and live happily ever after?"

She had that hurt look in her blue eyes that always tugged at his gut, but there was only so much he could tolerate, even from Clara. "You're mocking me, but yes, I believe they can," she said.

"It will never happen."

She whirled away from him and strode to the other side of the room, her voice angry. "In all these years of snubbing Forsythe and denying him your technology, has any of that really made you feel better? Has any of it worked to calm the roiling pit of anger inside you?"

How innocent she was. How simplistic and naive she was if she thought saying a few prayers to Jesus could solve the tragedy of what had torn his family to pieces.

"Actually, yes . . . denying my technology to Forsythe has made me quite happy," he said. "Every time I read that Forsythe needs to prematurely replace his rails, it makes me happy. Every time I read that he has to pay a fortune to stationmen along his line because he can't buy my timing switches, *it feels good*. It's worked like a charm, Clara."

"But would you try, Daniel? You've never had a chance to learn about God or Jesus and you can't dismiss it out of ignorance." She softened her voice. "Would you try for me?"

When she looked at him with her eyes shining in appeal, he wanted to go to the moon for her, but he couldn't grant her this request. It wasn't ignorance of religion that caused him to reject it. His mother had done an extraordinary job of sharing her faith with her children, and look at all the good it did for her. When he was growing up he had read some of the Bible but never found it particularly moving or helpful. Same thing for her father's sermons. Going through the motions of attending services with Clara and allowing her to believe she could transform him into a wholesome Christian would simply raise her hopes and, ultimately, be more cruel.

He tried to sound lighthearted. "Clara, you are obviously too good-hearted to recognize an unrepentant sinner like me."

"Please, Daniel. Please have a little bit of confidence that I know what I'm talking about. I want to help you."

He knew she did. From the first time she had let him use her piano to the time she rushed into the middle of a riot to rescue his sister, Clara had been the epitome of selfless loyalty.

"Clara, I adore you," he said simply but truthfully. "Back when I was a dirty-faced kid, you were like a ray of light in a very grim world. You were so fine that I never dared hope I could be worthy of a girl like you. I dreaded getting older, knowing that each day I was one step closer to losing you. One step closer to the day when you would look around and meet some man of your own class who would marry you and shut me out of your life forever. And then I would go back to the steel mill, to the boilers and coal wagons."

Daniel moved across the office to stand near her shoulder, so close he could smell the scent of her perfume. "And then a miracle occurred. I figured a way to earn lots of money and buy a fancy house with a grand piano and suddenly that blue-eyed girl with the golden hair was no longer so far out of reach. And when I saw her again, after all those years . . ." Did he imagine it, or were tears welling in her eyes? It was impossible to tell because she turned and faced the window.

"When I saw you again that day at the Opera House, you were so beautiful you took my breath away." Those words seemed so inadequate for the longing that raged inside him. In every hour of each day since he had seen her again, Clara had been a constant in his thoughts, a dream he fell asleep to at night and the inspiration he strove to be worthy of by day. "But now I find that another bar has been set for me," Daniel said. "Earning money and building a fine house was easy. Now she wants me to go out and transform my entire soul."

She turned to face him. "Yes, that's what I want."

He folded his arms across his chest and locked eyes with her. "I adore you, Clara. I always have, and if I live another hundred years, on my deathbed it will be you who fills my thoughts in my last hour. But I won't be your lapdog. I've worked and slaved and suffered to get to this point, and I'm proud of what I've accomplished." His gaze flicked over his office. His immaculate, freshly cleaned and tidied office. Not that it had mattered to her one bit. "If you can't accept that, I need to know it now. There is no point in prolonging this misery if you can't take me as I am."

He could see the play of emotions flickering across her face, disappointment warring with the determination to keep fighting. He held his breath, fearing that he pushed too hard and she would turn around and walk out of his life forever. His dearest friend, his brightest dream. He clenched his fists, fearing if she left him, the scar on his soul would never heal.

She lowered her head so all he could see was the top of her glossy blond hair parted neatly in the middle and pinned in an elegant twist. So wonderfully prim, but typically Clara. How desperately he wanted to run his fingers through those silky strands, bury his nose in the softly scented hair.

"I can't force you to change," she finally murmured softly.

"Only God can do that." When she raised her head to look at him, her eyes were hopeful. "But will you at least listen to me? This is a huge part of my life, and if you dismiss it like it is an annoying bother, I don't know that there is much hope for us."

"I've always listened to you, Clara." From the moment he met her, her opinion was the one that mattered most in the world to him.

At last, the creases on her forehead eased; she straightened her shoulders and looked back at him. Her voice was nonchalant when she finally spoke. "Then what time shall I meet you for your sister's tennis match this weekend?"

And Daniel smiled. He knew he had won.

CHAPTER 10

Bane tucked away his research on Daniel Tremain and the Baltimore harbor before going downstairs for the Professor's meeting. The more he learned about Baltimore, the more Bane was convinced it would be a fine city to serve as a base for criminal operations. When he went to carry out the Professor's errand against Tremain, he really ought to capitalize on the opportunity by laying some groundwork for future endeavors.

"Well, well, the little prince has decided to join us."

Bane ignored Rick Collier's taunt as he strolled into the Professor's spacious library. Everyone in the room knew the Professor considered Bane the heir apparent to the criminal empire, and Bane was fiercely resented by the men who had far more experience in the murky world of the illegal opium trade.

"And how are you this morning, Mr. Collier?" Bane asked pleasantly. How easy it was to irk the man simply by using the word *mister*, since it emphasized that Bane was still only a teenaged boy. The fact that he was also the most trusted of all the Professor's criminal lieutenants was doubly insulting. Rick Collier, Sammy Bennington, and Michael Green were all jealous of him, but these men had had plenty of opportunity to impress the Professor. They simply had been no match for the child who had been kidnapped at the age of six, yet managed to figure out a way to survive and then thrive in the Professor's strange world. Eleven years after the Professor had snatched Bane out of his mother's arms on the streets of San Francisco, he still treated Bane like a son. Now the teenaged, golden boy's power was gathering momentum as the Professor turned ever-increasing responsibilities over to him, and his fellow partners in crime did not like it.

"Just shut your pretty mouth," Collier growled. "The Professor isn't here to appreciate you kissing up to us, so stow it."

Bane made eye contact with Michael Green, the smartest of the three other men in the room, and smiled as he shrugged his shoulders helplessly. For months he had been courting Green's loyalty, and Green was smart enough to play along. Collier and Bennington still stupidly thought the way to win the Professor's admiration was in proving how tough they were. Nothing could be further from the truth.

Bane's eyes scanned the walls of the library, lined from floor to ceiling with thousands of rare books, treasures collected from all over the world. The key to the Professor's esteem was right here before them, wrapped in leather-bound casings and oiled with care. Professor Van Bracken *respected* power and ruthlessness, but he *loved* his books. Only people who shared his passion had any hope of earning the Professor's trust. The mansion was kept perpetually chilly, the optimal temperature for preserving old books. So much did the Professor love being surrounded by his cherished books that he insisted on all his important meetings taking place in this room.

And today's meeting was of the utmost importance. Only the Professor's top lieutenants were allowed to know the location of his Vermont mansion. The hundreds of henchmen and small-time smugglers who were foot soldiers in this criminal empire did not even know the Professor's name. Instead, the Professor had a small group of trusted lieutenants who had been assigned control of the opium trade in specific regions of the country. Bane controlled New England, Sammy Bennington was responsible for the port of Halifax, and Michael Green controlled the entire West Coast. For the past year, Rick Collier had been managing the smuggling from the coasts into the heartland. And at the center of the complex web of operations sat the Professor, spinning his master plan with flawless precision. Every few years the Professor orchestrated a shift in his entire smuggling business in order to stay ahead of the authorities. He called in lieutenants from all corners of the country to strategize how the new procedures would work. Although opium was a legal substance in the United States, taxes on the drug were more than three times the actual value of the raw opium. The high taxes and portable nature of opium made it an irresistible target for smugglers.

The door to the library opened, and every man stood at attention as the Professor entered the room. As always, Professor Edward Van Bracken was meticulously groomed, his salt-and-pepper hair smoothed back with Macassar oil, his beard neatly trimmed, and wearing a custom-tailored suit with a silk vest and starched white collar. But Bane noticed something alarming almost immediately. As the Professor strode into the room, he looked each man in the eye as he greeted them, took his seat, set a stack of papers on the table, and adjusted his jacket. But during the entire exchange, he had failed to blink even once.

It was an odd habit, and one Bane had noticed when he was still a child. Whenever the Professor was in a seething rage, the only indication was that lidless stare in which he rarely blinked. None of the other men in the room seemed to be aware of it, and Bane was not the sort of person to share these little tidbits of insight.

"Well, now," the Professor said in a smooth voice, "let's square things away quickly so we can move on to more important matters. We have already agreed to shift our West Coast operations out of San Francisco and into Vancouver. I have not yet decided on the best new port to use on the East Coast. I would like to hear all of your thoughts on the matter."

Bane was determined for it to be Baltimore. Ever since the Professor had tasked him with extracting Daniel Tremain from Carr & Tremain Polytechnic, Bane had made a great study of the city. It was essential to have a thorough understanding of any city in which he did business, and he was impressed with the infrastructure of the port of Baltimore. He had already been to Baltimore on other business ventures and knew it would be an ideal base for smuggling.

The Professor was waiting for each man's input as to the new port, and Collier had a firm opinion. "Easy," Collier said. "If we can't use New York anymore, we go to Boston. The railroad system in Massachusetts is perfect for what we need, and big enough for us to get lost in." Others in the room nodded their heads. The Professor turned toward Bane.

"Bane? What are your thoughts?"

For the Professor's benefit, Bane cast an apologetic nod toward Collier. "I'm sorry, Mr. Collier, sir, but I think Boston would be suicide."

"And why is that, golden boy?" Collier said.

"The port of Boston has a major naval base," Bane explained. "A new admiral has just been appointed to the Navy Yard. Five men were arrested last month for accepting bribes, and he isn't finished cleaning house yet. I don't think Boston is a good bet until we know more about the new admiral."

The Professor nodded. "Excellent observation. Where do you suggest, Bane?"

"Baltimore," Bane said without hesitation. There were howls of disapproval from the men for the unconventional choice, far south of anywhere they had ever operated, but Bane maintained his composure. "Baltimore has an excellent deep-water port, and it will allow ready access not only to New England but the Caribbean, as well." He looked to the Professor. "We haven't done as much as we could with Cuba and the West Indies. Baltimore will let us ramp up our operations. Most importantly, Baltimore does not have a reputation for smuggling. No one will be on the lookout for us if we move our East Coast operations there."

The Professor said nothing, just turned that lidless stare on Collier and raised his brow. Collier seemed to shrink in his chair. "Crazy," Collier said. "Baltimore is too far south."

"Is that the best argument you can summon to counter Bane's proposal?" When Collier said nothing, the Professor merely sighed. "When a boy of Bane's tender years shows more insight and strategic analysis than a man twenty years in the business, it gives me cause for concern."

Collier was under pressure, but this sort of exquisitely mannered questioning was standard for the Professor. It was the fact that the man was barely blinking that had Bane concerned. There was no telling *who* had set the Professor into a simmering rage, and Bane could not rest easy until he knew.

Green and Bennington both weighed in with their opinions, and ultimately Bane's recommendation was adopted. Collier relaxed as soon as the decision was made, but Bane kept his guard up. Whatever was bothering the Professor was bound to rise to the surface soon.

The Professor reached inside his tailored frock coat and retrieved a small card. "I received a telegraph message this morning from Halifax." Sammy Bennington immediately went on the alert, as Halifax was his territory. "It appears that the kidnapping of young Timothy Snyder was not all that it could have been. In short, the attempt to snatch the boy from his private school was thwarted."

The Professor swiveled his lidless gaze to Bennington. "Now I ask you, Mr. Bennington, how am I to have open access to the port of Halifax if the harbor master continues to accept bribes from my rivals while failing to show me similar consideration?"

Bennington's face had gone pure white. "We'll get the boy. We can try again. Immediately."

"My contact tells me the boy now has a bodyguard."

"I'll double up the men on the job. Triple them," Bennington stammered. "The bodyguard won't be a problem."

"Hmm," the Professor said, clearly unimpressed. A smile that wasn't a smile curled the corners of his mouth. "We are all part of a team here, Mr. Bennington. If one part of the team fails to perform, it hurts the entire team. And it doesn't seem fair for all of us to be let down because one team member did not know how to manage a job. I'm not interested in *why* someone failed, or *how* he plans to do better. He simply can't be part of the team anymore."

The door to the library opened, and four of the Professor's henchmen walked in, their sleeves rolled up for business. One of them was carrying a sledgehammer.

"I can't have that sort of carelessness among my top officials. It sets a bad example," the Professor said reasonably. "You know what this means, Bennington."

"Please! Please, Professor, no!" Bennington made to bolt for the door, but the henchmen restrained him. Bennington was a huge man, and there was a good deal of scuffling as bodies struggled against one another, but eventually he was hauled back into his chair.

"Please, Professor, just don't hurt my family," he said in a voice shaking with fear.

"Now, Bennington," the Professor said coolly. "Have I said anything about little Polly and the way she takes her puppy for a walk every afternoon right when she gets home from school? Although I must tell you that a loving father would have forbid his children to fall into such predictable patterns. It makes them so much more vulnerable, doesn't it?"

Bennington swallowed hard. "I'll do whatever you want. Polly is a good girl and doesn't deserve any of this."

"But I am sure little Timothy Snyder is a good boy, and you had no qualms about arranging for his kidnapping, correct?"

Sweat was pouring off Bennington, soaking his shirt and filling the room with the pungent odor of fear. Bane remained motionless in his chair, but closed his eyes in disgust. This was the game the Professor used to keep his men living in terror of him. Sometimes he might lash out at a man's family, while other times he would simply laugh and deliver a vase of flowers to a man's wife. It all depended on whatever fickle mood the Professor was in. Bane's fingernails bit into the palms of his hands, hoping his revulsion was not showing on his face. One of the things the Professor respected him for was his coolness under pressure. Long ago, Bane had perfected the art of appearing utterly serene, no matter how revolting the provocation.

The Professor sighed. "I'm sorry to see this pattern of careless behavior, Bennington. First with failing to secure Timothy Snyder, but especially with leaving your own child so vulnerable to whatever sort of riffraff that might have it out for you. Really, if anything bad should happen to poor Polly, the fault lies solely with you, don't you think? So I'm going to ask my men to take you out in the yard and teach you a bit of a lesson. Then I'll make my decision about poor Polly. What do you say? Is it a deal?"

A hint of relief crept into Bennington's face. If he accepted his punishment without a fuss, perhaps the Professor would have mercy on Polly. "Yes, sir," Bennington said. "Yes, sir, I think it is a good plan. A very good plan."

A moment later Bennington was escorted from the room by the four guards. In all likelihood, the girl would be fine. Otherwise the Professor would already be planning her demise behind those lidless eyes, but Bane was relieved to see that he was finally blinking again at the same rate as a normal human.

Not that there was anything normal about Professor Van Bracken. There was something wildly off-kilter about the Professor, but the man held the keys to the kingdom, and Bane wanted access to those keys. The Professor *owed* him those keys. Because of the Professor's actions, the only life Bane was suited for was operating within this shadowy criminal racket. And he was good at it. Actually, his skills for managing operations, commanding obedience, and using trickery were nothing short of impressive. The Professor had told him so often enough, and it was why Bane would be entrusted with the Vancouver operation as soon as he could prove his mettle by carrying out the Tremain affair.

The Professor took his seat. "Now that that bit of unpleasantness is behind us, let's have Mrs. Garfield bring us a nice meal, shall we?"

CHAPTER 11

Clara watched in amusement as all the other spectators craned
their necks back and forth, following the flight of the tennis
ball as it was smacked to-and-fro across the court. Only she and
Daniel were completely oblivious to the play. They spent the entire
afternoon recounting the long years that had separated them, filling
in the gaps and fleshing out the details. Only when Kate Tremain
came out to play did they force their attention down to the court.

Daniel's sister was the only woman playing today, but she had
as much spirit as her male competitors. Kate was at a distinct disadvantage because of the slim, form-fitting dress she wore, but she was
more nimble than her competition. She had just finished playing
her final match when two young men stepped up for their round.

"That's Jamie Carr," Daniel said as a young man stepped up to

ELIZABETH CAMDEN

play a match. "My partner Ian's son. Kate beat him in last month's match, and he's still smarting over it."

Clara nodded. "It can be very difficult for a man to compete with a woman. He'll seem churlish if he wins, but unmanly if he loses."

"That's why Kate is trying to persuade more women to join the club. She will no doubt ask you sooner or later."

Clara watched the two men vault across the court, swinging small wooden rackets with an odd combination of grace and vigor. Clara shook her head. "I've never been terribly athletic. I'd be more likely to smack myself in the head with that racket than succeed in getting the ball over the net."

Daniel had been excessively polite to her ever since picking her up this morning. She suspected he was trying to compensate for his stark refusal to consider some of her religious convictions, as if holding doors for her and sending her admiring glances could help soothe her concerns.

But Clara was patient. Daniel had just come back into her life and she would not abandon him so easily. It was through daily interactions such as these that she could teach him by living the example of a godly life. She had begun to pray every night that Daniel's heart would soften enough for him to be open to God's grace.

They sat together and watched Jamie Carr play, but Daniel showed little interest in the match.

"So tell me why you never married," he asked. Most men would have danced around the sensitive topic with exquisite delicacy, but leave it to Daniel to simply ask in his charmingly frank manner.

156

She smiled at him. "No one showed any interest? I'm slinking into spinsterhood due to inherent mediocrity?"

"Quit fishing for compliments. No less than half a dozen men have been ogling you from the moment we sat down. So why haven't you married?"

The abundance of male attention she had been receiving was probably due to the fact that very few women were in attendance at the sporting event, but her father taught her it was impolite to refute a compliment. And his question was a legitimate one, however bluntly it had been posed. "Have you ever heard of Nicholas Spencer?" she asked.

"No. Should I have?"

"Well, if you lived in London you'd probably know the name. He was a member of Parliament when I met him, very bright, very ambitious. We hit it off quite well, in fact." Nicholas had a charm and reckless self-confidence that had instantly reminded her of Daniel, which was why she felt so drawn to Nicholas. "He supported my working for *The Times*. Most men thought being a journalist was shockingly unladylike, but Nicky thought it made me clever. He didn't particularly like my political views, but then, I was not wild about his, either."

"In any event," she continued, "Nicky was appointed to the position of Assistant Viceroy of India. It was a terrific honor, and something he was quite well suited for. The problem was that I did not believe I was suited to be the wife of such a person. I've never thought much of England's involvement in India, and I dreaded the prospect of living there. I told him so, too. It didn't go over very well." That was an understatement. It was the raging argument they'd had that night that had led to their broken engagement.

"After a long argument he suggested we reconsider our betrothal, and I agreed. It quite shocked him, I think. I'm almost certain he expected me to agree to anything in order to proceed with the marriage. I guess he didn't know me as well as he thought. That was three years ago."

Daniel was looking at her with curiosity. "You speak of this so casually . . . do you still think about him?"

She had been devastated at the time. Clara remembered barely being able to get out of bed the days after Nicholas had broken their engagement, but now it was hard to remember what was so extraordinary about him. "I think the fact that I was willing to leave him rather than move to India was a sign that he was not the right man for me."

The way Daniel's eyes narrowed with a speculative gleam made him look like a panther getting ready to pounce. "Now, Clara," he drawled. "We can't have you getting the reputation of being a jilted woman. People would talk, and think how terrible that would be."

"No one knows about it here. Unless you start blathering about it."

"Nevertheless, it's a terrible thing to be alone at your rapidly advancing age. I'm willing to help you out in this matter."

A grin spread across her face. "And how precisely do you plan on helping me out?"

"For a start I will begin by calling on you. And taking you out to venues such as this where everyone can see you have a doting admirer sitting beside you."

The heat rushed to her cheeks. "I hardly see how that would help my reputation. I've heard from a number of respectable sources that you terrify polite society." If the grin on Daniel's face was any indication, he did not mind his alarming reputation. "Besides, I can't imagine you 'doting' over anyone," she said as she turned her attention back to the tennis.

"Really? What about if I put my arm around your waist, like so." She felt the pressure of his hand as it settled on the side of her hip. If she looked down, she would draw attention to his forward behavior, but a thrill went through her at sitting within the circle of his arm. It felt . . . well, it felt simply delicious.

"Daniel, you should stop," she said in a hushed tone.

"Or perhaps a little kiss," Daniel said as he ignored the urgency in her voice. "A respectable kiss, of course. Nothing tawdry here." He kissed the side of her cheek, so fleetingly that she barely registered the touch of his lips, but after he withdrew, the spot on her cheek tingled with awareness. Her gaze flicked about the other spectators in the bleachers, but all of their heads were swaying in that back-and-forth manner as they watched the tennis ball volley across the court. "Daniel, you are terrible," she said in a fierce whisper, but she couldn't help a smile from curving her mouth.

"That was terrible? Oh my, I'd best try this again." The arm around her waist tightened as he drew her firmly against the side of his body. From thigh to shoulder they were pressed together, and Daniel placed a kiss on the top of her cheekbone, then another on the corner of her brow. And then he casually withdrew his arm, shifted back to his seat, and turned his attention back to the tennis as though her heart wasn't pounding and sensation wasn't racing through every nerve ending in her body.

"Horrible form on that return volley," he said casually. "Jamie had best improve his backhand if he has any hope of keeping up with Katie. Now, back to the far more interesting topic of how you are to be properly courted. We've yet to discuss the matter of gifts. Did this Nelson fellow shower you with gifts?"

"Nicholas. And no, he was very thrifty."

"Thrifty, was he? Alas, I am not quite so *thrifty* when it comes to women I cherish. I've always thought you have the most glorious hair. Why you insist on hiding it beneath a bonnet is beyond me. Perhaps some pretty clips for your hair would be nice. With sapphires, to match your eyes. Not terribly thrifty, so poor Nigel would disapprove, but I think they'd be just the thing. Now, give me your hand."

"What for?"

"Why must you always fuss? Your hand." When he said it in that authoritative, infinitely self-confident manner, Clara was helpless to resist. He covered her hand and something cold and hard was pressed into her palm. When she opened her hand, two gold hairclips, covered with sapphires and tiny seed pearls, twinkled in her palm. Her gaze flew to Daniel's face, and her breath caught at the tenderness gleaming in his eyes.

"They are beautiful," she breathed. "But, Daniel, it wouldn't be right for me to accept them."

"Nonsense," Daniel said. "If you recall, I destroyed several of your hairpins the day we rushed downtown during the riot. Simply replenishing your supply."

It was so overwhelming. A smile hovered on the corner of Daniel's perfectly formed lips as he awaited her reaction. When he looked at her like that, it made her heart ache with longing. "Daniel, these aren't the kind of gifts one accepts from a friend. They are much too dear."

"Then perhaps it is time I become more than just a friend . . . that way I won't tarnish your reputation. Spinsterish as it is. Now, let's get this hideous bonnet off your head and see how they look."

They were in the middle of a tennis match, with spectators on all sides of them. "I can't take off my bonnet and let down my hair here. It would cause a scene."

"Very well." Daniel rose to his feet and held a hand out for her. She remained frozen on the spot, certain that wherever he planned to lead her was going to push her in a direction she had been hoping and fearing in equal measures.

"Sit down, man!" someone hollered from behind them.

Daniel waited patiently while calls of frustration mounted behind them. "Clara?"

It was hopeless. She knew Daniel would continue to cause a scene until she left with him, and in truth, she *wanted* to follow wherever he led her. Placing her hand in his, he guided them down the narrow row toward the aisle. The tennis courts were in the middle of a large field behind the clubhouse and there was nowhere to go for privacy. A moment later Daniel led her beneath the stands.

The smacking of the tennis balls continued, but she could not tear her gaze off Daniel as he stood before her.

"Be a sport, Clara. Try these on." His long fingers were already pulling the bonnet from her head. After it was removed, he contemplated the coils of hair arranged in twisting ropes at the back of her head. Grasping her chin between his fingers, he tilted her head forward and back, studying the complicated hairstyle with the intensity of an engineer scrutinizing a design he wished to dismantle.

A gleam of satisfaction lit his face as he removed the single pin at the top of her head, causing the coiled mass to tumble about her shoulders. She ought to be embarrassed. The heat of Daniel's gaze was nearly incendiary as he took in the fall of her hair spilling across her shoulders and down to her elbows. It was a look of sheer masculine appreciation that caused her to blush straight down to her toes. And yet, she reveled in it.

"Satisfied?" Clara asked serenely.

"Delighted. Now hold still." She felt him lift the length of her hair above one ear and fasten it with one of the sapphire pins. No man had ever dressed her hair before, and the moment felt oddly intimate as she stood beneath his raised arms, feeling him arrange her hair and pin it into place. The other side received the same treatment.

Daniel dropped his arms and studied her. "Breathtaking," he said, and Clara knew he was not referring to the hairclips. A burst of applause rose from the stands above, signaling the end of the game, but Clara stood frozen beneath the warm approval that smoldered in Daniel's gaze.

"The match must be over," she said.

His gaze did not waver. "Yes." He cupped her face between his hands and took a step closer to her. The lapels of his jacket brushed against her chest and she could scarcely breathe. Clara lowered her lids, and he needed no further invitation. His lips covered hers, drinking gently from them. She turned to fit her face closer alongside his, and he responded by locking his arms tighter about her waist. The length of him was pressed against her body and the intimacy was enthralling. When he lifted his lips from hers, he kept his arms locked firmly around her.

"I'm glad you came back from England, Clara," he said gently. "I was starting to wonder if you ever would."

The longing in his voice was unmistakable. "Daniel, you said that it was a good thing I went to England. That we were headed for trouble. Is that where this is leading?"

"Trouble? I certainly hope so."

He said it in jest, but Clara was wise enough to know there was plenty of trouble on the horizon. Daniel was the best friend she had in the world, but could never be more than that if he could not share her faith. Surely if she was patient, he would come to share her faith, wouldn't he? She would wait for Daniel until the moon fell from the sky if that was what was required of her, but in the back of her mind she knew she was playing with fire. Given how her entire world was beginning to fall into orbit around Daniel Tremain, she was playing with an *inferno*.

She pushed the dark thought away and forced a glimmer of light into her voice as she cupped his face between her hands, raised herself on tiptoe, and kissed him squarely on the mouth. "I hope *not*. Just to be contrary." The way his eyes gleamed when he looked at her, as though she was a precious treasure, made her want to melt in his arms.

"Daniel? Daniel, where are you?" Kate's voice sounded from the other side of the stands, but Daniel kept her snared in his gaze. A surge of exhilaration pulsed through Clara and she had the irrational wish that she could freeze this moment for all time. "We should probably go," she said.

"I know." He made no effort to move, just kept looking at her with that gentle smile playing about his mouth.

Kate was still calling out for her brother. "Daniel Tremain, if you left me here to walk home alone, I'll smack you all the way to China."

At last Daniel turned. "Over here, Kate," he yelled. He turned back to grin down at Clara and whisper in her ear, "If my sister weren't ten feet away, I'd fling you over my shoulder and carry you off with the worst of intentions."

"What on earth are you doing down here?" Kate asked as she twisted her way among the pilings.

Daniel straightened and removed the arm from her waist. As Clara replaced her bonnet, she watched in fascination as Daniel's demeanor shifted from reckless flirt into protective older brother in the space of an instant. As they walked toward the carriage, she savored the delicious knowledge that she was one of the few people in the world who had the privilege of knowing all the sides of Daniel Tremain.

CHAPTER 12

Clara scrutinized her father's face as his gaze tracked across the lines she had written, awaiting the first glimmer of either endorsement or dissatisfaction to show on his stern, impassive face. Would there ever come a time when she could function without the approval of the Reverend Lloyd Endicott? No matter how angry she was with him, no matter how many years she had worked as a journalist, she still felt the pathetic need for his approval as he read the article she had written for *The Christian Crusade*. She brought her article here to his study and sat in the exact same spot on the sofa where she had waited for him to review her schoolwork.

Lloyd tossed her pages down on the table and removed his spectacles, his face still wearing that frustrating blank look that was impossible to read. "It's a good article, Clara. Persuasive, articulate. A little strongly worded, perhaps."

She raised her brows. "An article should be strongly worded." Her editor in London had nothing but scorn for "namby-pamby" journalists who were afraid to take a position. Labor relations were on the verge of boiling over once again, and the public needed to be fully informed of the process by which wages were set and work conditions determined. Her access to Alfred Forsythe and Daniel Tremain had given her exclusive insight into two of the most important players in Baltimore.

"Let me rephrase this," Lloyd said carefully. "I believe you are letting your personal disapproval for Daniel's actions influence the tone of this article. It is as though you are using this article as an attempt to prompt him to change his ways, rather than inform the public about details relevant to the case."

"Daniel is not the least bit reluctant to let his enmity toward Alfred Forsythe be public knowledge," she said. "He is proud of his position. I don't see how shining light on it is unfair."

Her father picked up the pages again and scanned through her words. "What about this passage here? You write, *'Mr. Tremain has withdrawn his company from consideration to become a publicly traded company on the New York Stock Exchange, based solely on his refusal to license his technologies to any company who pays the qualifying fees.'* " Lloyd looked up at Clara. He was no longer her father; he was the editor of a newspaper in which she hoped to publish. "Do you know this for a fact, Clara? Surely, there could be a multitude of reasons a man might wish to keep his company in private ownership."

Clara shook her head. "I know it for a fact. He told me straight out that it was the restriction relating to Forsythe Industries that was the deal breaker. And I know he and his partner could use the money the public stock would bring them. They are both strapped for cash." Lloyd continued to scan the pages, and the first hint of disapproval registered on his face.

Clara pulled down the pages and leaned forward to speak directly to Lloyd's face. "Everything I wrote is true," she said. "Every word of it can be verified. All my instincts are screaming at me that this is a fair evaluation of the state of affairs."

"But how will Daniel respond to this? Your oldest friend in the world?"

Daniel had always been shockingly blunt with her and appreciated her forthright nature. "Daniel isn't afraid of the truth. When I couldn't write fast enough, he even slowed down to let me catch up. He knew I was interviewing him for an article and freely shared all this information. Of course he expects me to use it."

Lloyd picked up the pages and turned them over and over. "You have years of experience as a journalist, and I'm willing to trust your judgment on this. It will appear in next week's issue."

Clara smiled. Next week she would begin to help heal this useless vendetta that had been destroying Daniel's soul.

❧

Clara pulled a slug from the stem of the clematis vine and dropped it into a can. The vines grew along the fence that bordered the back of her rented townhouse, and Clara wondered how such a delicate vine could support the profusion of violet blooms. She loved these early mornings when she could tend to the vines. Probably some sort of frustrated maternal urge, but it felt right to care for these vines that must have been growing along this fence for decades. Clara straightened the edge of her wide-brimmed straw hat to block the angle of the early morning sun, then turned her attention back to the curling vines climbing the fence.

She heard Daniel before she saw him. Booted feet were slicing through the tall grasses that grew in the side yard. She looked up from the vine and saw his face, white with anger, and his tall frame rigid with tension. Rolled in his hand was the just-released issue of *The Christian Crusade*. Daniel covered the expanse of the lawn in only a few strides, and the way he drew his arm back with the offending paper made Clara fear he was about to strike her with it. Instead, he threw the paper at her, its pages flying as it hit her dress and tumbled to the damp lawn.

She blanched, but was proud of the way she kept the tremor from her voice. "I see you've read the article."

"Is that what you call it?" he bit out. "*An article?* I call it a stab in the throat."

The fury in his eyes was like nothing she'd ever seen. This wasn't the Daniel she knew; this was the face of unadulterated rage, and it frightened her. She adjusted the brim of her hat with trembling fingers, anything to give her a moment to gather her scattered thoughts. "I'm sorry you didn't like it," she stammered. She backed up a step, but the wall of clematis vines prevented her from putting much space between them. "When you've had a few moments to calm down, perhaps we can talk—"

"How dare you, Clara? How dare you attack everything I've ever worked for when you were born with a silver spoon in your mouth? Every tutor, every book, everything was handed to you, and now you've got the gall to attack what I have earned. Why did you do it, Clara? When you realized that you couldn't be the next Chopin, did you decide to make a name for yourself by becoming the biggest muckraker in journalism?"

She hoped he could not see her trembling, but refused to break eye contact with him. "I didn't write anything in that article that wasn't common knowledge."

Daniel nearly exploded, pushing away from the fence and stalking across the lawn. "You wrote about why we withdrew from the public offering! That was private information and you had no business publishing that!"

"But . . . but, Daniel, you told me all about it that day in your office. You knew I was there to interview you about your company. Did you think I would not use it?" she asked incredulously.

Daniel swallowed hard and for the first time she saw a flicker of uncertainty cross his face. "No, I didn't know," he said.

For all Daniel's genius in the world of technical invention, he had always delegated the business side of affairs to his partner. Daniel remained relatively unsophisticated in the ways of business and journalistic ethics, and it had just gotten him into trouble. And it had been at her hands. Her father had been right; she had betrayed her best friend. She had not intended to, but it was how

Daniel viewed her actions, and in truth, she had not been as careful as she should have been. She never considered Daniel's naïveté in working with journalists.

"I treated that interview just like any of the dozens I have done over the years," she said cautiously. "I think you treated it as a conversation between friends, but I saw it as a conversation for publication." Daniel's hard glare did not soften, but he did not deny her comment, either, and she knew her assessment was correct. Perhaps it was arrogant to believe she had the power to help mend the rift between Daniel and Forsythe, but the damage had been done, and the only way to make anything positive out of this debacle was to keep urging Daniel toward a just resolution of the issue.

"Daniel, you have been very forthright about your determination to ruin Forsythe. You have never failed at anything in your life, and I have every confidence that you will ultimately succeed in driving Forsythe Industries into the dust. Sooner or later you will shut his company down, just like you shut down his college." It hurt to see Daniel's smoldering anger directed straight at her, but Clara drew herself to full height and walked toward him, praying she would be capable of penetrating his animosity. "But while you are digging Forsythe's grave," she said quietly, "you may as well dig your own because you are *destroying yourself.*"

"I don't care," he said ruthlessly. "This is something that's been driving me for years, and it feels right, Clara."

"It feels *right* to allow Forsythe's employees to scrape by on pitiful wages? It feels *right* to destroy a college Forsythe planned to build? Daniel, what kind of man are you?"

Daniel froze, and Clara's heart nearly broke wide open when she saw the pain her questions caused him. "I'm the kind of man who has always trusted your judgment," he finally said. "When you were hauled up on charges in England, I never doubted you or spilled poison about you in the press. I just shelled out whatever payment it took to get you the best lawyer in England to fight on your behalf."

Clara's eyes widened in astonishment and the breath left her body in a rush. Never had she tried to discover the anonymous benefactor who had arranged for Mr. Townsend's staggering legal fees, and now that she saw the truth of the matter on Daniel's face, she wanted to weep. "That was you?" she asked weakly.

"That was me."

She held her hands outward, palms up in a mute appeal. "Daniel, I don't know what to say . . . how to thank you . . ."

If anything, her words seemed to make him angrier. "I don't want your thanks; I want your *loyalty*. I want to know how a woman I idolized more than the sun and the stars rolled together now thinks I am not worthy to be operating a business in this city."

His face remained shuttered, and Clara scrambled to find some way to reach him before he ruined every bit of goodness in his soul. Nothing she said made a dent in his bitterness. The man who now showered fury down on her head was not the friend she had known all these years. The garden bench was just a few steps away, and she managed to reach it before the strength in her knees gave way.

Daniel stood motionless; his face was carved in stone and he looked like a stranger. Daniel always seemed so strong and confident. Was that why she didn't expect him to be damaged by her actions?

Rather than help mend the situation, her recklessness had thrown oil on the flames of his discontent. The realization left her drained and exhausted. "I wrote that article because I hoped you could see how you're affecting yourself and thousands of innocent people." She turned her tortured eyes to him. "I'm sorry for what I did, but I fear you are about to ruin any chance you and I might have for happiness, for a marriage. For children together. None of those things will ever be possible if you pursue this obscene need to punish Forsythe. When Jesus hung on the cross, He forgave the people who crucified Him."

The moment she said the word *Jesus,* what little tolerance was left in Daniel evaporated. "No preaching, Clara," he warned.

"I wanted to save you," she said weakly.

"It didn't work."

He turned on his heel and left her sitting among her clematis vines.

Mrs. Lorna Lancaster, born Lorna Tremain, had the exact shade of gray eyes as her brother, but that was where the resemblance ended. Lorna's hair was a rich auburn she had twisted atop her head, and she wore a smartly embroidered peacock blue jacket and skirt. With a skirt so narrowly cut that she walked in delicate little steps, it was hard to envision Lorna growing up in the same squalid tenement alongside Daniel. Today, Lorna looked the picture of well-bred elegance as she sipped coffee at the Belgravia Coffee Shop in the historic section of Baltimore. The café had brick walls and ancient plank floors that leant itself to intimate conversations.

Clara was grateful Lorna had agreed to meet with her. After the publication of her article in last week's edition of *The Christian Crusade*, she feared she might be *persona non grata* among the entire Tremain clan. She had not seen Daniel since he stormed out of her garden that awful morning, and he'd ignored the series of conciliatory messages she had sent him in the following days.

Lorna was nonchalant about the article. "Business as usual," she said lightly. "Daniel has always carried on that relentless grudge against Alfred Forsythe. I lost interest years ago."

As the oldest of Daniel's sisters, Lorna was the person most likely to have insight into his character. For a man to be so brilliant, so talented, and yet suffer from such a profound lack of moral compass in his business operations was intolerable. It appeared everyone in Daniel's company and family simply accepted his vendetta against Alfred Forsythe as naturally as the sun setting in the west. Clara could not simply overlook the effect Daniel's anger had on his soul, and Lorna was her best shot at trying to unravel the complicated threads of Daniel's life during the long years she had spent in England.

"Daniel was always outrageously protective," Lorna said. "I knew we didn't have much money when we were growing up, but he shielded us from that fact. We were never hungry and he always had something for us on Christmas morning. A hair ribbon or a bar of scented soap. The only time I realized how close to the edge we lived was one morning when I noticed the Ansonia clock was missing from the wall in the kitchen. I thought we had been robbed and told Daniel about it when he returned from work that night. The look that came over his face . . ." Lorna's voice trailed off and her brow furrowed at the memory, but at last her voice continued. "He looked so ashamed. He had pawned the clock and hoped to earn it back before any of us noticed it missing. It was a valuable clock, and he never got it back, but a week later a new one was hanging in its place. It had a cheap oak frame and the hands were made of iron, but that clock means more to me than if it were made of solid gold. I still have it in my new home."

The cloud that had crossed Lorna's face cleared. "But enough of those dreary memories. Daniel always provided quite well for us. He made sure we went to school and studied hard. He sent us to church every Sunday. Our clothes were always clean—"

Clara's eyes widened in astonishment. "Daniel took you to church?"

"Well, Daniel didn't, but he made sure Mrs. Hershberger, who lived down the hall from us, came and took us with her to services each Sunday."

Clara leaned forward, hope surging in her heart. This was the first she had heard that Daniel had any regard for religion whatsoever. "Why didn't Daniel take you?"

"He was never particularly religious."

"But he thought it was important for *you* to go."

"Oh yes. He was adamant that we attend each week." Lorna

poured another cup of coffee, and offered some to Clara, who accepted in order to prolong their meeting. "I remember there was an Easter morning and I asked him to go with us," Lorna said. "The choir always sang such lovely songs on Easter, and I thought that he would enjoy that. When he said no, I pressed him. I didn't want him sitting alone in our apartment when I knew how much he loved music." Lorna poured a bit of cream into her cup. "Anyway, he got very angry and told me never to pester him about it again. There were very few things that Daniel forbade us to discuss, but the way he shouted at me that morning made me afraid to ever bring it up again."

"What else did he forbid you to speak of?" She ought to feel embarrassed asking a virtual stranger such intimate questions, but her journalistic instincts told her she was on the verge of something very important.

The sigh that came from Lorna was heavy with years of sorrow. She twirled a spoon in her coffee and her eyes grew distant. "Do you know how my mother died?" she finally asked.

Clara remembered that it had been Lorna who found her mother's body hanging in their tiny kitchen. "Yes, I know," she said softly.

"Daniel was horrified by what happened," Lorna said. "It was even worse because he knew all of us had seen Mother dangling there before he could come home and get her down. As soon as my mother's body was carried from the apartment, Daniel tried to close the door on what happened . . . pretend that we never saw her hanging there. It was as if he thought that by refusing to discuss it, we would forget." Lorna idly stirred her coffee as she stared into the cup. "I suppose that was probably true for Katie. She was only three when it happened, and she didn't really understand. But I remember."

The wistful expression on Lorna's face tugged at Clara's heart. She knew what it was to lose a mother at a young age, but she could not pretend to know anything of the sorrow that must have surrounded Mrs. Tremain's demise. She reached out and covered Lorna's slim hand with her own, wishing there was something she could offer beyond mere sympathy.

"In any event, Daniel started making good money after he filed his first patent. Two years after Mother died he rented a house for us, one that had a bathroom with running water in it and a front yard. We felt like it was a castle. He bought houses for both Rachel and me when we got married, and I expect he plans to do the same for Katie, although I gather ready cash is a bit tight for him these days."

The unspoken thought hung in the air. If Daniel allowed his company to become public, he would become one of the wealthiest men in the country. As it was, he was scrambling to ensure his sisters maintained the lifestyle which he had been able to provide for them.

The bell above the entrance rang as a man, out of breath and sweating, burst inside. "Trouble brewing down on McNeill Street," he said.

The proprietor standing behind the service bar tossed his towel down. "Not again," he growled.

Clara gritted her teeth, but sent a reassuring squeeze through Lorna's hand. "None of the recent demonstrations have been violent," she said. Lorna had heard all the details of the day three weeks ago when her sister had been trapped by the riot downtown. In the past week there had been daily demonstrations that marked a souring of relations between the railroad workers and corporate owners. And much of that hostility had been directed straight at Daniel. "Nevertheless, we should probably move on," Lorna said.

✦✦✦

The carriage Clara took home dropped her off two blocks from her rented townhouse, where she was dismayed to see an overturned fruit cart and the awning over a fish market that had been pulled down. Had her article played any role in igniting this riot? Words were powerful weapons, and her article had launched a potent broadside at the two industrialists who employed so many of Baltimore's workers. She nearly staggered under the thought that she might have played a part in this. Her articles were intended to spark *dialogue*, not vandalism!

Clara saw a woman scrambling to retrieve fruit that had rolled into the street while her small son trailed behind her, holding a basket. The anxiety on the little boy's face made Clara's mouth thin in anger. She was just about to join the boy in gathering fruit when she saw her father walking toward her.

"My heavens, what happened to your forehead?" she gasped.

Lloyd held a handkerchief spotted with blood to his temple. "Caught a bit of flying apple with my face," he said with remarkable good humor. "If you had been here ten minutes ago, you would have seen far more excitement. I had forgotten how hard young boys can hurl projectiles."

Clara was flabbergasted. "They threw apples at an *old man*?"

Lloyd winced. "Nothing hurt quite as much as that statement, Clara. Now show me to this townhouse you and Clyde are renting."

Clara grasped her father's arm and walked with him the two blocks to her townhouse. He seemed steady on his feet, thank goodness, but there was something particularly terrible about seeing an elderly man with blood on his face. Once inside, she sat him down at the kitchen table, fetched some water, and dabbed at the cut on his forehead as gently as she could. It was a tiny scratch, but she remembered Clyde saying that head wounds always bled more profusely.

"I wish Clyde were here; he would know what to do," she said as she pressed the cloth to his head and applied pressure.

"You are doing perfectly well. Besides, it was not Clyde I came to see."

She suspected as much and sank into a chair opposite him. Her father had not been seriously hurt—it was only the slightest cut—yet the thin sheen of perspiration on his skin and the shakiness in his frame alerted her to the fact that the incident had been stressful on the old man. Seeing her father in such a condition rattled her, and she imagined how terrible she would feel if he had been seriously hurt and she was allowing this ridiculous rift to languish between them.

"What did you come to see me about?" she asked.

Lloyd pressed the towel to his forehead and the glint of humor came back to his eyes. "I heard there was rioting in this part of town, and I was rushing to your rescue, my dear."

Clara's heart turned over. "Oh, Father, truly there was no need . . ."

"I can see that now, but one of the quirks about parenthood is that the impulse to protect a child can't be suppressed, even after the child is completely grown. And daughters are especially likely to fuel this quirk." The smile he sent her held a world of sadness behind it, and she knew exactly what he was thinking. No matter how wrongheaded she believed him to be, there was no question in her mind that her father believed he had been acting in her best interest by separating her from Daniel all those years ago.

She leaned back in her chair and fixed him with a quizzical stare. "Isn't it odd that I have been nagging Daniel about his inability to forgive those who have sinned against him, while at the same time I took myself off to the other side of Baltimore rather than confronting my own issues with forgiveness?"

"I am not foolish enough to risk commenting on Daniel Tremain's qualities or shortcomings at this particular juncture. As to the second part of your question, I would more than welcome your returning home to bat about issues of forgiveness with you at greater length."

It was likely to be the only apology she would ever get from her father. But what had she expected? Lloyd Endicott was not a man who would reverse his convictions and come racing across town just because she had left his house in a snit. And what if he had been killed today? What if instead of an apple, it had been a rock that had struck him and sent him crashing to the ground? She would never forgive herself if her father had died while she had made no effort to mend the rift between them. Daniel would never get an apology from Alfred Forsythe, and she would never get one from her father. They both had to accept that.

She covered his hand with hers. "I'll be happy to come back home," she said.

CHAPTER 13

Bane lounged against the wall as the Professor rifled through the assorted ties, cravats, and opera scarves hanging in his oversized dressing room. Finally, the Professor found a white silk cravat that pleased him.

"Now pay attention, boy. A man who can't tie a cravat is a pitiful sight." The Professor tossed another cravat at Bane, then walked to a mirror above his dressing bureau. He settled the strip of fabric around the back of his neck and waited for Bane to do the same. "Now take the long side and cross it over the short side. Be sure you cross it over the top, just like this."

Bane mimicked the actions, wearing the brand-new cutaway jacket, silk waistcoat, and slacks the Professor had had tailored for him. Not for any special occasion—the Professor had simply said it was time for Bane to have a formal suit. The Professor's words still rang in Bane's ears. *"You are the closest thing I will ever have to a son, Bane. You must look the part."*

Bane soon had a perfectly tied cravat. He raised his chin a notch, liking his reflection in the mirror. He looked like a man of consequence, not like a powerless idiot who would let himself get snatched off the street.

"Why white silk instead of black?" he asked. "I thought black was the most formal color."

"Not for evening wear," the Professor said. "White is the most formal color in the evenings, but you must never wear it before six o'clock. Remember, your appearance and the manner in which you present yourself is of the utmost importance. There will be times when you will need to mingle among high society, and your manners must be second nature. Effortless."

"Sprezzatura," Bane said, hoping he was pronouncing the Italian word correctly. From the dazzling smile on the Professor's face, he knew he had.

"I see you have been reading Castiglione," the Professor said with admiration in his voice. "Excellent. The quality of *sprezzatura* will help any man who wishes to accomplish great things while appearing utterly nonchalant. You have already shown impressive skill in this area."

Bane adjusted the crisp silk as it rested against his chin, careful to keep the excitement from his voice. "Speaking of business within respectable society . . ."

The professor raised a brow. "Yes?"

"I have completed my research on Daniel Tremain and am ready to go into action."

The Professor's eyes gleamed. "Tell me your plan, son." As Bane outlined his technique, the Professor's eyes warmed in approval. Although smuggling opium was a lucrative trade, it required a massive network of shipping contacts and took months before the payoff. The Professor's criminal empire was highly diversified, and when the opportunity to earn a quick, untraceable ten thousand dollars had presented itself last month, the Professor had asked Bane to manage the task.

Not that Bane had any hostility toward Daniel Tremain. If anything, he admired a self-made man, but this was the test the Professor had set for him, and he would succeed in stunning fashion. It was important to demonstrate not only his cunning and agility but his ability to do so in an utterly calm, ruthless fashion. He knew what the Professor admired, and he would deliver it without a qualm. After all, Canada awaited him.

"What men have you arranged to take with you?" the Professor asked.

"Bill Richards, Scot McGahee, and the Castellano brothers."

"Are you sure about McGahee?" the Professor asked. "That baby face of his is not very intimidating." It was true, but Bane appreciated the value of being underestimated due to appearance. After all, for most of his life he had used his veneer of prettiness to lure a victim in until he was ready to reveal his true colors.

Bane said nothing, he just calmly turned to face the Professor, locking him in a motionless stare before morphing it into a hard glare.

For a moment the Professor seemed taken aback, and then a huge grin spread across his face. "Excellent!" The Professor clapped Bane on the back. "Bane, that is quite the most chilling look I've ever seen. Always remember, it is far better to be feared than loved. Keep your subordinates terrified of you. Someday a traitor might try to get the better of you, but stark terror will cause others to curry your favor by ratting him out." The Professor turned to look in the mirror as he began trimming his beard with a pair of tiny silver shears.

Bane returned to lounging against the wall and stared at the man who had once so frightened him. It had taken years to conquer that numbing sense of terror, but he had managed to accomplish it. He was still too young to contemplate taking on the Professor—there was far too much he needed to learn before he dared such a thing—but he could conquer Daniel Tremain. Everything he knew about Tremain indicated he was ruled by emotion, which was a hot, unwieldy instinct difficult to control. Cold logic was more lethal than a hot temper. Logic versus passion. Bane smiled, knowing in this upcoming battle with Tremain exactly which quality held the upper hand.

"You will do well, boy," the Professor said. "When you return, we must prepare you to undertake your new position in Canada."

Bane could hardly wait.

CHAPTER 14

The day after Clara returned to her father's home she spent the afternoon helping him pack his bags for a trip to New York. That evening he would depart for a conference of the American ministers who were working toward educational reform. It seemed such a shame that she had only just returned to her father's house before he had to dash off on business, but after all, he was the Reverend Lloyd Endicott, and a man of his position had important responsibilities.

Clara also found refuge at the piano, hoping the lyrical melodies of Franz Schubert could soothe the tension that had gripped her ever since she'd seen her father wandering down the street with a bloodied forehead.

On some level, she felt responsible for the ongoing unrest, since her article calling attention to Daniel's peculiar business practices had helped to reignite simmering labor tensions. Riots had been occurring once or twice a week when she arrived in Baltimore, but now they were a daily event. For most of his career, Daniel had been able to avoid troubles with labor since his employees were limited to a handful of engineers and innovators who worked alongside him in his wonderfully eccentric laboratory. That had changed five years ago when they diversified their business by purchasing railroad lines. Now Carr & Tremain had hundreds of employees working on the lines, replacing railroad ties and soldering new rails. Thanks to Clara's article, these workers were only just learning of the profit Daniel was rejecting by refusing to license technology to Forsythe Industries. Some of that money could surely have been used to supplement their wages. The smoldering embers of discontent were stoked as the workers realized they were the pawns of wealthy men in a private feud.

And this morning's newspaper brought another salvo in the war between Daniel and Forsythe. On page two of *The Baltimore Sun* was a full-page advertisement bearing the logo of Forsythe Industries and block text calling for Daniel Tremain to relent in his retaliatory business practices. A table beneath the text contained current wages paid to Forsythe workers, and another table outlined what he could pay should his company have access to Daniel's technology. Alfred Forsythe's advertisement would only further inflame the public's animosity toward Daniel. She lowered her head. Was she any better than Alfred Forsythe? It made her cringe to realize that her article, well-intentioned though it had been, was little different from Forsythe's in laying the blame at Daniel's feet.

When Clara's father saw the advertisement, he agreed with her. "I'm sorry Forsythe placed this advertisement, as I don't think it is helpful in easing the current tensions," Lloyd said. "Unless Daniel relents soon, this is the sort of thing that will only fuel the flames of discontent."

"But do you really think Forsythe would pass that profit on to his workers?" Clara asked. "He is not as wealthy as Vanderbilt, and that fact keeps him awake at night. He has the reputation of bleeding his workers white in order to increase his earnings."

Lloyd took the newspaper from Clara and adjusted the spectacles on his nose as he studied the columns in the advertisement more closely. Finally he shook his head. "Now that Forsythe has gone public with what he is prepared to pay should this feud come to an end, it will be hard for him to back out of it," Lloyd said. "He wants to run for governor, and if he rescinds this promise, his political career would take a thrashing from which he could never recover. It is Daniel's move now."

Clara let her gaze drift to the fading light outside the window, and a horse and rider pulling up before the house caught her attention. He was a nattily dressed gentleman, but Clara was certain she had never seen him before. "Do you know this man, Father?"

Her father knew half of Baltimore, but he failed to recognize the man, either. When they answered the three brisk knocks on the door, the man did not even bother to introduce himself.

"I am here to see the editor of *The Christian Crusade*," the man said abruptly.

"That would be me," Lloyd said.

Before her father had even completed his sentence, the stranger thrust a roll of papers into Lloyd's hands. "You are hereby notified of a pending lawsuit in the Circuit Court of Baltimore. I wish you a good day, sir."

The moment the door closed behind the officious stranger, Clara and Lloyd unrolled the thick stack of documents. Clara gasped in shock.

"We are being sued by *Daniel*?" she gasped. Clara felt the beginnings of tunnel vision, but forced her gaze to keep scanning the pages. A multitude of legal terms smacked her in the face: slander, libel, interference with a private corporation, invasion of privacy. Each word sliced at her like an ice pick. They were the same charges she had faced in London, only this time it was her father's newspaper she was sinking. A long list of attorneys' names, lined up like soldiers ready to do battle, was affixed to the document.

"Well, he certainly is thorough," her father said. His normally brisk voice sounded thin and tired.

Clara's legs felt too weak to support her. "I'm so sorry, Father," she whispered through pale lips. She had hoped her article would help bring this feud to an end, but Daniel was just getting started. He was barricading himself behind a team of lawyers and banishing her from his life. She should have known when she saw the cold steel in his eyes the morning he confronted her in the garden. Daniel was finished with her. He had flung her out of his life in the same abrupt manner in which he walked away from Forsythe Industries.

She knew the way Daniel's mind operated. If she didn't do something to stop him, the wall he was building to shut her out of his life would calcify into a structure nothing could tear down.

❧❧

The setting sun was casting long shadows across the downtown streets, and Clara hurried to reach Daniel's office before he left for the day. It made no sense to confront him at his home, where he could easily toss her off his property. It would be much harder to make a scene at his office with dozens of employees as witness. Not that she didn't think he would hesitate to do it, but she might have a few seconds to break through to him before he surrounded himself behind his squadron of attorneys.

She was surprised at how easy it was to get into his office. Perhaps he had not expected her to seek him out because no one tried to stop her as she strode across the oversized laboratory and knocked on the door of his private office.

"Come in," she heard him say from behind the heavy door. Clara leaned her forehead against the door and prayed for strength. She took a deep breath and pushed her way inside.

Daniel's eyes widened in surprise, but he quickly masked any sign of emotion as he turned his attention back to the papers on his desk. The white-hot fury of last weekend was gone, replaced by icy formality.

"We have no business to discuss," he said without looking up from his papers. "The names of my attorneys are on the papers you received this morning. They are the appropriate people to discuss your concerns with from this point forward."

She tried not to flinch as the coldness of his words sliced through her. "Stop it, Daniel. I won't let you talk to me like that."

"Like what?"

"Like you despise me," she said. "I hurt you and I understand why you are angry with me, but I know you don't despise me. Had I known you wanted that information kept private, I would have respected your wishes. Is there any way you can stop seeing me like a reporter you resent and return to treating me like a friend who cares about you?"

"You gave that up when you published that article." The way he twirled a pencil between his long fingers might fool a casual observer into thinking he was bored, but Clara saw the anger in his clenched jaw.

"I'm not leaving until you at least *look at me*, Daniel."

He dropped the pencil and finally looked up at her, but still maintained the coldly impersonal tone. "I see from yesterday's newspaper that your father has called a meeting for all your wealthy parishioners to pray that Forsythe and I seek wisdom and understanding. Do you realize how insulting that is?" he said in a silky voice.

Clara stood a little straighter. "I know that my father has the best of intentions, but you are still looking for bombs to throw at Forsythe. This behavior does not flatter you."

"The best intentions," Daniel said with perfect equanimity.

"This is the man who stole our letters and then dares to preach to me about godliness. The two of you are responsible for stoking the fire of this mess, so let's not hide behind schoolmarm reprimands, shall we?"

It was so hard to keep looking at him. He had the same face, the same slightly tousled black hair . . . but everything she knew and loved about Daniel seemed to have disappeared.

"Why don't you come to the prayer meeting?" she asked impulsively. "It would at least show people that you are open to listening to their concerns."

"One thing you need to understand," Daniel said. "This isn't England, where disputes can be politely handled in a court of law. Nor is it a prayer meeting where we all hold hands and hope Jesus will help our enemies see the light. This is a tough, gritty world where arguments are settled with fists, and riots are broken up with bayonets."

Daniel stood and strode around the desk, clamping the palm of his hand around her elbow. "Come along," he said. "There is someone I want you to meet."

Clara was so startled she let him pull her along as he strode out of the office, across the length of the laboratory, and down a long corridor filled with private offices. He gave three quick raps on a closed office door, then opened it and pushed her inside. A startled man looked up from behind his spectacles to stare at them both.

"Clara, meet Lou Hammond, my attorney. Any further conversation you wish to have with me will be funneled through Mr. Hammond's office. Good-bye, Clara."

When the door slammed behind her, Clara knew she had failed. Daniel had gone back to building his wall between them.

∗∗∗

Something caused her to rouse from her heavy slumber.

Clara rolled over in bed, her mind groggy with sleep. Her bedroom was dark and still, nothing to cause alarm. But then she heard it, a clanging sound coming from far away. The urgent, rapid-paced ringing of bells was echoing through the night air.

She rose from her bed and rushed to the window, unfastening the latches and pulling the casement up. Now it was easier to hear the bells, coming from the north side of town. Riots? She waited to hear the distinctive one-five-one sound of bells that signaled a riot. But the clanging of the bells was a steady, ongoing staccato, indicating a fire, not a riot.

She went to the window on the far side of her room and could see the eerie red glow lighting the horizon. The fire was up on the high end of Guilford Street, where lots of well-to-do homes had been built in the last few years. It was where Daniel lived.

A sense of foreboding enveloped her. There were many houses in that part of town; any one of them could be on fire. But Daniel was one of the few company owners who lived that far north, and the one most likely to be a target should this be related to the recent troubles.

She hadn't even finished the thought before she was pulling on a shift and overskirt. She would have to ride her father's horse in order to get there. She would rather handle a nest of live hornets than mount a horse, but it couldn't be helped. It was possible this would be a pointless ride that would end in nothing more than a lost night of sleep, but sitting here in this bedroom when there was a possibility that Daniel was in trouble was inconceivable. It took her less than two minutes to dress and be out the door.

Her father kept his horse at a private stable two blocks away. Clara hiked up her skirts and ran, breathless by the time she arrived at the stable. Then came the far more daunting task of saddling Old Soldier. She refused to let this ridiculous dread of horses stop her if Daniel was in trouble. Old Soldier did not like being pulled from sleep and kept drifting to the far side of the stall each time she tried to heft the saddle over his back. Twice the horse tried to push Clara into the side of the stall, nearly knocking the wind from her body, but at last she got him saddled, mounted, and grudgingly moving north.

As she approached Guilford Street and the pungent scent of smoke tinged the air, Old Soldier got skittish and began sidestepping her attempts to move him forward. This was the point when she normally would give up and let the horse win, but Clara shortened the reins and squeezed her knees with every fiber of muscle she possessed, then squeezed again. At last she succeeded in spurring the reluctant horse forward.

No ride had ever taken so long, but she finally arrived within two streets of Daniel's house. People were pouring onto the street, hauling buckets of water to douse their own homes and shrubbery lest the fire spread. The sound of the bells grew louder and finally Old Soldier refused to move any farther. She leapt from his back and secured him to a fence post before running the final few blocks to the site of the fire. The air got hotter as she rounded the corner and finally saw the source of the fire.

Daniel's home was completely engulfed in flames.

She stood frozen as she watched men lift heavy canvas tubing from the water truck to shoot water at the houses on either side of the fire in a desperate attempt to stop the blaze from spreading. No effort was being made to salvage Daniel's house. The fire had already eaten through most of the exterior woodwork, exposing the frame of the building. It was a waste to pour water on Daniel's home when the neighboring houses might be spared.

Even worse than the heat of the fire were the sounds. The tinkling noise of glass as the windows shattered in their frames, the sound of wood popping and groaning as it twisted under the weight of the roof. The house was going to collapse soon, and firefighters were trying to move the crowd of onlookers farther back to a safe distance from the house.

Clara prayed that Daniel and Kate had escaped. She frantically searched among the crowd, but the glare from the fire made it hard to see any more than darkened silhouettes of people standing before the glare of the fire. Most of the bystanders were standing alone, but one man had his arm around a young woman . . . surely that was Daniel and his sister.

Clara raced toward them and grew dizzy with relief when she recognized Daniel and Kate. Daniel was staring at the fire as though hypnotized. His face was streaked with sweat and soot, but his eyes reflected the eerie flickering orange glow of the fire. "Daniel, thank God you are all right." She stepped forward and laid a hand on his arm, but he pulled away from her and hugged Kate tighter to his side.

"Get out of here, Clara," he said blankly. "This is no place for you." He did not break his gaze from his burning house, just kept staring at it as pieces of timber dropped from the roofline and sent showers of sparks into the air when they hit the ground.

"You'll need a place to stay," Clara said gently. "Come to my father's house. You can stay for as long as needed."

"So that you and your father can preach to me about wisdom and understanding? Trust me, I understand the message that was sent tonight, so what more do you want, Clara? The sins of my riches are all burning before your eyes."

She took a step back. "You know I had nothing to do with this."

"Do I?" His voice lashed out like a whip and he turned to look at her for the first time. "I was never despised by the working people until you came here and started whipping up sentiment against me."

Now Kate was looking daggers at her, as well. Clara straightened her shoulders. "I can't leave until I know you have a place to go," she said.

"Lorna will put us up," Kate said. "At least we've always been able to depend on family."

Clara did not miss the pointed barb. "You can depend on me," she said firmly. Daniel had turned his gaze back to the fire, ignoring her, but Clara moved to stand directly in front of him and grabbed his shoulders. His face was steeped in resentment, but at last he met her eyes. "I will never turn my back on you," she vowed in a fierce voice, loud enough to be heard over the menacing blast of the fire. "You are the best friend I've ever had and I won't abandon you no matter how angry you become. I *understand* you, Daniel. I understand why you hate Forsythe and I understand what this house meant to you." The glare he sent her at the mention of his house was scalding, but she wouldn't give up. "I even understand why you are furious with me," she continued. "No matter what terrible things befall you, I won't ever abandon you. You can throw me off your property, or you can sue me to kingdom come. You can take out advertisements in every newspaper in the land proclaiming me a muckraking idiot, but I will *always* consider you my greatest friend."

A tremendous groaning sound came from the house, and she saw Daniel's eyes widen in disbelief. She swiveled her head just in time to see the entire roof collapse into the house, shooting a blast of sparks into the sky like fireworks. A wall of heat rushed outward and she took a step back. They were well away from danger, but it was an instinctive move as the blistering heat magnified and the blaze consumed the house.

Daniel's attention had gone back to the house, ignoring her and his sister, as well. She laid a hand on his arm. "It's going to be all right. It is only *things* that have been lost. Nothing that can't be bought again."

Daniel's face looked to be carved from flint, a muscle ticking in his jaw as he clenched his teeth with anger. "Get out of here, Clara."

The quiet intensity of his voice made her want to flee. Instead, she stood up and kissed him on his cheek. "I'll be waiting for you when you are ready to come back to me," she said.

And then she turned and left him standing before the ruins of his house.

CHAPTER 15

Maguire would not have done it," Manzetti said with confidence. "Oh, he'll burn things down, but he provides plenty of notice before he does it."

Daniel sat at the table in Lorna's kitchen, an untouched cup of coffee before him. All he cared about was hunting down who was responsible for last night's fire, and the list was endless. Manzetti had risen through the same rank and file of steel workers as Daniel, and they were both personally acquainted with many of the men who now led the newly resurrected labor movement. If the fire related to labor, Eddie Maguire was the logical suspect. He was the leader of the cannery workers, and they had been known to organize riots in sympathy with other labor unions. Plus, he had a reputation for violence.

"Can I get you another cup of coffee?" Lorna asked softly. He shook his head no, and Lorna withdrew to the far side of the kitchen. His smoldering anger was making her timid, but for once in his life he couldn't rein it in to give her comfort.

"I still think it was Alfred Forsythe," Daniel said. "What better time to strike at me than when he can point the finger of blame at labor? The instant I withdrew the company for sale, he knew he would have no chance at licensing our technology. If I were removed from the scene, the deal would have gone through."

Manzetti shook his head. "But why burn your house? You said three shots were fired before the flames started burning. It sounds like whoever started it was providing a warning . . . making sure you were awake and could get out. If someone was trying to murder you, you'd have been killed before the flames were set. I think this is labor, not Forsythe."

Daniel shot to his feet and began pacing in the small confines of the kitchen. "That doesn't make sense," Daniel said, his voice slashing through the air. "Labor hasn't had enough time to issue their demands. You do not start burning houses until negotiations break down. We weren't even close to that point."

Manzetti kept talking, but it was hard for Daniel to concentrate. It wasn't just a house that had burned down last night, it was the culmination of his dream. When Clara had stated he could simply buy new things to replace what was ruined, he'd had to fight the impulse to bodily throw her off the property. That house contained every musical score he had ever written. It contained the first rudi-mentary drawings for his patents and the original prototypes of his inventions. And it had the only photograph left in existence of his parents. The picture of his deliriously happy mother with her crown of daisies was burned and gone.

Perhaps that was for the best. Whenever Daniel looked at that photograph of his mother's face bathed in joy, he wondered if it would have been better for her to have been struck dead that very day. How much better would it have been for her to die when she was happy, rather than sink into the wrenching despair that caused her to abandon every scrap of responsibility for her children and commit suicide? Did her goodness even count? Did the fact that she was a good Christian who loved her children even matter? From the day of his mother's suicide, Daniel had never set foot inside a church. To do so would mean confronting those awful questions and abandoning his thirst for revenge. Pursuit of Alfred Forsythe had been the fuel that had motivated him all these years, and he had no desire to set it aside.

His mother's suicide was just another curse in the long line of events that led back to Alfred Forsythe. His gut was screaming at him that the blame for last night's fire also lay with Forsythe. At the root of most of the tragedies in his life lay the slithering ambition of Alfred Forsythe, and this had the same stinking air. Forsythe had been on the verge of wrapping his claws around Carr & Tremain, so close he had no doubt been counting the revenue that would soon be flowing into his coffers.

He pierced Manzetti with a hard stare. "We need to find out what Clara Endicott knows. She has been talking with Forsythe, and I would not put it past her to have begun speaking to labor organizers, as well. Bring her to my office so we can talk." The very thought of Clara being entangled in this made his anger burn brighter. Clara had always represented a sanctuary where he could flee the responsibilities that weighed on him; now she was cavorting in the gritty underbelly of the world with his enemies.

The memory of the foul way he had treated her seared his mind. Last night he had given vent to the anger that festered inside his soul, but despite all that, she had vowed eternal loyalty to him. The sight of her anxious, sweat-stained face as she dared to confront him before the ruins of his house would stay with him the rest of his life. He had made no attempt to rein in his unwieldy temper, lashing out at her with reckless disregard. Somehow, he needed to figure out a way to keep the anger and pollution inside him from damaging the precious, gilded thread that tied him to Clara. If he did not protect that bond, it was in danger of snapping.

At noon the following day Clara heard the sound she had been dreading. The distinctive one-five-one pealing of alarm bells signaling another riot had begun.

It could not have come at a worse time. This morning she had received a message from Daniel requesting a meeting. Mr. Manzetti was slated to arrive within the hour to escort her to Daniel's downtown office, where she hoped they could begin piecing together the wreckage of their relationship. Whether the meeting was to discuss the breakdown of their friendship or the trouble brewing for his company didn't matter. It was all bound up in the same tangle of old history that needed to be resolved before Daniel could move forward.

Clara sat on the porch swing, waiting for Mr. Manzetti's arrival. Clyde whittled a piece of driftwood with an impressive-looking knife. "Are you sure this is really an offer of truce Tremain is planning? He is a master at holding grudges. Not so much for extending an olive branch."

"Then I'll bring the olive branch," Clara said. She swiveled on the porch swing so she could see him better. "Clyde, if you could have seen how proud Daniel was of his house, you wouldn't be so flippant. He poured himself into every line of the design and filled it with things that can never be replaced." Like a simple sketch on the back of a napkin that he had framed and displayed in a place of honor, and music he had written for her when he was still just a boy. "And it was more than just the things," she continued. "I think Daniel was proud of the fact that he had been able to give his family a sense of security they never had. That was what the house represented to him."

Clyde seemed unimpressed. "I've lived in a tent or under the stars for most of the last ten years. Forgive me if I'm not swamped with sympathy because your robber-baron boyfriend will have to buy himself a new mansion."

She was spared a sharp retort when the distinctive clop of horse hooves signaled Mr. Manzetti's arrival. She wondered if he would be as hostile as Daniel and his sister, but he sprang down from the carriage and tipped his hat to her as he approached the porch.

"Trouble brewing down by the mills," he said, "but they won't dare spill into Calvert Street where Tremain's office is. Are you still willing to go?"

The newspapers warned civilians to stay safely inside when the riot alarm sounded, and it only made sense to be afraid of a riot, but nothing petrified her as much as the thought of losing Daniel forever. She lifted the hem of her skirt as she marched down the stairs. "Just try to stop me," she said as he helped her into the carriage.

The carriage was sleek and well-sprung, but the interior smelled of smoke damage. She remembered that Daniel kept a stable a few acres down from his house, so at least his horse and carriage had been salvaged.

The roll of the carriage slowed as they traveled east on Mulberry Street. Clara sent a worried glance out the window, but aside from a snarl of carriages, there didn't seem to be untoward trouble. The city was growing so rapidly that this type of traffic was becoming increasingly common. The little window at the top of the compartment slid open and Mr. Manzetti called down to her, "I'm heading down Greene Street to bypass this mess."

Clara had been absent from the city for ten years and trusted Mr. Manzetti to know traffic navigation better than she, but on Greene Street carriages were caught up in something more ominous than an abundance of midday travelers. The riot alarms were sounding closer, and panicked pedestrians were hurrying amid the horses and carriages. Clara thought she heard a thump as something struck the carriage. She was about to lean forward and try to contact Mr. Manzetti when the carriage door was wrenched open.

A young man, or boy really, hurtled into the carriage. "Sorry, ma'am. Can I take cover in here?" He pulled the door shut behind him and slid into the seat opposite her. "The shops are all locking their doors and I've got nowhere to go."

Despite the sheer panic written across his face, the boy was possibly the most beautiful youth she had ever set eyes on. White-blond hair framed a face with Nordic features and crystal blue eyes. It was impossible to tell his age, but she could detect the barest hint of whiskers on his smooth white skin. The boy looked fearfully out the window. "The trouble is headed this way," he said as he pulled the lock closed on the carriage door. "It's a good thing your driver turned around, or you'd be headed straight into the thick of it."

Mr. Manzetti had turned the carriage with alacrity, sliding up onto the sidewalk in order to make quicker progress as they headed back up Greene. Clara tensed her fist in frustration. If she thought she could walk to Daniel's office, she would do so, but it was several miles away, and it was impossible to know what sort of chaos lay between here and there. Heaven only knew how long Daniel's conciliatory mood would last, and she had to get through to him today.

"Thank you for taking me in, ma'am," the boy said. "I've never known the rioting to get this far north."

The barest hint of a tremble shook the boy's voice, and Clara felt a surprising maternal instinct to comfort him. "You don't need to be afraid," she said soothingly. "We may be stuck here for an ungodly amount of time, but we will survive."

She was trying to remember how Daniel had jimmied those locks with her hairpins. If need be, she'd get out and find a way to seek shelter for herself and the boy in one of the locked buildings. A hint of relief flickered into her companion's blue eyes as he sent a nervous smile at her. This boy could probably slay girls clear across the Atlantic with that smile. "My name is Clara Endicott," she said, trying to ignore the increasing chaos outside the carriage window. "And who might you be? I must say you have a rather dramatic way of making an entrance."

"Sorry again for that," he said. The Adam's apple in his thin neck bobbed as he nervously swallowed. "I'm Alex."

The butt of a rifle smashed through the glass of the window and a thick arm reached through the opening, sliding the bolt and wrenching the door open. The boy hurtled across the carriage and clung to Clara as three men forced themselves inside. The carriage plunged to one side and almost toppled under the weight of the massive intruders.

"Get out of the carriage," Clara said to the boy. "*Move!* They don't want us, they want the carriage." She tried to push the boy toward the door, but a Colt revolver was shoved in her face, freezing her movement.

"You're not going anywhere, lady," the man said in a voice that sounded like gravel. The revolver traveled closer to her nose, and she leaned back in her seat, the boy still clutched in her arms.

"Pointing a gun at women and children," she said, amazed at the calm tone of her voice. "Your mother must be so proud."

The other two men laughed, but Clara noticed they were armed to the teeth, as well. She didn't know a simple belt could hold so many knives, clubs, and holstered guns. The carriage continued to careen down the street, and Clara had no idea if Mr. Manzetti was still in charge, or if he had leapt off to safety long ago.

The man pointing the gun found no humor in her comment and narrowed his scowl at her. "You don't like a gun pointed in your face? Fine. I'll keep it on the kid. See if that shuts up that smart mouth of yours." And with that he shifted the gun to point directly between Alex's terrified blue eyes. The boy's fingers tightened around her waist, but he bravely met the gravel-voiced man's eyes.

"You d-don't have to hurt either one of us," Alex said through white lips. "Just let us out of here."

"Why don't the two of you shut your face and enjoy the ride. We've got a ways to go."

Now Clara was certain that Mr. Manzetti was no longer driving the carriage. They were flying through a back alley completely devoid of protesters. When the gravel-voiced man noticed her looking out the window, he nodded to one of the other men, who pulled the muslin shades closed. Somehow being inside the darkened carriage with nothing to see but the three terrifying men was even worse. Clara's eyes drifted closed, and she sent up a prayer. *Yea, though I walk through the valley of the shadow of death . . .* She drew a blank on the next line. For years, she had recited Psalm twenty-three when troubled, and now when she was most in need, the lines escaped her. *Just please keep the boy safe.* She was old enough to fend for herself, but this poor child was out of his element and completely petrified. She was, too, but somehow it was easier to endure terror as an adult than as a boy barely old enough to shave.

She shifted and swayed in the seat as the carriage swerved

through the narrow city streets. She kept her arm around Alex's slender shoulders, occasionally sending a reassuring squeeze his way.

At last the carriage slowed to a halt, and Clara felt her mouth go dry. She was about to find out if all they wanted was the carriage, or if they intended to murder her and poor Alex on the spot.

The door was pulled open from outside and the men began filing out. No rays of sunshine leaked though the open door, and when she stepped outside, she was amazed to see the horse and carriage were inside a huge, mostly vacant warehouse. Alex got out behind her, but she was too busy looking for Mr. Manzetti to focus on anything else. Another giant ox of a man was in the driver's seat of the carriage, and there was no sign of Mr. Manzetti anywhere.

"Move out" came an order from behind her. Immediately the men assembled into a formation, and like a phalanx of Venetian soldiers, they boxed her in and forced her along with them as they strode deep into the warehouse. The echo of footsteps clattered throughout the cavernous space, and only a little weak light filtered through the dirty windows several stories above them.

At the far end of the warehouse a table and few chairs littered the corner. Crates were stacked up to enclose the space almost like a private room. Clara was shoved against a chair, which she took to be a request for her to sit. She did, not that she had any choice in the matter. Directly across from her the men were lined up as though in formation, arms folded across their beefy chests as they seemed to have no purpose other than to stare at her. There was no sign of Alex.

"Where is Mr. Manzetti?" she asked. "And Alex? What have you done with them?"

The gravel-voiced man stepped forward and grabbed a handful of her blouse, hauling her forward until she was nose to nose with his sweaty face. "I told you before to shut up, and if I have to remind you again, I'm slicing that tongue out of your head and sending it to Tremain and see if he'll pay ransom for that much, at least. Have you got that through your thick skull?" With one arm he shook her like a rag doll, and Clara felt the coils of her hair coming loose and tumbling down the back of her head.

"Richards, knock it off."

The cool voice came from the far side of the warehouse and her tormenter immediately dropped Clara back into her chair as a glimmer of fear shone in his eyes. "Sorry, Bane," he mumbled. "It won't happen again."

Clara looked toward the voice, and her eyes widened in shock as Alex strolled forward, his beautiful face a portrait of serenity as he casually pulled out a chair opposite her. "Bring us something to drink; our guest looks thirsty. McGahee, get rid of the carriage and set the horse free."

The men turned to do his bidding, but Clara could not tear her eyes off the boy. He seemed so young, and yet he calmly ordered men who were twice his size and age with the ease of a prince born into power. She couldn't lose her nerve now.

"I'm not interested in something to drink. I'm interested in what you've done with my driver, Alex."

"My name is Alex Banebridge, but call me Bane; everyone else does," he said calmly. "And you really shouldn't open your door to strangers, Clara."

"You forced yourself into my carriage!"

"Let's not split hairs. Do you care for coffee or tea? I've got both."

She ignored the question. "So what is the plan? Are you hoping to ransom me back to someone? I'll make it easy on you. My father will pay; Tremain will not."

A smile lit Bane's face, revealing an array of perfectly straight, gleaming white teeth. "Thank you for that piece of information, but we are planning on killing you, so there will be no need for any messy ransom notes. Paper trails are so bothersome."

The breath froze in her throat and she stared in disbelief at the slip of a boy sitting before her. "Are you serious?" she finally managed to stammer.

"Afraid so. But don't worry. I'm good at this and it won't hurt. I can be very quick." One of Bane's thugs set down a pot of tea and two teacups. She watched in fascination as Bane leaned forward and poured out a carefully measured dose of tea and slid it across the table to her. He poured one for himself and took a sip. Surely he would not be drinking from the same pot if the tea were poisoned.

"It would be rude not to join me," he said. He withdrew a watch from his pocket and noted the time while drawing another sip of tea.

"And you are such a stickler for manners, I see. Do you always take tea before bedtime? Am I to read you a story, as well?" She was surprised to see nervous glances being exchanged between the thugs who surrounded the table. Did they really fear this boy so much? She didn't believe he was capable of killing her . . . if he wanted her dead, she would already be dead.

She took a sip of tea. It tasted fine, so she downed the entire cup. This kidnapping business had made her extraordinarily thirsty. "So who paid you to kidnap me? I've never seen you before, so someone must have put you up to this."

"Obviously."

"Who?"

He leaned back in his chair with feline grace, that creepy little smile back on his pretty face. "I don't give information away for free; it is not good business."

She was still thirsty and reached to pour another cup of tea, but Bane's hand locked around her wrist like an iron band and slammed her arm to the table before she could touch the pot.

"No more tea," he said.

"Stingy, are we? And you are about to come into such riches from your criminal enterprise today."

One of Bane's goons leaned forward. "I've seen Bane break a man's leg for that kind of wise crack. You'd better watch it, lady." Bane neither confirmed nor denied the comment; he just remained watching her so calmly it was impossible to read what was going on behind that oddly beautiful face.

But strangely, she didn't really care. A rather delightful pressure settled on her shoulders and chest, making her feel expansive and brave. She glanced at the teapot and Bane's hand still keeping her wrist locked to the table.

She had been drugged.

"So what was in the tea?" she asked calmly. It was easy to be calm, since nothing really mattered anyway. "Am I going to die from it?"

Instead of answering her, Bane opened his watch again. "Two minutes," he reported, and one of his goons made a notation on a small notepad. "This batch is stronger than the last, so we ought to fetch at least ten percent more."

"You drank it, too," she said inanely.

Bane looked amused. "Of course I didn't. The powder was in the bottom of your teacup before I filled it. Opium is a nasty habit. I don't indulge."

Bane kept talking, but she had quit listening. She was grateful the chair had a back because holding her head up was getting to be too much work. She slumped against the back of the chair and her head lolled to her shoulder. She kept her eyes open, though. The thugs were putting little gray cakes on the table, and Bane was grinding them into a powder. Was he some kind of drug runner? The way he took a tiny little instrument and held the powder to the light made him look like some kind of scientist. A dazzling, wicked scientist.

Her left side felt very heavy, and the floor was beginning to look more comfortable than this straight-backed chair.

"Better catch her," she thought she heard someone say. But it was the last thing she heard before everything went dark.

CHAPTER 16

Daniel pounded on the front door of Clara's house. He could have been polite and knocked like a civilized person, but there was very little civility left in him. Clara should have been at his office hours ago, but she hadn't shown up. He might have understood if Clara had refused to meet with him as agreed, but Manzetti's simultaneous disappearance was ominous. There had been some minor rioting downtown this afternoon, but that had dispersed almost as quickly as it had arisen. And still no sign of either Clara or Manzetti.

Daniel pounded on the door harder. If Clara was safely holed up in her house, Daniel didn't know if he would embrace her or shake her until her teeth rattled. Finally the door was opened by

Clyde. Or someone who mildly resembled the Clyde Endicott he had once known.

"Is Clara here?" Daniel asked bluntly.

Clyde took his time peeling an apple with a small hunting knife. "Who wants to know?"

It had been twelve years since they'd laid eyes on each other, but Daniel was certain that Clyde knew precisely whom he was speaking to. "It's Daniel Tremain, Clyde. Clara was supposed to be at my office at two o'clock, and there was never any sign of her."

Clyde merely shrugged. "Maybe she decided she had better things to do than listen to her supposed 'best friend' accuse her of inciting arson. Can't say that I blame her." Clyde propped a shoulder against the frame of the door and flicked the long curl of apple peel into the garden. He was about to slice a wedge from the apple when Daniel's fist closed around his hand and wrenched the knife away.

"I sent my man to pick up Clara just after lunch, but they never showed. An hour ago my carriage was discovered abandoned near the canneries, with a broken window and shattered glass inside. Clara's reticule was on the floor of the carriage."

Clyde straightened to his full height, the nonchalance replaced by fierce concentration in those pale blue eyes. "What do you need me to do?"

"I need a fresh horse. I'm heading to Manzetti's home next. I have already traced the route they would have taken to my office, and there was no sign of them. Manzetti's is the next logical place to look."

Clyde strode to the hallway closet and nearly wrenched the door from its hinges as he flung it wide. A moment later he had a leather satchel that he threw over his shoulder. "I'm coming with you."

It took twenty minutes for the men to reach the three-story townhouses where Manzetti lived in one of the city's middle-class neighborhoods. After receiving no answer to their pounding on the front door, Daniel made short work of the lock and pushed his way inside.

The interior of the townhouse was eerily silent as Daniel strode through the ground floor. Clyde vaulted up the stairs, calling for Clara. An open-faced newspaper was spread on the kitchen table and a canvas bag of laundry hung on the coatrack, awaiting the regular Tuesday pickup. Aside from that, everything was in perfect order. Manzetti took great pride in his home, keeping the hardwood floors polished with a regular fresh coat of wax and the interior immaculately tidy.

Clyde was coming down the stairs when Daniel pulled open a drawer from the front hall table. "His riding gloves are gone," he said. Now he knew for certain that Manzetti had taken the carriage to pick up Clara, as the only time the man wore riding gloves was when he was handling a team of horses. Nothing short of an onslaught of violence would have knocked Manzetti from his mission. Manzetti wasn't simply a bodyguard; he was a three-hundred-pound force of nature who could intimidate lesser mortals who dared to interfere with his duty. The thought that Clara could have been the victim of random violence when Manzetti was with her was unthinkable. Daniel shoved the thought away and tried to think of the only logical explanation for their disappearance.

"I think we need someone posted at both of our houses to await a ransom demand," Daniel finally said.

Clyde's eyes widened. "Our family is not the sort who would attract that kind of attention."

"But I am," Daniel said flatly. "There are enough people in my inner circle who could have guessed that Clara meant more to me than a casual friendship. They knew I would pay." Although anyone close to Daniel would also know of his affection for his sisters, and Kate's penchant for sporting events would have made her a much easier target. He scanned the room, looking for anything out of the ordinary, or something that could shed the tiniest light of insight into what had happened to Manzetti. But everything looked in its place. The stack of newspapers he rarely threw out, the tidy arrangement of furniture, the little lace doilies he had covering all his tabletops because he thought it looked like the way well-to-do people decorated their homes.

The roll of money on Manzetti's desk was out of place. Manzetti had grown up in the same hollow-bellied poverty as Daniel, and would never have left money lying so casually about his home. In two strides Daniel had reached the desk and weighed the hefty roll in his palm.

"That's a fat wad of bills," Clyde said. "How much is there?" Daniel unrolled the stack of dollar bills and fanned them out to count them.

"Two hundred dollars." This didn't make sense. Daniel did not pay Manzetti in cash but arranged for a regular deposit to be paid into his bank account every two weeks. What would Manzetti need this much cash for? He knew the man had been hankering after a new horse, but that would cost less than a hundred dollars.

"What kind of purchase would require that much money in cash?" Clyde asked.

"Precisely what I was thinking."

Clyde dragged a hand through his hair. "Could he have been blackmailed into something? Or bribed?"

The thought was repugnant. Daniel trusted Manzetti as he trusted that the sun would rise in the east tomorrow morning. He paid the man a small fortune for the unswerving loyalty he had shown to Daniel throughout the last decade. But Clara was missing, and Manzetti was the last person she had been with. Had her involvement in the war between him and Forsythe reached out to drag her down? His anger at her evaporated and it hurt to even draw a breath, knowing that Clara was in danger and even now might be struggling for her very life.

"Start looking through his desk," he ordered quietly. Clyde began with the papers on the desk, while Daniel sat down and tugged open the drawers. He cursed under his breath when he saw so many of the documents were written in Italian, but he scanned them, looking for any words that might relate to Clara. He had moved on to the next drawer where there were primarily financial records, and thankfully, most of them were in English. If Manzetti was moving money in order to make a large purchase, perhaps there would be some indication of it here. Daniel was plowing through the second stack of documents when he realized that Clyde had not moved a muscle but was staring at a document lying on the top of the desk. His face had gone white.

Daniel stood to examine the note, written in an exact imitation of his handwriting, which was brief and damning.

She's coming to my office this afternoon. I want her finished by nightfall. Half now, half after the job. Tremain.

When Clyde turned to face him, his eyes were murderous. "Her little articles bothered you that much?" he spat.

Daniel could not respond. He could not even *breathe*, seeing his deepest fears confirmed in writing before his eyes. Someone had kidnapped Clara, and he was being framed for the deed. His sweet, precious Clara had been assaulted and dragged to some godforsaken place. If she was still alive, she would be terrified and desperate for help while Daniel had been wasting time rifling through Manzetti's house.

He closed his eyes and drew a steadying breath. Clara needed him, and Daniel would somehow find the rationality necessary to unravel this mystery and have Clara safely back in his arms. The first thing to do was calm her brother and get him working toward a common goal.

"Do you think I'd be so stupid as to sign my name to a note like that?" He closed the desk drawers and arranged the items on the desk exactly as they had been. "Leave everything here, untouched. Whoever planted these things probably didn't expect them to be uncovered so quickly. Let's get back to my office and start laying out a strategy for getting Clara back."

She was thirsty.

Clara tried to move, but there must have been some sort of weight on her head, because even her eyelids seemed too heavy to lift. But nothing was worse than the thirst. It felt like her mouth and throat were filled with cotton, making her tongue thick. She wondered how long she'd been sleeping to provoke this aching thirst and why she couldn't rouse herself to go to the kitchen for some water.

The floor was grainy beneath her cheek, and the sound of muffled voices came in the distance. Memories crashed down on Clara like the worst sort of nightmare. This nightmare was *real,* and she recognized the sawdust scent of the hideous warehouse she'd been brought to. She wondered if she had been restrained, as the horrific weight on her head felt unnaturally heavy, but then she remembered the drug. It had been in her tea that evil boy made her drink.

She cracked her eyelids and light streamed into them. The men were close and she could hear their voices as some sort of argument seemed to be taking place. It was probably best to keep feigning sleep, and she let her lids drift shut, leaving only a sliver open to see. If she could learn what their intentions were, perhaps she could bargain for her release.

"Please, Bane," she heard a voice beg. It was the gravelly voice of the man called Richards, his voice vibrating with fear. "I know I messed up, but it was dark. I looked as long as I dared before people started coming out of the house and I had to get out of there. Besides, the gun can't be traced back to us. No harm can come from it."

"No harm? I run a clean operation, Richards, and I don't like my associates leaving a gun at the scene of a crime." The voice had the tranquil clarity of a crystal bell. Such a soothing tone and lovely to hear. It made the contrast with his words all the more terrible. "It could not have been all that dark if the house was on fire, now, could it? I can't have that sort of carelessness among my crew; it sets a bad example. Back you go to the Professor," Bane said.

Now the man looked terrified. "Please, Bane. Don't send me back to the Professor," Richards pleaded. "He'll kill me; you know he will."

Bane shrugged. "Don't be ridiculous." He looked at the other two men. "Get him out of here," he ordered. Clara wondered who the Professor was, and what could be more terrible than being under the mercy of this pitiless boy.

A tear leaked from the corner of her eye, but she dared not lift a hand to wipe it away. She needed to survive this ordeal so she could return to Daniel and make amends. It was unthinkable that the last time she should lay eyes on Daniel this side of heaven would be as he raged at her in front of his burning house. That was *not* the way their friendship would end.

She forced the tension to fall from her face and tried to assume the slack look of a drugged sleep. The longer she could avoid inter-acting with this hideous boy, the better off she would be.

❦

Clyde was a good man to have covering his back. One would never have guessed the small, wiry body could contain such a fierce warrior, but that was what Dr. Clyde Endicott was.

Exhaustion was beginning to pull on the edges of Daniel's consciousness, but he forced the feelings away. He'd spent hours last night at the Baltimore Police Department, laying out precisely what had occurred and offering a huge bonus to the department if they could locate Clara. Not that he intended to rely on the police to solve this crime. He and Clyde had ridden directly from the police department to his offices on Calvert Street. There he was met by the small army of guards he had hired this month to secure his railroad lines during the recent unrest.

"I want Alfred Forsythe's house watched," he told Micky O'Shea, the foreman of the crew. "Have at least six men covering the house. If anyone leaves, I want him tailed. I want men stationed at Forsthye's offices and steel mills, as well. The men need to be armed and ready to take action. Anyone who is squeamish about firing shots at Forsythe's henchmen can stay home. I am demanding cold, steel-eyed determination."

"Done," O'Shea said.

As soon as the men were deployed to strategic locations throughout the vicinity, Daniel began the toughest part of the evening—calling on the heads of all the labor unions in Baltimore's tough lower south end. Eddie Maguire was captain of the local cannery union and lived on the same gritty block where Daniel had spent the first twenty years of his life. The scent of the wet bricks and coal dust brought back sharp memories. He understood the hardscrabble outlook of the men who lived and worked in this part of town where the sun rarely shined above the bleak tenements.

It took some coaxing to get Eddie Maguire to the front door, and Daniel talked quickly once the burly man stood before him. "There is a meeting at the stockyard beside Camden Station tomorrow morning at ten o'clock," he said. "The war between me and Alfred Forsythe just got a lot more personal. Send out the word that anyone who cares about moving the cause of labor forward should show up. I'll make it worth your while to be there."

As Daniel and Clyde moved from street to street, they used a list of names supplied by the Baltimore Police Department. A hefty bribe had yielded the names of all known union organizers, ranging from the steel workers, cigar rollers, cannery workers, and ship builders. And, of course, the railroad workers.

At two o'clock in the morning, Clyde asked if they should stop until daylight, but Daniel flatly rejected the notion. "The message will carry more urgency if it is delivered under cover of darkness and with little forewarning. Trust me, I know how this will be received."

The sun had barely cleared the horizon when Daniel finished contacting all the names on the list. When he looked at Clyde's haggard face and bloodshot eyes, he figured he probably looked at least as bad, but this was no time for resting. They had three hours before the meeting at the stockyards and more work to do. They mounted their horses and headed back toward Daniel's office on Calvert Street.

"That last issue of *The Christian Crusade*—the one with Clara's story in it—do you have any more copies?" Daniel asked.

Clyde straightened in his saddle. "Father always holds a few copies back. I think he also has a box for shipment overseas, but those have not been sent yet."

"Where are they?"

"The printer delivers the entire run to his house. They are in the storage shed, all boxed up for shipping."

"Get them," Daniel said. "I don't care if you have to beg, borrow, or steal a wagon to get them down to the Camden stockyard, but this little chat we have with the unions will go much better if we blanket the crowd with that rag your father publishes."

Clyde needed no further prompting. He wheeled his horse around to head for his Bolton Hill home, and Daniel headed toward his bank on Charles Street. He'd greased a number of palms overnight, and this morning he would no doubt be offering more bribes to whoever could help him in turning this city inside out and upside down in his quest to shake Clara loose from wherever she was being held.

Shortly before ten o'clock in the morning Daniel arrived at the Camden Station stockyard and was relieved to see a healthy crowd had already gathered in the open space that was used as a holding area for cargo ready to be loaded onto the trains. Hundreds of hardened workers mingled with curious boys and other onlookers. Word about Daniel's strange midnight communiqué had spread like a blaze through parched grasses in summer. As Daniel scanned the crowd he saw policemen lurking along the edges, and he gritted his teeth in annoyance. The sight of the uniformed men was likely to inflame the already suspicious crowd, but the damage of the police presence had already been done. He would just have to work that much harder to earn these men's trust.

At the far end of the stockyard he saw Clyde navigating a wagon through the crowd of workers and stacks of freight containers. Daniel sprinted through the crowd, grabbed hold of the horse bridle, and helped move the wagon directly into the center of the crowd. When the wagon was positioned precisely where he needed it, Daniel sprang aboard and used a crowbar to pry the lid from the first crate of newspapers. A curious red-haired boy climbed up on the side of the wagon to watch. "My dad said you are Daniel Tremain, but I don't believe it," the boy said.

Daniel stared at the child. The boy was wearing the exact same type of bandanna tied around his neck as Daniel had once worn. All the boys working in the steel mills wore them to keep the sweat from their faces from staining the front of their shirt. "I'm Daniel Tremain," he said, and the boy seemed to light up as though he had just confessed to being the president of the United States.

"I work at the Forsythe coal room in the steel mill. The men in the mill said it is the exact same room that you used to work in."

"That's right," Daniel said. What an odd sensation, to look at this younger version of himself. Daniel reached inside his pocket and pulled out a five-dollar bill. He pressed it into the boy's hand. "Start blanketing the crowd with these newspapers," he told the boy. "When you finish, come back for more newspapers, and there will be another five in it for you."

The boy had probably never seen such a fortune in his life, and within an instant the bill had been shoved deep into his pants pocket before he scooped up the newspapers and began handing them out to the crowd.

By ten o'clock the newspapers had been distributed and the workers were getting restless. Daniel stood in the center of the wagon, Clyde standing guard with a long-barreled shotgun resting on one shoulder. With his frontier garb and long braid of hair, Clyde looked more like a barbarian than a doctor, but Daniel was grateful for his presence. Daniel grabbed a railcar train horn and squeezed off a few blasts to signal that the meeting was about to begin. The throng of workers settled into an uneasy silence as they waited for Daniel to speak.

"I know these stockyards well," he called out in a voice loud enough to echo off the brick factory walls. He pointed to the northeast corner of the stockyard. "I grew up two streets down from here, and lived under the same roofs, drank the same lousy well water, and worked for the same wages you work for." At the mention of wages, a rumble rippled through the crowd, but Daniel didn't stop.

"I've pulled myself up and out of here, and plenty of you think I've done so by stepping on your throats on my way up." A smattering of applause sounded from the back of the crowd, but the men standing before him remained still, with arms folded across their chests and faces rampant with skepticism. "One of the people who thinks I have treated you unfairly wrote the cover story on the newspaper that is floating around amongst you." There must have been close to a thousand people gathered in the yard now, and only a few hundred newspapers scattered among them. Still, even as he spoke, Daniel saw a number of the papers being passed hand-to-hand through the crowd.

"Clara Endicott wrote the story condemning the way Alfred Forsythe and I have been conducting our business, and the only reason she cared was because of the effect that it has on you and your children's lives. Clara Endicott was driven out of England because she spent two years crawling through the underbelly of the coal-mining industry, trying to protect children from the abuses of the mine owners. She risked her safety; she risked her security on behalf of children whose names she did not know. She published stories in the London newspapers that brought the rage of mine owners down on her head." A low murmur of approval began to roll through the crowd, and Daniel had to raise his voice to be heard.

"And now Clara has come back to the United States. Once again, she is working toward the betterment of the laboring classes, and she has taken up your cause—" Now the crowd was stamping their feet, rumbling with approval. Daniel had to struggle to be heard, his throat raw from calling out over the din of the crowd. "Clara Endicott has taken up your cause, but someone doesn't want her to succeed, and as of last night, she has been taken from us and held without communication."

The crowd fell silent, and Daniel could feel the heat of every gaze in the crowd focused directly on him. "Clara Endicott has only two known enemies in this city. Myself, and Alfred Forsythe. And I'm not the sort to make war on a good woman. I don't know if Forsythe is behind this, or some other corporate titan who does not want to see Clara Endicott do to the corporations of this city what she tried to do to the mine owners in England. All I know is that someone in this town knows where Clara is and who took her. And, my friends"—Daniel leaned forward and strengthened his voice—"*I will pay well* for this information." His vow was met with the stamping of feet and a few fists raised in the air.

Daniel held aloft a copy of the newspaper for all the masses to see. "Clara Endicott wrote this story for you, and now she is suffering for it. This is a woman who will fight to see that you earn a fair wage and your children have food in their stomachs every night." Once again a roar of approval began moving through the crowd. As Daniel stared into the gritty, sweat-streaked faces of the hardened men before him, he knew they were his best chance of rescuing Clara, his generous, foolhardy Clara, whom he loved more than life itself. The pain in his throat swelled and threatened to choke off his words, but he needed to keep pushing through for Clara. "This woman is generous and valiant, and if we can save her from whatever thugs have her, this woman will turn every ounce of her glorious soul into making your world a better place. This woman is the best friend that labor has ever had, and any man who can bring me news as to where she can be found will never know a day of poverty again."

The roar of the crowd was increasing, growing in volume and rhythm until it spilled over into a chant. "Clar-ra, Clar-ra, Clar-ra," they chanted. Daniel met Clyde's eyes, which were burning with confidence. If there was any union man in the city of Baltimore who knew where Clara could be found, they were on the way to discovering it.

Chapter 17

Clara had been feigning sleep for hours, even forcing herself to lay motionless when one of Bane's men occasionally nudged her with the toe of a boot to test her awareness. Would they kill her once they realized she was awake? She had been listening for any clue of their intentions, but all she heard was Bane discussing navigation routes and tidal schedules. She could make no sense of the discussion, and that left her mind to wander. She wished Daniel were here. What she wouldn't give to feel his arms around her and listen to the confident tones in his voice. Whenever she had been timid or afraid, he could always tease her out of it.

A lump formed in the back of her throat. She would probably never see Daniel again. Clara felt the terror begin in her spine and work its way up to her throat. Begging for mercy was useless with this boy, for he was utterly, entirely without a conscience. Her wrists were bound and she lay on the floor of an abandoned warehouse, she was still sluggish from the opium, and she was surrounded by henchmen who were at the command of an insane adolescent. She would never escape this place alive.

I can do all things through him who strengthens me.

The words came unbidden to her mind. In this moment of inconceivable fear, the comfort of the passage reached out and soothed the worry that threatened to cripple her. Even in these darkest of hours, she knew that Jesus had not abandoned her. Her life was unfolding as God wished it to, and she must not yield to the soul-destroying effects of despair.

"Well, well. Sleeping Beauty has decided to rejoin us."

Clara's gaze darted to Bane, who was watching her through those crystal blue eyes. She struggled to push herself upright. Her newfound courage took a hit when she saw him approach her. How was it possible that she had once thought him fine looking? There was fierceness behind the boy's icy blue eyes, a feral quality that sliced through the air and robbed her of composure. Bane hauled her upright and then squatted down beside her to look directly into her eyes. "I imagine you are thirsty," he said, not unkindly.

Clara wouldn't take a drink from this boy to save her life. Her tongue felt so thick she doubted she could speak, but when she managed to make it move, all she could say was, "I'm still alive."

"For the time being." Bane's arm locked like a manacle about her arm and he pulled her to her feet. The ache in her head pounded and Clara felt herself sway, but Bane propelled her toward the table and chairs in the corner of the warehouse. She flinched at the sight of the small knife in Bane's hands, but all he did was slice through the rope that bound her wrists. She sank into the chair, feeling the pressure in her head increase and slide about inside her skull. What a hideous sensation, but worst of all was the plaguing, unrelenting thirst. Bane pushed a pitcher of water toward her, and Clara had to clasp the seat of her chair to stop herself from grabbing it between both hands and swallowing from the pitcher until it was empty. She clutched at the chair until her knuckles went white, and Bane seemed amused by her plight.

"It's plain water; I haven't drugged it."

Droplets of condensation rolled along the outside of the pewter pitcher, looking like the coolest, purest water she had ever seen. "I would drink the sweat from a horse before I drank anything you served me."

A smile turned up one corner of Bane's mouth, giving him an almost unearthly beauty. "While I would find it vastly amusing to watch, there's no horse readily available. I suggest you drink the water."

How cool the water would feel sliding down her throat. The cotton in her mouth seemed to swell, and Clara longed for nothing so much as the clean, tempting water just inches away from her.

She forced her gaze away from the water, and her eye was snagged by the form of a man curled atop a cot in the corner. His face was turned toward the wall, and unlike Bane's other henchmen, this one was dressed in fine clothes. A dark suit and well-made leather shoes.

"Mr. Manzetti?" she asked as she rose from her chair. The man remained motionless, and her horrified gaze slipped to Bane. "Is he dead?"

Bane shrugged. "I certainly hope not, as that would upset my plans. He is enjoying the same narcotic you recently had."

When she listened carefully, she could hear the slow wheezing of Manzetti's breath as he slumbered. It was hard to remain standing on her weakened legs, and she sank back into the chair.

"What are you planning on doing with us?"

"I am planning on killing you, but Manzetti has other uses." He tossed off the comment as though it were of no more consequence than what he intended to eat for dinner. Clara pushed back the wave of fear that threatened to clog the working of her brain. She had to reach behind that cool facade Bane wore so effortlessly and figure out who this boy was if she was to have the tiniest prayer of survival. What did he value? What had corrupted him at so young an age?

Bane poured himself a glass of water from the pitcher and drank deeply. The ache of thirst intensified as she watched him swallow, and he caught the look of pure longing on her face when he set his glass down. "It isn't drugged," he said. "That is the last thing I would do to myself in the middle of a business deal."

She believed him, and she simply could not function until she quenched this agonizing thirst. Before he had finished his sentence she picked up the pitcher and swallowed directly from it. She sucked the life-saving water down her throat, savoring every second as it cleared the cotton from her throat. She tipped the pitcher higher, and water rolled down the front of her dress, but it didn't matter.

When she had drained the pitcher she set it down, feeling well enough to do battle. Find out who Bane was, his weaknesses, his needs. "Do you use narcotics at other times?" she asked.

"Never. I've seen what opium does to the mind and have no interest in turning into a drooling idiot."

"And yet you sell it," she said. She had seen him that first night weighing and measuring the drug like a shopkeeper sacking up bags of flour.

"I have no qualms about making money from other people's weaknesses. All over the world there are people willing to pay solid gold for the opportunity to snort, drink, smoke, or inject this poison directly into their veins. If I don't ship it to them, someone else will."

A curious turn of phrase. Someone who merely sold it on the street would not speak of "shipping" a drug. Baltimore had a harbor that reached the entire East Coast and Europe, as well. If Bane was using the Baltimore harbor to ship drugs, he was far more powerful than she originally thought.

Her gaze strayed to Mr. Manzetti, still lying unconscious on the cot. Bane may be a drug runner, but somehow she did not believe her kidnapping related to drugs. What was it that Bane had punished Richards for doing? Something about leaving a gun at the scene of a fire. And she knew of only one fire in recent days.

"Did you set the fire at Daniel Tremain's house?" she asked.

"Personally? No."

"But you were responsible for it." She remembered Daniel's face as he watched his home become engulfed by the flames. It was infuriating that Daniel had suffered at the whim of this terrible adolescent sitting before her. "What on earth did you gain from such a thing?"

"I was handsomely compensated."

"By whom?"

"You don't need to know that."

"Was it the same person who paid you to kidnap me?" she asked.

His casual shrug was maddening. "Once again, you are asking questions I have no interest in answering. It's getting a little tiresome. Now it is my turn to ask you a question." There was something disturbing about those fine-looking eyes as he scrutinized her. Bane had the face and voice of an angel, but his eyes had a piercing intelligence that made it hard to look at him. "Tell me this," he said silkily. "Why does Tremain have such animosity toward Alfred Forsythe? If the reports I have read are true, he has lost a fortune over the memory of a dead man. That seems a little off-balance, don't you think?"

"Daniel loved his father very much. Why would such a thing surprise you?"

Bane shrugged his shoulders. "It just does. I've never met anyone who would walk away from that much money over a principle." Bane's eyes narrowed in thought. "In a way, I suppose it is admirable."

Yet he sounded sad when he spoke the words, and for the first time, Clara saw a trace of softening in the cold marble of his face. She was still terrified of him, but her best chance of survival was in trying to understand him. "Has there been no one you have ever cared about?" she asked. "No one you would sacrifice for?"

A bitter smile twisted Bane's mouth. "The man who is the closest thing I will ever have to a father is not the sort who would inspire lifelong devotion. If someone ever bumped him off, the only thing I'd feel would be relief."

Clara's eyes widened in shock. "You would not mind if your own father was killed?"

Bane shook his head. "My *real* father died long ago. I'm speaking about the man who raised me. He is a dragon, and I won't shed any tears if he comes to a bad end."

When Bane spoke, the revulsion in his voice was plain, but it masked the tiniest trace of anxiety. "Is he the person who is paying you to do all this wickedness?" she asked. "Burn down Daniel's house and kidnap me?"

Several moments passed before he answered her. "You know, Clara, the less you understand about what is going on, the greater the likelihood you'll be allowed to survive this ordeal."

"I thought I was as good as dead anyway."

"I did, too." Bane almost looked surprised when he made the statement, but the look quickly vanished to be replaced by his usual nonchalance.

"What has changed your mind?"

He narrowed his eyes as he considered her. "I like you," he said abruptly. "You stood up to Richards when he burst into your carriage. I didn't expect that." Clara remembered the incident when Richards had first shoved that imposing revolver in her face. *"Pointing a gun at women and children. Your mother must be so proud,"* she had said.

"Is that what it takes to impress you?"

"The only thing that impresses me is someone who has the guts to face down their fears. Maybe you qualify."

"And if I do? Is it going to save my life?"

Bane shrugged. "Maybe, maybe not."

Keep him talking, just keep him talking, Clara thought. "Do you believe in God?" she asked suddenly.

The question seemed to take him aback, but he gave it consideration. He leaned back in his chair and folded his arms across his chest. The way he stared at her was unnerving, but she didn't let herself look away. Finally he answered. "Maybe."

"Why do you say that?"

"Because I believe in the devil. And if the devil exists, I suppose God probably does, too."

Looking into those vacant eyes and hearing him proclaim his belief in the devil was chilling, but she could not afford to stop. "What makes you believe there is a devil?"

That peculiar smile spread across Bane's face, revealing a row of white, perfect teeth. "Because I've met him, Clara." He gave a snort of laughter at her shocked expression. "You may think I'm wicked, but trust me, the man I work for reeks of brimstone."

It was too hard to continue looking at Bane. Fear was crawling up her spine again, and her stomach was filling with acid. She looked at the crates stacked up around them, forming a makeshift room in the corner of the huge warehouse. Contained in these crates was the recipe for unmitigated human misery. How many thousands of people would imbibe this poison after it left the warehouse?

Marriages would crumble, children would suffer as their parents slipped into a narcotic haze, fortunes would be lost. All so that Alex Banebridge and his crew could line their pockets.

I can do all things through him who strengthens me.

She straightened her shoulders and forced herself to look back at Bane. "Why do you always let the devil win?"

Bane stared at her blankly. "What?" he finally asked.

"Why do you let the devil run your life? Wouldn't it be more of a challenge to stand up to him? You said the only thing you are impressed by is someone who has the guts to triumph over their fears. And yet you succumb to the devil rather than stand up to him."

"Don't tell me you are one of those dreadful missionaries. And I was starting to like you, too."

She leaned forward across the table. Getting this close to Bane made her flesh crawl, but it had to be done. "Just how brave are you? Brave enough to walk away from all this"—she gestured to the crates—"and give yourself over to God? It wouldn't be easy, Bane."

"Is it true you are the daughter of some fancy minister?"

"Yes."

"I suppose that accounts for this prissy God-talk." Bane took out the knife and began twirling the point into the wood surface of the table. The gleam of the metal sent flashes of light about the warehouse. "Some people just aren't cut out for walking with the angels. I've been destined for the darker side of life since I was six years old and was hand-delivered to the wickedest man in the world."

She glanced around the warehouse. "Is he here?"

"No."

"Then you have no excuse for your behavior. Don't defend yourself by telling me about a tragic childhood; you are old enough to be making your own decisions. There is nothing in the world to prevent you from walking out that warehouse door and starting a brand-new life today, Alex."

"Bane."

"What?"

"I prefer to be called Bane."

"Let's see how brave you really are, Alex. Wouldn't your life be a little more interesting if you started challenging this belief that you are intended for more than to unleash evil on the world? Wouldn't you respect yourself more if you had the nerve to stand up to this devil you claim to believe in?"

Bane twirled his knife even faster as he smiled at her. "I have never lacked for self-respect. I am pretty much my favorite person, come to think of it."

"That does not speak well for the company you keep."

If possible, the amusement in the boy's eyes grew even stonger. "At last, you have made a statement I whole-heartedly agree with."

"Then why don't you *do* something about that?" Clara looked pointedly at the crates of opium that surrounded them. "If you destroyed the opium in these crates rather than shipping it out to exploit the weakness of men's souls, it would be a fine start in a new direction. You can begin your life again and carve out a new path for yourself."

At mention of destroying the opium, the amusement fled Bane's face. "If I destroyed this opium, the price on my head would have every criminal in America out for my blood. I suppose that would certainly be a new path for me, just not one I want to be on."

"It scares you, then? To stand up to this man you say is the wickedest man in the world?"

Bane just shrugged. "Someday I will be a match for him. Not yet, though."

She reached across the table and grabbed his hand, surprised at her own daring. "The Lord will protect you, Alex. I don't know what sort of appalling circumstances put you into that man's path when you were just a child, but you are strong enough to walk away. Do it today, Alex."

He snatched his hand back as though he had been burned. "You can be really annoying; do you know that?"

"I'm not going to give up on you, Alex. I am not going to calmly sit here while you destroy the lives of thousands of people with those drugs and drag your own soul through the muck while you do it. God has given you the freedom to simply walk away. *He will forgive you.*"

She could not pinpoint when it happened, but there was a shift in the atmosphere. The knife Bane had been twirling dug a gouge into the surface of the table, and his fingers were clenched tight around the handle. "All your pathetic God stories make me sick," he said. "You brainwash children into believing goodness and sunlight and mercy swirl around them like fairy dust. In the real world, children can be snatched from their mothers' arms and plunged into a pit of corruption where no trace of sunlight can ever penetrate. Where is God in a scenario like that?" Contempt dripped from his voice, but Clara would not let it dissuade her.

"I'm not blind to the evil in the world," she said. After all, it was sitting not five feet away from her. "And I am not blind to the fact that I have been given gifts you never had. Living a godly life was expected of me, and it was an easy path for me to follow. No one ever had such expectations for you. For you to embrace the Lord at this point in your life would be nothing short of heroic, Alex. It would take an act of such strength and courage that it would be humbling for all who have ever known you. You can begin building a life of valor *today*."

Bane stood up and walked to the makeshift counter where food and supplies were kept. "You ought to listen to what I say. Cut out the God-talk."

For the first time since he had revealed himself as the mastermind behind this criminal enterprise, the coolly remote look on Bane's face was gone, replaced by anger glittering in his eyes. Bane had been drenched in evil and vice from the time he was a child. Of course he was going to struggle against leaving that life behind, but the fact that he hadn't killed her yet meant that on some level she may have broken through to him. "God made you for a purpose, Alex," she whispered. "I have no idea why you were steeped in such violence for most of your life, but it is not too late to turn this around. It would take the courage of a gladiator to turn your back on all this. Just how brave are you willing to be?"

Bane turned to face her. "Don't say I didn't warn you." The cool, blank look was back on his face again, as though no earthly cares could ever bother him. He pulled out a chair and sat beside her at the table. Before she could gather her thoughts, Bane yanked her arm down on the table and locked it into place with his forearm. With his other hand he shoved a needle into her arm, and pain shot up her nerves like a bolt of lightning.

"Time to say good night," Bane said as her world grew dim.

CHAPTER 18

It was a full thirty-six hours before a credible lead emerged, and in that time Daniel had not known a moment of rest. He remained stationed in his office, keeping a central command post where anyone could bring information.

Exhaustion poured from him in waves, but each time he felt himself slipping, memories of Clara blazed to the surface, searing him with anxiety and forcing him to keep turning over leads in a desperate attempt to find her. Was there ever a more delicate, dainty woman than Clara? She was afraid of everything from horses to speaking in public and everything in between, and yet for years she had been facing down those fears to do what she believed was right. What she believed God wanted of her. Now she was suffering for

Daniel's sins. He didn't know who had taken her, but Daniel was certain it was his fault.

The memory of Clara's face illuminated by the light of the fire that had destroyed his home haunted him. He had all but accused her of inciting the fire, even as she had vowed she would never give up on him.

And by all that was holy, he would never turn his back on her again, either. As the sun darkened on the day Daniel had made his impassioned plea in the Camden stockyard, his hope for a quick solution to Clara's disappearance dwindled. A handful of people had come forward with flimsy tips. All of them were being investigated by men Daniel had hired, but it was apparent the people who had given them the leads were more interested in the financial reward and had nothing of substance to offer.

He clasped his hands together and prayed. *Please, God*, he thought. *Please keep Clara safe. I've never been able to pray to you before, because I don't even know if you exist . . . but Clara believes, and that's good enough for me.*

He had a mild feeling of guilt, knowing that he had only turned toward God when he was out of options and his back was to the wall. But it was for Clara—he asked nothing for himself, only that a woman of Clara's startling goodness should not be punished.

The next day passed in the same endless torment. Lead after lead filtered in, and each time a man walked through the door, Daniel's heart surged in his chest, hoping that *this* time the lead would prove solid. It wasn't until the sun was low in the sky on the third day of Clara's disappearance that the first credible lead came in the form of a nervous Eddie Maguire.

It seemed odd to see a man of Maguire's size and reputation appear to be intimidated, but the sheen of perspiration on the man's skin as he twisted a rumpled bandanna in his hands made his anxiety evident.

"This is an anonymous tip; is that clear?" Eddie stated as he sat in a chair opposite Daniel's desk. Clyde came around the room to scrutinize Eddie as the grim-faced leader of the cannery union cleared his throat several times before proceeding.

"I'm bringing this news from one of my men," he said. "He is sick to his guts over being pinned as the man who squealed. He doesn't want any reward for this, because he is afraid it might give him away. All he wants is to help the lady, since she seems like someone who doesn't deserve to be mixed up in whatever foul deed Bane has up his sleeve."

Daniel pierced Eddie with an intense gray stare. "Who is Bane?" he asked quietly.

Eddie shifted in his chair. "I'm not really sure. Nobody I know has ever seen him, but he runs a tight operation, and anyone who crosses him doesn't live long enough to brag about it. I heard that he comes from somewhere out west . . . California maybe. He controls the opium shipments in and out of New England." Eddie swiped his brow with the bandanna and Daniel could detect a tremor in his hand.

"Go on," he prompted.

"Anyway . . . this man I know said he heard that Bane is using a warehouse down near the Locust Point harbor. He heard they were stocking it with supplies because they were going to be keeping a couple of hostages there for a while."

Daniel leaned forward. "Which warehouse?"

"I don't know."

"There must be hundreds of warehouses down near that end of the harbor," Clyde ground out in frustration. "Tell me the name of this guy and I'll pin it down more."

"You just don't get it, do you?" Maguire broke out. "This man has a family. He took enough of a risk to tell me what he knew, and I'm not going to roll over on him so Bane's jackals can peel the flesh from his body." Eddie Maguire stood up to his full height and glared at Daniel.

"I only came here for the lady, not for you. For today, I hope you get her back, but tomorrow you and I are at war again. I want you to forget who told this to you. And if you are going to take on Bane, you'd better have an army when you do it."

CHAPTER 19

This time when she came out of the opium-induced stupor, Clara had a better idea of what to expect. Her head was filled with pressure, and the raging thirst made it hard to move her tongue in her mouth. Lifting her eyelids was even a struggle, but there wasn't much point anyway. She could still smell the sawdust and knew from the grainy texture of the concrete floor beneath her exactly where she was. The worst was the awful, repetitive sounds of banging that made the pain in her head reverberate with each *whack*.

When she finally managed to open her eyes she could see the source of the noise. Bane and that awful person named McGahee were nailing crates shut. She scanned the area and saw Mr. Manzetti, still drugged and motionless on the cot, but something was different.

LIZABETH CAMDEN

She turned her head and noticed the dozens of crates that had been stacked around them were gone. The warehouse was almost empty.

She pushed herself into a sitting position and leaned against the brick wall behind her. "Where is the opium?" she managed to ask in a ragged voice.

Both Bane and McGahee glanced her way. "It's out there in the world now," Bane said, a couple of nails clenched between his teeth. There were still plenty of crates scattered across the floor, but McGahee was filling them with bottles of whiskey, and Bane was nailing them shut. Propped up on the far wall were bolts of fabric, dozens of bolts of silk and calico and muslin. She must have been deeply drugged to have remained insensible while so much cargo moved in and out of the warehouse.

"There is water on the counter if you want it," Bane said. "It is not drugged." Somehow she believed him. Of all the horrific things Bane had done in the few hours since she had known him, he had not lied to her. Not that she put it past him, but the bruise on her arm was proof that Bane could easily drug her without resorting to tricks. She carefully walked to the counter and drank. Just getting on her feet and quenching her thirst helped ease the pounding in her head. She studied Bane as he unpacked new crates of contraband, and for the first time noticed a diamond winking in his ear. The fruits of his ill-gotten gains, no doubt.

Her gaze strayed to Mr. Manzetti, still unconscious on that cot. She did not know what the reaction would be if she attempted to tend to him, but decided to find out rather than ask permission.

Bane ignored her as she kneeled beside the cot and put a gentle hand on Manzetti's shoulder.

"Mr. Manzetti? Can you hear me?" She nudged him harder. His face remained slack, his mouth hanging open as gentle snores continued.

"It's pointless, girl," McGahee growled. "Bane shot him up with enough dope to keep him dreaming for days." She looked to Bane for confirmation, but he didn't stop filling the crates with bottles.

She sent a glare at Bane. "I'm no expert on opium, but I've experienced enough of it to know that abusing Mr. Manzetti with an endless stream of the stuff can't be healthy. You ought to be ashamed of yourself."

Bane continued to nail the lid on a crate without breaking rhythm, but he snickered at her. "You sound just like a schoolmarm. Why are you so worried about him in any case? You are the one who is about to meet your maker."

The thought had not left the forefront of her mind since the moment she'd been kidnapped. "So I ought to be measured for a casket; is that what you're saying?"

"Sit down," Bane ordered. She sobered at the pair of handcuffs dangling from his fingers. Her gaze flew to his. "I'm not going to kill you, but I've got to help McGahee get these bolts of cloth out of here. Give me your hand." And with that she found herself manacled to a pipe that ran along the side of the wall. The warehouse doors were slid open and a horse pulling a wagon was led in by some of the men she'd seen the previous day. "Don't get any bright ideas about screaming while those doors are open, or I'll break your neck before you can utter a sound," Bane said.

For the next few minutes she watched while more crates of whiskey were unloaded from the wagon and bolts of cloth were put in their place. When the fabric was loaded, Bane ordered the men to take it to the Camden train station. He closed the warehouse doors behind the wagon, and she was once again alone with Bane. The boy used a crowbar to pry the lid from the new crates and began removing bottles of whiskey, which he loaded onto the table.

"Why are you unpacking all those bottles? Aren't you just going to crate them up in different boxes?" That seemed to be what he had been doing all morning.

Bane shrugged. "This shipment is headed out west, and I don't want anyone to know where it originally came from."

"Why should that be a secret?"

Bane looked at her like she was a simpleton. "Taxes, Clara. I'm not a big fan of paying taxes."

"Oh," she said, feeling rather foolish. Someone who stooped to arson and selling opium surely wouldn't shy away from a little smuggling. There seemed to be no end to the criminal endeavors Bane indulged in, but she knew she had to keep him talking. The more they talked, the more likely it was that he would regard her as a human being who should not have her neck snapped. Yesterday she thought she saw a tiny glimmer of humanity lurking deep within him, and her only hope of survival was finding that spark and nurturing it forth.

Clara leaned her face against the side of the pipe she was chained to. Her body still felt as if sludge was moving through her veins, and the support of the cool pipe against her overheated face was welcome. "I'm sorry you sent the opium out," Clara said. "A lot of people are going to suffer because of that."

Bane pried a lid from a crate. "Don't tell me you lose sleep over what a bunch of dope fiends choose to do with their bodies."

Clara needed to talk to Bane, and he kept turning away from her to mess with those crates. She was trapped against this pipe and needed to get to where she could look him in the eye. "If you unlock these handcuffs, I'll tell you why you should care about all those dope fiends."

He snickered again. "That ought to be some fairy tale."

"Unlock me and I'll prove it to you. I swear I won't try to escape."

Her vow must have been good enough, because Bane strolled over and unlocked her handcuffs.

"It isn't just dope fiends who get hurt," Clara said as she rubbed the circulation back into her aching wrist. "When I was in London there was a terrible story of what a mother did to her own daughter." Clara remembered clearly because the story was so horrible, some of the people at *The Times* thought it was too gruesome to print.

"There was a woman who was living in India because her husband was a sergeant with the Royal Brigade. Mrs. Stockton was her name, and she had a six-year old daughter named Hannah. When her husband died of a fever, Mrs. Stockton decided to return to England, but there wasn't a lot of money. The Crown would provide passage for her and the girl on a navy ship, so there should have been no problem. But Mrs. Stockton had developed a terrible dependency on opium while living in India. She bought as much as she could before her journey to the port at Mangalore, but by the time she arrived in the port city, she was already running low on the drug, and she feared running out during the passage at sea. It takes over a month to arrive home, you see."

Bane had stopped his hammering and was watching Clara. The sudden silence felt odd in the cavernous warehouse. "Mrs. Stockton sold Hannah to an Indian brothel in exchange for two pounds of opium," she said quietly.

The hammer slipped from Bane's hands and clattered to the floor, but he remained motionless as he stared at her, his face stamped with revulsion.

"It took a while for her crime to be discovered," she continued. "When Mrs. Stockton returned to England she took up work as a prostitute to feed her habit, but eventually her husband's family sought her out and inquired what had happened to the girl. When she could provide no explanation, they turned to the police, who launched an inquest and discovered that Hannah had not been aboard the ship when it sailed for England. Mrs. Stockton was arrested and placed in prison, where the depth of her fascination with opium became apparent. She confessed to what she had done, and then hanged herself with a bedsheet." Clara rubbed the raw spot on her wrist where the handcuff had marked her, feeling foolish for complaining about this minor irritant when that precious child had endured unspeakable depravities. She looked back at Bane. "I always wondered if she hanged herself because of what she had done to her child, or because she knew prison would deprive her of opium. I suppose we will never know."

"What happened to the girl?" Bane's voice was tense, and his knuckles were white as he clenched his hands into fists.

"No one ever found her," she said softly. "By the time Mrs. Stockton's crime had been discovered, almost a year had passed. A search was launched in Mangalore, but the child was long gone, leaving no trace whatsoever."

A transformation had come over Bane. A muscle throbbed in his jaw and his eyes were narrowed in anger and a hint of . . . remorse? It was hard to tell because he turned away from her and began pacing the warehouse, his spine rigid with tension.

"So you see it is not merely the dope fiends who suffer from the sale of narcotics," Clara said. "For each dope fiend there is a child, or a parent, or a spouse." She glanced around the near empty room. "How many pounds of opium were in the crates you just shipped out?"

She did not expect him to answer, but he did. "Nine hundred pounds."

Close to *half a ton* of opium. But perhaps it was not too late; perhaps Bane had the power to stop the avalanche of human misery he had set in motion. His face was still tense and shuttered. For some reason the story of little Hannah Stockton had knocked him off-kilter, and she would never have a better time of reaching him than right now.

"Where is it headed, Bane?"

"Some to Cuba. Some to New Orleans."

She was surprised he answered, and kept pressing for more. "How is it going to get there?"

"Forget it, Clara. It's out of my hands now."

"But you know where it is. How is it going to get out of Baltimore?"

"There is a ship in the harbor called *The Albatross*. It sails in eighteen hours on the morning tide."

Clara straightened her spine. "Then we have eighteen hours to get it off that ship. You can't let this sort of stain pollute your soul. You can begin turning your life around right now, and I will help you do it. I think the Lord would be very proud of you for taking such a fearless step."

Bane picked up the crowbar and went back to unpacking his newly delivered contraband. "Don't get started on the God-talk again." He had turned his back on her, but Clara walked over to kneel in front of him.

"Look, Clara, I'm in way too deep to just walk away from all this," Bane said. "I'm sorry about what happened to that girl. It is true that I never thought about the effect the opium business has on innocent kids."

This time when he looked at her, the regret in his eyes was plain. "Clara, if I thought scuttling this deal would help that girl in India, I would do it in a heartbeat, but it is too late for her and it would probably get me killed."

"You know too much?"

"I know *everything*. If I tried to cut loose, there isn't a rock in this entire country he would not turn over and smash open in order to search me out. So drop the God-talk, okay? I'm in too deep and it is not an option for me. If that opium disappears on my watch, I'll be dead before the next full moon."

She handed him another nail. "I thought you said the people you respected most were those who could face up to their fears. I should think stopping *The Albatross* might fit into that category."

"It would fit into the category of sheer insanity," Bane said. He finished pounding a row of nails into the crate and shoved it into the corner, but Clara did not miss the introspective look that lingered on Bane's face long after she stopped talking.

Bane spent the better part of an hour repackaging the whiskey. With each crate that was repackaged, Bane made precise notations on a document he was keeping. "Even criminals use bills of lading," he had told her.

Suddenly, he stopped and stared her straight in the face. "Have you ever been in love?" he asked.

She turned the question around on Bane. "Have *you*?" she asked him.

Bane stared at her, the oddest expression in his eyes. "Been in love? Maybe. I don't know."

Keep him talking, Clara thought. "Tell me about it."

Bane shifted in his seat, and judging by the flush on his face, he might actually be embarrassed. "I'd rather you go back to your God-talk."

So as Clara concluded her first experience in black-market

shipping, she talked to Bane about salvation. As she spoke, the tension of the last few days began to drain away as a sense of peace and warmth swelled within her. She was doing exactly what God wanted of her. She was trying to save a boy who had brought an unimaginable amount of destruction into His kingdom and turn that energy and intelligence into something positive.

Bane held up his hand. "If what you say is true, I can hop off this train of destruction I've been riding, and God will greet me with open arms so long as I vow to quit my wicked ways."

"That's right. If you want salvation, you can have it today," she said earnestly. "Just walk away from this life and never turn back. I can help you get started in a life that is new and clean and worthy."

Bane shot to his feet and began pacing again. "If I walk away from this web of pure evil, every crime lord on both coasts will be salivating for my blood. I know where all the bank accounts are stashed, where all the skeletons are buried. I know the distribution channels for every shipload of opium that enters and leaves this country. You are asking me to walk into the jaws of certain death, Clara." Despite the dark words, Bane's face was bright with excitement. She could practically see his sharp mind rattling through his options, and she knew she was on the cusp of swaying him.

"I know it will be frightening," she said. "But the Lord will welcome you back into His fold and protect you. No matter the stain on your soul or the darkness of your life, He will never abandon you. If you give your life to God, He will shield you through whatever terrors plague you."

Bane turned to face her and looked her straight in the eyes.

There was a resolve in his demeanor she had never seen before, and then he uttered two words she never expected him to say.

"Prove it."

The question took Clara aback. "How?"

The intensity of his stare was frightening, but she was mesmerized and could not tear her eyes away. Bane grabbed a knife, and with a violent lurch that stunned her into immobility, he stabbed the document that recorded his opium shipments to the table. The knife vibrated from the force long after Bane took his hand away.

"If you truly believe the Lord will protect those who do His work, I want to watch *you* walk into the jaws of death," Bane said as he leaned in close to her. "I want to watch *you* walk onto a ship swarming with hardened criminals and dump the opium into the bay. Tonight. Prove that you really believe God will protect you. Prove that *you* have the courage to do what you are asking of me."

The force of what he said was like a fist in her chest. The dare he just tossed in her lap was so terrifying Clara could not even draw a breath to respond to the stunning challenge; she just stared at him in openmouthed astonishment. "I can get you to the docks and on board the ship," Bane continued. "I want to watch you walk into the middle of a drug deal and scuttle it. If you truly believe that God led you to me in order to make the world a better place, you don't get to bail out just when things get interesting. I'll get you onto *The Albatross*, and I want you to dump the opium in the bay." His smile widened. "I'll even go with you. If you say this is what God wants me to do, I'll do it. But you are coming with me, Clara. Every step of the way."

Clara had seen those crates, more than thirty of them. How on earth could she dump thirty crates loaded with opium and escape without notice? Her heart pounded and the heat of the warehouse made her feel light-headed. "Bane, I don't know anything about ships. . . ."

"I'll be right there beside you." The smile Bane sent her was grim. "You go in this with me . . . or the deal is off."

Bane strode to the far side of the warehouse, and with a mighty heave he slid the door wide open. The clatter of the door rumbling on its rails made her flinch. Sunlight streamed into the dusty confines, and the din of street traffic filled the air. "You are free to go, Clara. I won't stop you. But if you walk out this door, *The Albatross* and all its cargo will set sail with tomorrow's tide, and I will know precisely which sort of Christian you are."

The sounds of children laughing in the street and the call of a fruit peddler selling oranges filled the air. If she walked out that door she could be safe at home within the hour. This nightmare would be over and she could go about her life and make amends with Daniel.

And she would also know that when she had been tempted, she had failed. At this moment she had the power to help save a young man from pursuing a life of rampant crime, and she needed to delve deep within her soul to find the courage to see it through. But what Bane was asking of her was so terrifying her voice box had gone mute.

Clara tore her eyes away from the sunlight streaming through the open door. Her breathing felt choppy and the muscles in her legs tingled as she fought the temptation to sprint out the door and into freedom. It would take only a few seconds, and Bane promised he would do nothing to stop her. He was awaiting her answer with an odd combination of mockery and hope on his face, but Clara was still paralyzed by fear.

I can do all things through him who strengthens me.

Once again the verse arose in her mind, and she knew precisely what she needed to do. There was no point in fretting or doubting; she was simply going to trust in the Lord and submit to His will. She turned to face Bane. "You make the plan," Clara said, "and I'll carry it out."

❧

Bane dumped another three spoonfuls of sugar into the cup of thick black coffee, then slid it across the table to Manzetti.

"Drink up," he said casually, but covertly Bane was scrutinizing the man's every movement. The wobbling of the coffee as Manzetti raised it to his lips was less noticeable now and his eyes were more alert. They could not leave until Manzetti was completely sober, and Bane had spent most of the afternoon on the task. After six hours, the opium was finally wearing away. Between cups of coffee, Clara had been coaxing Manzetti to walk about in the confines of the warehouse, stretching his abused muscles and exercising his lungs. When Manzetti was finally roused and in control of his faculties, the news of what had transpired over the last few days did not go over well with the man.

Manzetti gaped at Clara in disbelief. "This pretty-faced brat tries to kill you, and now he wants our help undoing the mess he dug himself into? I'd rather rip his arms off."

Bane remained unruffled. Anyone who grew up in the Professor's household was not intimidated by someone whose only weapon was brute force. "Think of the mess," he said blandly.

Manzetti stomped across the floor and shoved himself into Bane's space, standing so close Bane felt the heat from Manzetti's breath. He refused to flinch or to take a step back, even though Manzetti was more than a foot taller than he. "If Clara wasn't watching, I'd be feeding you to the fish in the Baltimore harbor," Manzetti said in a voice that reeked with loathing.

Clara intervened. "Mr. Manzetti, the plan is for you to drive us to the docks. The men guarding *The Albatross* know Bane and will follow his orders when he tells them to leave the ship while we dump the opium."

Manzetti's voice was dense with skepticism. "What kind of guard leaves the ship?"

"They will do as they are told," Bane said. After all, every one of those men knew Bane was the Professor's heir apparent and gave him their unquestioning obedience as they rushed to do his bidding. Bane had fought hard to earn his reputation for cold, ruthless efficiency. How strange that now all he wanted to do was destroy that reputation in exchange for the salvation Clara described.

"I don't trust him," Manzetti said. "You expect me to believe this truant is prepared to walk away from thousands of dollars? All on a dare?"

Bane turned away to sprawl back in a chair, negligently dangling his shoe off the end of his big toe as he studied Manzetti. "Money does not have any allure for me," he said slowly. "I'm far more curious to see if Clara has enough backbone to see this through." Bane straightened and tugged the shoe back on his foot, analyzing the way Clara was chewing the corner of a thumbnail in anxiety.

Don't back down on me now, Clara, he silently urged. No matter how conflicted she was, he must not pressure her. He wanted to know . . . he *needed* to know if she really believed what she had said about salvation.

"Clara and I will board the ship, while you divert the attention of the guards on the docks," Bane said.

"No way," Manzetti said to Clara. "Daniel will skin me alive if I let you walk onto that ship like a lamb to be sliced, diced, and slaughtered. If anyone boards the ship with this brat, it will be me."

Bane shook his head. "Nope. It has got to be Clara. No one else will do."

"Bane says I can pass myself off as a boy when we board the ship," Clara said. "His clothes will fit me, and I'll be able to hide most of my face from them because of the sack I will be carrying on my shoulder. There is no way I could pass as a boy if I'm the one manning the wagon where the sailors will be told to wait. You will have to do it, Mr. Manzetti."

Manzetti turned his steely glare on Bane. "I'm doing this for *her*, not for you."

At Manzetti's capitulation, Clara's smile widened and her eyes sparkled. She was quite possibly the first truly good person Bane had ever met in his life.

There was only a sliver of moonlight casting a weak glow over the city as the wagon bumped along the cobblestone streets toward the harbor. The clomping of the horse's hooves and roll of the wheels seemed unnaturally loud in the silence of the night, but surely that was just paranoia. Why should anyone take notice of a wagon with a couple of passengers and a few bags of wadded-up material?

Because they were on a mission to outsmart a passel of hardened criminals, and Clara was certain the entire city could hear the pounding of her racing heart. Manzetti was in front driving the rig, while she sat curled beside Bane in the back of the wagon, swaying in tandem with him at every dip of the wagon as they moved closer to the docks. Never in her life had she worn boy's clothing, and it felt odd to see the outline of her legs stretched before her. A baggy shirt, a vest, and her hair twisted up beneath a cap completed the look. Bane had rubbed some damp coffee grounds over her face to get rid of that "lily white look" no respectable boy would have.

"Do you really think this is going to work?" she whispered as she saw the harbor ahead of them. To her criminally inexperienced ways, Bane's plan seemed like a good one, even though he had armed himself to the teeth before they left the warehouse. A revolver was in the holster at his waist, a switchblade tucked in his boot, and in his pocket he was carrying some device the size of an apple that would *create quite a show.*

Bane was back to his remote, unnaturally cool demeanor. "We'll pull this off," he said confidently. "I figure we will both survive this night, but my odds of making it to Christmas don't look so good."

Clara felt her mouth go dry. How odd that not even two days ago Bane had completely terrified her, and now she deeply cared about what happened to him. "Is that because you didn't kill me as planned?"

Bane snorted. "No, that's nothing. It's the guy who owns this opium who is going to be the problem."

"He is the criminal emperor you were talking about?"

"Yup." Bane gave her a sad little smile. "I want you to know, no matter what happens, I'm glad you are willing to go on that ship with me. You have given me something to believe in. I've never really had that before, and it feels so . . ." He appeared to be struggling to find the words. Finally he simply said, "It feels really good."

And then he turned to her, his face filled with concern. "Look, Clara. Don't ever tell anyone what you've done tonight. The dragon who owns this stuff is going to be out for blood, and he's not someone you want on your tail. I will go to my grave swearing that I acted alone on this. I need you to promise me you won't put yourself in danger by trying to tell this story to the world. It's not worth it."

Looking into that beautifully sculpted face, it was hard to believe that Bane was still little more than a boy. His eyes were old, filled with anxiety on her behalf. "I promise, Alex."

He laughed a bit at the use of his given name. "You just don't give up, do you?"

She curled her hand over his. "I will never give up on you, because you truly are a hero, Alex."

CHAPTER 20

With Eddie Maguire's lead about the Locust Point harbor, Daniel armed himself with a contingent of hired guards to search through the warehouses that rimmed the waterfront. There were over a hundred buildings, each standing between two and four stories in height, each containing dozens of rooms where a small, frightened hostage might be stashed away.

Clyde and Daniel spent the day going from building to building, searching through hundreds of storage rooms. Each time they forced their way into a building, a terrible squeezing pressure clenched Daniel's chest. He didn't know what he was looking for—Clara and Manzetti bound and gagged in a corner? A bloody spot on the floor? It had been almost four days since Clara had been kidnapped, and the likelihood of finding her alive was dwindling with each hour, but he forced his mind to remain rational. Methodical.

It was past midnight when they discovered the warehouse where Clara had been held captive. The oversized room looked like dozens of others they had searched, but the canary yellow dress, crumpled in a wad in the corner, had belonged to Clara. On shaking legs, Daniel knelt on the dusty floor and held the dress to his face. He was too late. He closed his eyes and tried to draw another breath into his tortured lungs.

"That was the dress she was wearing when Manzetti picked her up," Clyde confirmed, his face white as parchment. Everything was here—her corset, her petticoats. Even her dainty suede pumps were tucked beneath the dress.

Clyde snatched the dress from Daniel and held it up before a flickering lantern. "There are no bloodstains here. And the buttons are not torn or missing."

On some level that ought to be comforting. Clara had not been bleeding or thrashing about when those animals had stripped the dress from her. She would have to be unconscious or dead to have permitted those dozens of tiny buttons to be unfastened without a struggle.

Before the white haze of rage could cloud his mind, Daniel pushed himself to his feet and began pacing the grim warehouse, scanning the empty crates and makeshift kitchen area, anything that might give a clue as to where the occupants had come from or where they went.

"Check everything here," Daniel ordered. "Open every crate,

look through every pile of garbage. Look for papers, receipts, maps . . . anything that might show where they came from or where they are going next." Daniel strained to see in the flickering light of the lantern, sickened that this filthy hole was where Clara had been forced to spend her last hours on this earth. His gaze was snagged by something odd on the table. A knife pinned a single sheet of paper to the scarred wooden surface.

He pried the knife free and held the document before a lantern. It was a bill of lading for the HMS *Albatross*. Clyde moved to stand beside Daniel.

"*The Albatross* must be a ship, correct?"

Clyde nodded. "Most likely. Those numbers are for the positioning of crates in the cargo hold. I've shipped enough medical supplies to know that."

Then the people who had been in this warehouse had either come or were going to *The Albatross*. It was all Daniel needed to set the next stage in motion. "Get some men stationed here to guard this space until the police can get here. We are going to the docks."

The Albatross was a two-masted brigantine and was still tied up to the dock. A network of piers stretched several acres out onto the harbor, a clockwork of right angles to which boats and skiffs and cargo ships were tied. Clara's and Bane's boots made hollow thudding sounds as they walked down the pier toward *The Albatross*. Over her shoulder Clara lugged a huge bundle, and Bane carried an even larger one. She clutched the burlap sack so tightly her hands threatened to cramp up. *I can do all things through him who strengthens me.*

There was that verse again, giving her comfort in surely the most frightening moment of her life. As she and Bane approached the ship, two faces appeared over the edge. The men had thick necks and suspicious eyes. Bane took off his cap, his white-blond hair glowing in the thin moonlight. "Zeidermann, get down here," he ordered.

"Yes, sir, Bane."

A rope ladder was flung over the side and the sailor made his way down the twisting ladder and hopped down onto the pier. Clara's heart sank. She had no idea she would need to climb a flimsy ladder like that while lugging this huge sack of wadded-up cloth. It wasn't heavy, but Bane had instructed her to hunch over as though she was burdened by great weight. Dead weight, as it were. As instructed, she turned her face toward the sack and tried not to wince at the sight of the blood soaking through the burlap. It was Bane's blood. He'd sliced the inside of his ankle and let the blood seep onto the fabric—*"for a little added authenticity,"* he had told her.

Mercifully, Bane had a solution to the problem of the flimsy ladder. "We need the gangway lowered," he told Zeidermann. "We've got too much weight here to climb a rope ladder. And listen, you and whoever else is on that ship need to get off for a few minutes. We don't need any witnesses."

Zeidermann hesitated. "I don't know, Bane. The cargo that's on board ought to have a couple of rifles guarding it at all times."

Bane's voice was silky in its calmness. "I don't want any witnesses while I take care of a private matter, Zeidermann. In the next fifteen minutes I need to dismember the contents of these two sacks into small, unidentifiable pieces. Then I am going to dump the pieces to the bottom of the ocean floor. Do you *really* want to witness this?"

The man's eyes grew round and color drained from his face. Bane tended to have that effect on people. Zeidermann cleared his throat. "No, sir. I suppose we can guard the ship from the entrance to the pier. Just a moment while I get the gangway lowered." He cleared his throat again. "Sir."

Zeidermann scrambled up the ladder, and within moments a gangway was lowered over the edge. Clara picked her way up the slatted boards, weaving as *The Albatross* rose and sank on the gentle waves. When she arrived on board she kept her eyes fastened on the deck, her face turned away from the crew. She could see three pairs of boots shuffling toward the gangway. One of the men was grumbling about leaving their post, but Zeidermann was adamant. "Just do it . . . don't ask questions, just do it," he said in a fierce whisper.

As the men hit the pier, Bane leaned over the edge and called a warning. "You didn't see anything. You didn't hear anything."

"That's right, Bane," a fear-roughened voice replied.

Two minutes after boarding *The Albatross*, she and Bane were alone. "Follow me," he said. The hold was only a few steps away, and immediately upon descending the short flight of steps, Clara was assaulted by the sweet, pungent odor she had come to know too well over the past few days. The hold was entirely dark except for the narrow rectangle of moonlight coming from the door behind her. Bane struck a match and lit a small kerosene lantern, casting an eerie yellow glow over the crates stacked in the hold.

"What now?" she asked.

"Can you lift one of these crates up to the gunwale on your own?"

"What's a gunwale?"

Bane sprang up the short flight of steps onto the deck, and rapped the uppermost rail on the ship's side. "The top edge of the ship," he clarified.

Clara wrapped her hands around the rough oak crate and waddled up the stairs. She lifted it to balance on the gunwale. Heavy, but manageable. She nodded to Bane.

"Good. Put it down, then, and we'll move the crates up to the portside of the ship where they can't be seen from the shore. Then we dump them all at once. Move."

Clara needed no further prodding. Navigating the stairs was easy in her boy's clothing, and she carried a steady stream of crates almost as quickly as Bane could move them. In less than ten minutes they had thirty-four crates of opium lined up along the portside of the ship, ready for pitching into the swirling waters below. Bane squatted down and lifted a crate, which he balanced on the railing of the ship. Just before tossing it overboard, he looked at Clara.

"I think this is the first purely decent thing I've done in my entire life," he said. His face wore a quizzical expression, as though it had never occurred to him that doing something positive with his life was in any way a worthwhile endeavor.

"Perhaps it will set a trend," Clara said. She prayed that it would. If Bane turned his skills toward the good, there would be no end to the things he could accomplish.

"Let's find out," Bane said as he heaved the first crate over the side of the ship. Clara winced at the splash, a crash of noise punctuating the night air. "Keep moving," Bane said. "They know to ignore any sounds they hear of cargo being dumped, but let's make this fast."

Clara wrapped her hands around another crate, wishing she had worn a pair of gloves as the rough wood cut into her hands. She had to stand on tiptoe to hoist the crate onto the ledge of the ship; then she shoved it forward with all the strength she could muster. A moment later came the satisfying sound of the splash as twenty-five pounds of opium dissolved in the salty water of the ocean.

Bane continued to heave crate after crate over the side of the ship. Clara tried to keep up, but Bane was dumping the crates at twice the rate she could manage. Just as they were nearing the end of the dumping, a terrible sound interrupted their rhythm.

A clattering of footsteps sounded behind her, and a groggy voice called out, "Zeidermann, is that you?"

Bane froze and his gaze fastened on someone behind her. "Keep your face turned to me," he whispered fiercely. Then he stood up and raised his voice. "And what are you doing here, Hansen? I told Zeidermann to clear everyone off this ship."

Fear kept Clara immobilized as she hunched over a crate. There were only two other crates remaining on the deck of the ship. Bane moved to stand before one of the crates, partially obscuring the view from whoever had just stumbled up onto the deck, but anyone with a functioning brain would be able to figure out what they were doing.

"I fell asleep in the forecastle and thought I heard something sloshing around," the blurry voice said. "What you got there, Bane?"

Bane's voice lashed out like a whip. "None of your business, Hansen. If you want to live another sixty seconds, you'll dive over the side of this ship. Otherwise, I'll shoot you where you stand."

She prayed the sailor would cooperate, but behind her came the dreaded sound of approaching footsteps. "Are you out of your mind?" the man said. "That's prime opium you are dumping. The Professor will have our heads for this."

And in an instant, Bane broke the tension. He shoved the revolver into his belt and reached down to hoist another cask. "You think I'm dumping opium? You idiot, it's the minced up pieces of what is left of that fool Richards. That's why I didn't want any witnesses." Bane tossed the crate overboard, and Clara did likewise with the crate she still clutched. One crate left.

But Hansen was on to them. He darted to the hold and tore open the door, revealing the empty cargo space. "You dumped the opium, you insane maniac!" Hansen ran for the side of the ship, cupping his hands around his mouth as he called out to shore. "Bane is dumping the opium! Get back here, you fools! Bane is dumping—"

Before he could finish the sentence Bane had rushed the sailor and flipped him overboard. Clara hoisted the final crate and tossed it over, then looked to Bane for instructions.

"*Run!*" was all he said. He tugged her arm so fiercely she thought it might be pulled from her socket as he yanked her to the gangway. She toppled down the gangway, landing on her knees on the pier, but Bane hauled her upright as they made a dash for the shore. Directly ahead of her were the four men from the shore who had heard Hansen's warning, running straight at them like a herd of enraged beasts.

Going the way they had come was suicide, and Bane dragged her down a different pier. The height of the ships tied along the docks made it difficult for their pursuers to track them as they darted through the maze of interconnecting piers, trying to find a way to reach the shore.

So fast were they dashing down the pier that Clara barely noticed that the planking abruptly stopped, creating a dead end. With another two hundred yards to the shoreline, they could proceed no farther and their pursuers were gaining quickly. Manzetti had seen what was happening and had moved the wagon into place, but reaching him was hopeless.

The only remaining pier that reached the shore was on the opposite side of the old schooner they were stranded beside. "We're going to have to climb aboard and make a leap for the opposite side," Bane said. Their pursuers were still trying to navigate the correct path through the maze of piers to reach them, but it would only be seconds before they figured it out.

Bane grabbed a rope and pulled himself upward to scramble aboard the schooner. Clara didn't know if she'd have the strength to haul herself up in a similar manner, but the sound of pounding footsteps on the planks behind her gave her the surge of energy she needed to heave herself up and swing a leg over the edge of the ship. Bane reached an arm around her waist and finished hauling her aboard. He pulled up all the ropes that dangled from the ship to the pier. "Quickly," he said the moment the last rope had been pulled up before they dashed to the other side of the ship.

The pier was at least ten feet from the side of the ship and Clara's heart plunged in defeat. "We'll never make it," she said, certain they would plunge into the bay no matter how hard they leapt away from the ship.

Bane grabbed her hand. "Trust me" was all he said. With the grace of a cat he leapt onto the lip of the gunwale and held a hand out for her to follow.

"I don't think I can do this," Clara said.

Bane didn't budge. "This time you are just going to have to trust me," Bane said. He bent at the waist and took her hand in his. Clara let him help her up on the gunwale of the ship. She could hear their pursuers trying to figure out a way to board the ship without the aid of the ropes.

"On the count of three, push off as hard as you can on your right foot," Bane said. "We'll keep our hands locked and make a flying leap for it. Either we both make it, or we both go in the drink."

And at that moment, with hardened criminals just a few feet behind her and the prospect of breaking her neck on the pier below, that odd sense of calmness settled over Clara once again. She smiled and nodded her assent toward Bane, and when he counted to three, she leapt forward with all of her strength.

Just as she was landing on the pier, her hands scraping against the rough, dry surface of the planking, the crack of gunshots rang out, and Clara looked in horror as Bane collapsed against her, a bloom of blood spreading across his shirt.

* * *

Daniel heard the smattering crack of gunshots before they had even arrived at the harbor. He leaned low over his horse's neck, urging the beast on faster. The thin moonlight made it almost impossible to see. Daniel squinted at the ghostly silhouette of ship riggings swaying in the harbor. Dozens of ships and a forest of masts lined the docks, making it impossible to tell which of these ships was *The Albatross*. They'd have to go ship to ship looking for it, just as they had done with the warehouses.

A clatter of horses' hooves and wagon wheels penetrated his senses. Daniel wheeled his horse to a stop, his eyes widening in disbelief as a wagon careened toward him.

Manzetti?

The giant of a man was standing as he cracked the whip over the two wild-eyed horses pulling the wagon. Manzetti barely spared him a glance as he passed them. All he did was point to the pier and cry out, "Clara!" Daniel's gaze swiveled out to the harbor, where he saw two figures in the dim light hurtling down the pier, one leaning heavily on the other. Before he could make sense of the pair, they stopped, and one of the men paused to toss something behind him before they turned and raced toward the shore.

The explosion lit up the sky. In that instant he could see everything perfectly, the silhouettes of the ships, the outlines of the planking, and two figures racing down the pier toward the shore, one man practically dragging the other.

Daniel spurred his horse forward to follow Manzetti, who pulled the wagon to a halt at the base of the pier. Manzetti leapt from the wagon to lower the back hatch.

Daniel gritted his teeth in frustration as he scanned the maze of ships and docking. "Where is Clara?" he demanded.

"On the pier! On the pier!" Manzetti shouted in reply.

Daniel squinted at the harbor, searching in vain for someone besides the two men running toward them. And then it happened. In the struggle to drag the man ashore, the cap fell from the smaller man's head and a tumble of golden hair fell down her shoulders.

"Clara!"

❧❧❧

The tremendous boom was so loud it hurt Clara's ears and drove both her and Bane to their knees. She caught herself on the palm of her hand, and Clara felt a shudder run along the planking of the pier. A shower of sparks fell about them like falling snowflakes and Clara feared the pier was about to collapse. When she turned to look behind her, she could see the section of the pier surrounding the schooner was completely destroyed, making it impossible for their pursuers to follow them to shore.

"Keep moving," Bane said. "I don't know how long the rest of this pier will hold."

A surge of excitement flooded through her. She and Bane had risked everything to take on the demons, and they had won. The shoreline was less than ten yards away. Clara braced her shoulder beneath Bane's arm and ran toward Manzetti, who was waving frantically at them. Her eyes widened at the sight of two men standing alongside him. It was hard to see in the dim light, but it looked like . . . could that possibly be Daniel waiting on the shore? His stance was wide and he was staring at her as if she were a ghost, and it made Clara run faster down the pier. *He had come for her!*

Before she reached the shore Daniel had snapped from his trance and bolted toward her. "Clara!"

He bounded to her and he cupped her face between both his hands. Whatever horrible anger had raged between them the night his house burned was obliterated by the pure relief of being alive. She ought to say something to reassure him, but the exuberance was still bursting inside her and she was shaking too hard to speak.

Manzetti showed up a moment later and scooped up Bane, taking him away to the back of the wagon.

At last Clara found her voice. "It's okay, Daniel, we got away . . . we got away. . . ." At least that is what she tried to say; he had wrapped his arms around her so tightly it was hard to draw a breath. Her feet left the ground as she felt herself being rocked in Daniel's strong arms.

"Oh, Clara, I love you more than life itself, and I'm getting tired of you leaving me."

Tears pricked the back of her eyes. "I love you, too, Daniel. I was afraid I would never be able to tell you that." His arms tightened around her, and she felt his ragged breathing against her neck. She wanted to stay here within the warmth and safety of his arms forever. She wanted to laugh and cry and listen to Daniel tease her. Tears spilled down her face, for even as relief washed through her, she knew she and Daniel would return to a life with all their old problems of faith and mistrust between them. But at least the Lord had given her the opportunity to try to repair that damage.

She swiped the tears from her face. "Alex is hurt and we've got to get him out of here," she said once she was able to pull out of Daniel's embrace. He gave a quick nod and strode with her to the wagon. By the time they reached the shore, Manzetti had already dumped Bane into the back of the wagon and was holding the reins of Daniel's horse, which was shifting and stamping nervously in the street. Daniel mounted the horse and then stretched a hand down toward her.

"Hop on up, Clara. You can ride behind me."

Clara paused just for an instant and cast a glance at Alex, who lay propped in the bed of the wagon. Clyde was squatting beside him, applying pressure to the wound in the boy's side. There was no room for Clara. The horse was twitchy, still spooked by the explosion. It would make the horse even madder when she tried to mount up behind Daniel, and she gazed longingly at the small seat in the front of the wagon.

"Daniel, I'm afraid of horses."

A pained burst of laughter came from the back of the wagon.

"What are you laughing about, brat?" Manzetti growled.

"Clara," Bane gasped. "After all you've been through in the past few days, you are too afraid to get on the back of a horse?"

It did seem ridiculous.

Clara's gaze flitted between Daniel and the horse. She straight-ened her shoulders. "I can do this," she said. "Help me up."

Bane tensed, struggling to remain still while the cart rocked with each bump along the cobblestone streets. Every jolt and lurch of the cart sent white-hot pain spiraling through his body. The man named Clyde, who Manzetti said was a doctor, kept a hand pressed over the bullet wound in Bane's waist. Maybe the pressure was helping, but from Bane's point of view, the hand pressing his wound was torture.

Just as bad as the pain was listening to Tremain gush over Clara. Ever since they had left the docks, there had been a steady stream of conversation coming from the pair riding on horseback beside the cart. It sounded like Tremain had it bad. He kept vowing never to let Clara ten feet out of his sight, telling her how beautiful she was, how brave, how precious.

"How long am I going to have to listen to that syrupy mush?" Bane asked Clyde.

"Tell me about it. She is my sister" was all he said.

Bane tried not to laugh. "I suppose that makes it even worse." But the doctor wasn't paying attention to him; he was taking Bane's pulse and concentrating on keeping steady pressure on the howl-ing mass of agony in his side. Bane closed his eyes, trying to blot out the blinding joy on Clara's face when she saw Daniel Tremain again. Bane had no business hankering after someone like Clara. It was not the fact that she was so much older than he that was the problem; it was simply that Clara was way too good for someone like him. That didn't stop the longing, though.

The cart hit a pothole, and Bane was embarrassed by the whimper that escaped his clenched teeth. Waves of pain rolled from his stomach, causing the beginning of a convulsion.

"Are you going to throw up?" the doctor asked.

The agony made it too difficult to reply. "Nod if you want me to roll you over," Clyde said. "I don't want you choking."

As bad as he felt, Bane didn't want the doctor to roll him over. Turning on his side would cause the pain to rip him wide open. "No," he managed to gasp. "I'm fine." He tried to concentrate on the stars overhead, anything other than dwell on the seething pain that radiated through his entire body.

Freedom had come to him tonight . . . hadn't it? No matter how grim his fate looked at this particular moment, he never had to return to that sinister mansion in the Vermont woods again. He had broken away from the Professor's iron fist and was now free to make his own way in the world. It was different than his original plan, but it was better. A smile curved his mouth, and a feeling of joy started to bloom as Bane experienced the meaning of *freedom* for the first time in his life.

"I'm going to lift my hand and check if you are still bleeding," Clyde said. Bane gasped as the doctor released the pressure from his throbbing wound. The stars tilted, grew dim, but then another rush of agony seized him as Clyde replaced his hand. "Still bleeding. Hold on there, son."

Bane tried not to smile. Did this man have any idea whom

he was talking to? Clyde's look of concern would probably turn to horror if he knew he was up to his wrists in the blood of a vicious criminal.

But that wasn't really true, was it? He was now walking a new path. He tried to remember how Clara had put it. *"You can begin building a life of valor,"* she had said. Bane fought against the wave of nausea that rolled through him. He was ready for his new life. He wanted that life of valor Clara spoke of. He wanted to slay dragons and climb mountains and do something noble with his life. The next few years would be consumed with simply trying to outwit the Professor's army of assassins, but eventually he would gain a foothold and stop running. The world Clara was showing him was too enticing to let the Professor ruin.

CHAPTER 21

Never in a million years could I be a nurse, Clara thought as she watched Clyde draw a needle through the torn flesh in Bane's torso. Her brother's face was expressionless throughout the procedure, which was easier than watching Bane's tense features as he gritted his teeth and clenched her hand with each pass of the needle.

The sun was rising by the time they had made it to Clara's Bolton Hill home. She hoped Bane would be safe here from the Professor's men for a day or two while his wound healed and he figured out where to go.

Manzetti had carried Bane into the guest bedroom right beside Clara's room, and Clyde had removed the slug from Bane's waist. Clara pulled a stool close to the mattress so she could hold Bane's hand throughout the ordeal. Clyde had offered Bane a hit of morphine to ease the pain, but Bane had refused. "I'll take it without the crutch," he had said. "I suppose I deserve whatever I have coming."

Even though Clyde assured her that Bane's wounds were not life-threatening, Clara could not abandon Bane, not when they had come so far together.

And not when Daniel paced like a caged lion right outside the door. Clyde insisted on having only one person in the room to assist him with the surgery, and Clara was glad that Daniel had been banished from the room. If Daniel had the least inkling about who Bane was, she wouldn't put it past him to tear the boy to pieces. Not four days ago Bane had ordered the fire that had destroyed Daniel's home, then had proceeded to orchestrate her kidnapping. She wanted Bane patched up and gone before Daniel's quick mind could put the pieces together.

"Hand me the scissors," Clyde said as he tied off another of the tiny row of stitches that tracked across Bane's waist. Clara pressed them into her brother's hand, then cleared away the water bowl that was tinged dark with Bane's blood. "That's the last of the stitches," he said. Clara could feel some of the tension drain from Bane when he heard the words. "I'll need Daniel in here to hold Alex up while I bind everything tightly."

She cracked open the door to ask Daniel to help. The moment the door opened, Daniel's drawn face appeared in the doorway. The frantic look she'd seen in his eyes earlier was gone, but still he snapped to her side the moment she asked for help. His face looked haggard and exhausted and she ached to take him in her arms and stroke the dark hair back from his forehead. It would have to wait until Bane was safely out of the house.

"Clyde needs your help to hold Alex up while he bandages him." She really didn't want Daniel anywhere near Bane, but it could not be helped. She cleared the stool from the bedside and stepped aside. "Be careful with him," she cautioned as Clyde and Daniel lifted Bane from the mattress. What little color was left in Bane's face drained as he was lifted upright to be bandaged, and Clara thought he might faint. Hoped he would faint, actually, so at least he would be out of pain for a short while. Clyde moved quickly and efficiently, and Bane was gently lowered back against the mattress.

She picked up the torn and bloodied shirt from where Clyde had tossed it to the floor. "I'll get you one of my father's shirts," she said. But she didn't want to leave Daniel alone with Bane. There had been no time to fill Daniel in on what had been going on over the last few days, and he was chomping at the bit for information. Under no circumstances did she want him talking to Bane unless she was there to mediate.

She opened the door and called out to Manzetti, directing him to her father's room to fetch a shirt.

"Try to get some rest," Clyde said once Bane was lying down. "It will be at least two or three days before you can be up and about. It is going to hurt like the devil for another week or two, but in a month you'll be good as new."

"Not good enough," Bane said tightly. "I'll be heading out by nightfall."

Clyde raised a brow. "Don't be a fool. I just spent thirty minutes putting in a row of stitches that are sheer poetry in their perfection. I'm not going to tolerate you ripping them out."

A smile hovered on Bane's face, and with the barest hint of movement, he shrugged his shoulders. "Have it your way," he said casually.

Clara knew he was lying. The moment no one was watching she was certain Bane would leave the house. Even now, there were probably dozens of people scouring Baltimore on a hunt for the most wanted man in the country. Clyde proceeded to outline how Bane's injury should be cared for, how the dressing should be changed and an ointment applied to the wound. As her brother talked about how the patient's movement should be limited and how much sleep he should be getting each day, her heart sank. Bane would not have the luxury of a soft bed or someone to help him change his bandages. Within a few hours he was going to be in a flight for his life.

A rap on the door was followed by Manzetti, who handed in a white cotton shirt. At least she could send the boy off with clean clothing. "Here's a shirt for Bane," Manzetti said as he handed the garment to Clara, then left the room.

Clara flinched at the rasp of indrawn breath.

"*Bane?*" Daniel said in a disbelieving voice. His entire body had gone rigid and his eyes were ablaze with anger.

Clara raced to stand between Daniel and the bed. "Actually, his name is Alex. Alexander Banebridge."

"Bane." Daniel spat out the word. Clara glanced at the bed,

where Alex calmly folded his hands across his chest, looking the epitome of serene relaxation.

"Yes, Bane," the boy said. "Clara likes to call me Alex because she thinks it is more civilized, but I prefer Bane."

Daniel shoved Clara aside and lunged toward the bed, hovering over Bane like an avenging angel. "I swear by all that is holy I'm going to rip you apart limb from limb."

Bane's smile was angelic. "Clara will never forgive you if you do."

Daniel froze. After a moment he reared upward and swiveled his gaze toward her. "Clara, do you know who this man is? That he orchestrated your entire kidnapping?"

"I know exactly who he is, and what he has done." She wondered if Daniel also knew that it was Bane who had reduced his home to a pile of ashes. She wasn't about to bring up the matter. Once again she inserted herself between Daniel and the bed. "Bane is sorry for what he's done, and I've already forgiven him. I expect you to do the same."

"Never."

"Bane has turned his life around. If the Lord can forgive him, we need to be able to do the same."

"He's a vicious, foul drug runner. He reeks of filth."

"Which is why his transformation is all the more remarkable."

Daniel's eyes were glittering with anger and he looked ready to spit nails. "Clara, do you realize that every time you open your mouth, he is smirking behind your back?"

She whirled around just in time to catch a glimpse of Bane's taunting smile before he wiped it clean. She turned back to Daniel. "Bane can be excessively annoying, I know. He's still learning how to be a decent human being and he has got a long way to go, but he has *earned* his right to have a clean start. I'm not going to let you ruin that, Daniel."

Daniel continued to glower at Bane. "He's doing it again." Clara did not even need to turn around to know that Bane was taunting Daniel with one of those smug grins.

"Stop it, Alex," she said in frustration. "How am I to broker some sort of truce between the two of you when you both act like children?" It seemed foolish to worry about protecting Bane when he was recklessly taunting Daniel. She strode to the door. "I'm leaving. Bane, you can fend for yourself."

❧

Daniel did not even let the door close before he came charging after her. Of all the reckless, dangerous situations in which Clara had placed herself over the years, this was certain to be the most foolish. Bane was the person who had Eddie Maguire quaking in his boots, and Clara was fussing over the scorpion like a mother hen? He strode after her and followed her into her bedroom.

He forced his voice to remain calm. "Let me be explicitly clear," he said. "Bane is the person who masterminded your kidnapping. He controls the entire drug trade along the East Coast. Did you know that?"

"Yes." Clara opened her wardrobe and pulled out a simple muslin dress. "I'm changing now, so you'll have to step outside."

She was still dressed in the pants, vest, and shirt she'd been wearing when she made a dash down the pier. The same pier Bane had blown up while she was standing on it.

"I'm not leaving you unprotected in this house. Not with that viper in it."

Clara hugged the dress to her chest. "Fine. Guard me from the other side of the door."

What he wanted to do was shake some sense into that lovely head of hers, but the sooner she was out of those pants, the better. He had a good suspicion about whom those clothes belonged to, and the sight of his dainty, delicate Clara wearing that snake's clothing was revolting. He stepped outside her bedroom and leaned his forehead against the closed door. This had been the longest four days of his life. His home was destroyed, someone had tried to frame him and take away his freedom, and the woman he loved more than life itself had nearly been killed. But he had Clara back. He smiled, knowing that all his other problems faded into the ether so long as he could have Clara at his side. Never in his life had he seen such splendor as when she came racing down that pier, her golden hair blowing in the wind and her eyes ablaze with excitement.

"Leave your hair down," he called through the closed door.

"That would hardly be proper." Her voice was muffled, as though she was tugging the dress over her head even as she spoke. He laid his palm against the door.

"Clara, it would send me over the moon if you would consent to being a little improper just for this afternoon. Let me see you with your hair down."

When she opened the door, his knees went weak at the sight of her. She was wearing a blue-and-white-flowered dress, her hair tumbling around her shoulders and a smile on her face as bright as the morning sun. He opened his mouth to tell her how beautiful she was to him, but it was as though he had been struck dumb.

"Let's go downstairs where we can talk," she said quietly. Her little hand slipped inside his as he walked down the staircase. The quiet elation of sharing this simple, domestic moment with her was astounding. All his riches, his renowned discoveries . . . all of it could crumble into the dust if that was what it took to simply share his life with Clara. He still needed to sort through the ugliness of what had caused her abduction and who was trying to frame him. And then he would ask Clara to marry him. If she wanted him to go to church, fine. If she wanted him to stand on his head and sing Handel's *Messiah*, he would do that, too.

"I need you to forgive Bane," she said, the moment the door was closed on the study.

Daniel closed his eyes as the weight of exhaustion sank through him to the marrow of his bones. It was hard to even keep standing, but if forgiving that holy terror was what Clara needed of him, he would find a way to do it. Daniel opened his eyes and looked at her, standing in the morning sunlight. Her expression was hopeful and her hands clasped together before her, as though in prayer. Her face looked luminous, and the delicate white skin of her arms . . . his eyes riveted to an ugly bruise on the inside of her elbow. He shot across the room and turned her wrist up to see the wound, mottled purple with a dark red spot in the middle.

Clara tugged her hand, but he kept her wrist in his hand like a manacle. "Who did this?" he rasped.

Clara did not meet his eyes when she whispered her reply. "Bane did it."

"It looks like a needle mark."

"It is."

He dropped her arm and paced the room, fighting the urge to spring up the stairs and choke the life out of the wounded man resting above. He leaned over her father's desk and curled his fingers around the edge to stop himself from bolting from the room. "What did he do? What *precisely* did he do to you?"

"It was opium," she said, and Daniel squeezed his eyes shut as waves of anger rolled through him. His sweet Clara, held down and drugged by that monstrous brat. "I'm still not exactly sure what his plan entailed," Clara continued, "but he was hired by someone to frame you and Manzetti for murdering me."

"It was Alfred Forsythe, wasn't it." It was a statement, not a question.

Clara shook her head. "I don't think so."

He stifled an angry snort. Clara was so naive in her desperate need to believe that a simple conversation could banish the enmity between him and Forsythe. She had no idea what a man would sink to if a fortune were on the line. Clara moved to stand before him. "Bane wouldn't tell me who hired him, but he said something about you needing better judgment about the people you surround yourself with."

He narrowed his eyes. There was a very small circle of people at the helm of his company, and Daniel would trust each of them with his life. "He is just trying to sow dissension between me and the people I have worked with and sweated beside for the better part of a decade. I know these people, Clara, and *I trust them*. That leaves Alfred Forsythe, who has spent his entire life cutting corners and cheating to get what he wants."

Clara shook her head. "I don't think it's Forsythe, Daniel. I really don't."

"Fine," he bit out. "Bane is not setting foot outside this house until he spills everything."

"That's fair enough." Her face softened and she placed her hand on his shoulder. "Daniel, there is more you need to hear." Her voice was so gentle, as though she were trying to comfort him, when she was the one who had been brutalized and deserved comfort. He turned to face her, removing her hand from his shoulder, and pressed a kiss into her palm. He breathed in the warm scent of her as he cradled her hand against the side of his face.

"Tell me what you need to say. I won't lose my temper."

She drew a deep breath. "Bane was the person who ordered your house to be burned down."

The breath left his body in a rush and he sat on the side of the desk. Clara kept talking, rattling on about how Bane didn't personally set the fire, but he had stopped listening. There seemed to be no end to the destruction that angelic-looking monster had introduced into both their lives, and heaven help him, he knew what Clara was going to ask of him. He knew it to the marrow of his bones, but he didn't know if he would have the strength to do it.

"He has changed, Daniel. I have forgiven him and I trust Bane."

He grabbed her wrist and turned her arm up to the light. "You would trust a man who forced drugs on you? Who burns down houses in the dead of night? What would you have me do, Clara . . . turn the other cheek? Do we offer him your father's house to burn down next?"

Clara pulled her arm away. "Don't you understand what I've been telling you? Bane has *repented*, Daniel. He was as hard and vicious as they come, but no one could do what he did last night if he were not truly prepared to walk away from that life forever." He listened as she told him of the opium Bane had destroyed, and in so doing how he had awakened a network of evil that even now was searching for him. "When a man repents his sins, God will forgive him and welcome him back. The Lord's capacity to forgive a person who is truly repentant is without limit, without qualification. We must learn to forgive Bane, as well."

Ever since she had returned from London, Clara had been badgering him about forgiveness. First Forsythe, and now Bane. He looked down into Clara's sweet, heart-shaped face, her vibrant eyes bright with excitement as she implored him to forgive his enemies. It seemed to be so easy for her, this willingness to let go of the sins that had been committed against her.

"This isn't easy for me, Clara."

She cradled his face between her hands. "I know what I'm asking of you. I know you've struggled and worked and sacrificed your entire life, which is why it is hard for you to forgive someone who cheats you out of what you have earned. But it is doing the hard things that makes a man great," she said. She stood on tiptoes so she could see him better. "Be a hero, Daniel. Be the kind of man who can weather the storms hurled at you and emerge stronger and better than before."

What kind of man did he want to be? A man so small he valued the bricks and mortar of his ruined house more than the love of this awe-inspiring woman? A man whose resilience paled in comparison to a seventeen-year-old street thug who had managed to turn his life around? He leaned down to Clara.

"If Bane is truly repentant, he is going to answer every question I have about who paid him to kidnap you."

"Agreed."

"And I swear on my father's grave, if Bane dares to implicate Ian Carr, I will know for certain he is on Alfred Forsythe's payroll. The two of them are likely thick as thieves."

Clara's eyes dimmed. "I don't think Bane has anyone left in the world." And as they left the room, Daniel knew that she was wrong.

Bane had Clara.

CHAPTER 22

D aniel stood in the corner of the room, his arms folded across his chest as he watched Clara sit at Bane's bedside, the young man's slim hand clasped between her palms. "You need to tell us the truth, Bane," she said softly. "I can't go through the rest of my life wondering when another attempt is going to be made on my life."

Bane was gazing at Clara with a dazed half smile. It bore no resemblance to the smirks and the nonchalant taunts he had seen on Bane's face earlier. If Daniel didn't know better, he'd think the boy was infatuated with Clara.

"I told you," Bane said. "Your robber-baron boyfriend needs to clean up his business affairs if he wants to keep you safe. I never would have been so careless with your safety if you'd been with me."

Daniel gritted his teeth. He would throttle the boy if he dared to make a false move toward Clara, or if he suggested that Ian Carr had betrayed him.

"A little more specificity would be a big help, Bane," Clara said.

Bane's lazy gaze traveled to Daniel. "You really ought to take a closer look at Ian Carr," he said.

"You're not even worthy to speak that man's name," Daniel ground out.

Bane shrugged. "Probably not. But Carr doesn't know much about raising a family. His son is a lazy waste of a man with a mistress he can't afford and a hankering for the finer things in life. When I talked to Jamie Carr, he was obsessed with all the riches you have cost him by refusing to sell stock in the company."

Daniel felt his eyes widen. It was true that Jamie Carr had always lacked the drive that made his father such an outstanding man of business. Ian had long despaired of his son's profligate ways, but how on earth would murdering Clara bring Jamie the fortune he craved?

"The plan was for me to kidnap both Manzetti and Clara," Bane continued. "I'd keep Manzetti drugged and out of commission for a few days. Long enough for us to bump Clara off and plant the evidence in Manzetti's house. We'd leave some incriminating evidence from Manzetti's house on Clara's body, as well as a fat wad of cash that had been withdrawn from your bank. We made a hefty withdrawal from your account last week. Forgery is one of my sadly underutilized talents, and it was laughable how easily your bank was deceived."

Clara shook her head. "How was framing Daniel for killing me going to make Jamie Carr rich? Surely all of Daniel's assets would have gone to his sisters."

Daniel felt the blood in his veins turn to ice. "If I were out of the company, Ian would have proceeded to take our company public. He would have sold our technology to Forsythe, and the company would have made a killing on the stock market. Jamie would have been as rich as any Vanderbilt or Carnegie." Instead, Jamie was going to prison, and Ian Carr was going to be destroyed seeing his only child taken from him.

"Bane, why did you burn down Daniel's house?" Clara asked. "How did that fit into the plan?"

The smirk was back. "Oh, that was my idea. I told Jamie no one would believe Daniel would take out Clara over a stupid newspaper article, and that he ought to make it look like he was mad at her over all the labor troubles she stirred up. If he believed your meddling articles caused his house to be burned down, well, that is the sort of thing that was liable to set a man off. From what I hear, he played right into my hands, shouting at you in front of dozens of witnesses the night of the fire."

Daniel's eyes drifted closed. Clara's life had been hanging by a thread, all on the whims of two adolescent boys, both acting for their own twisted means. And now that hatred and corruption was about to reach out and strangle Ian Carr, a man who had picked

Daniel up out of poverty and trusted him enough to make him a business partner.

He skewered Bane with a glare. "So what made you change your mind?"

The boy flicked a glance at Clara, and Daniel thought he saw a flush redden the boy's cheeks. "I just didn't feel like killing her, that's all."

Heaven help them all; Bane was in love with Clara.

❦

She heard the breath rush out of Daniel as he sagged against the wall. A combination of emotions warred across his face—disgust, anger, exhaustion. But mostly he simply looked bleak.

He pushed away from the wall. "I've had enough of this," he said and bolted from the room. He spoke the words in a voice so soft she could barely hear it. At first she thought Daniel was merely leaving the room, but she heard his treads on the stairway and then the slamming of the front door.

Clara bounded down the stairs and followed him outside, the glare of sunlight making her squint as she raced to catch Daniel. Her satin slippers were not meant for running, and tiny pebbles managed to work their way inside. She was limping by the time she caught up to Daniel on the cobblestone street.

He barely spared her a glance as he kept striding toward the end of the street. "You don't need to say anything, Clara. I know you want me to forgive Bane, but I don't know if that is possible. I will vomit if I have to spend one more second in his presence."

Clara reached out an arm to slow him. "Daniel, please. Tell me what I can do to make this easier for you." She didn't expect him to stop so quickly, and she nearly ran into him when he halted and turned to look at her.

"*You* offering me comfort . . . how rich," he said with a bitter twist to his mouth. "Don't you understand, Clara? I am responsible for this entire disaster. It is my fault you were kidnapped, my fault that Ian is about to lose his only son. It is all toxic poison from my private feud with Alfred Forsythe."

"Don't be ridiculous," she said. "This was *Jamie Carr's* doing. You can't accept responsibility for that."

"Fine, then. There is plenty of blame to spread around, but that doesn't change the fact that I'm at the center of this stinking heap." He faced her, and the anger drained from his face, replaced by a raw, aching agony in his eyes. The fingers of his hand were trembling as he laid them against her cheek.

"Clara, all I've ever wanted to do was make you happy, to give you a tiny shred of the joy you have shown me. Back when I was working in the steel mills, I wanted to lay the world at your feet, but I could barely afford the clothes on my back. There was nothing I wouldn't do for you, because Clara, from the moment I met you, your friendship has given me a glimpse of what paradise must be like."

She clasped his hand to the side of her face, fearing that the lump swelling in her throat was about to make her start bawling like a baby right there on the street, but Daniel hadn't finished speaking. "I've never done you much good," he said. "I got you shipped off to England when you were still just a child, and ever since you've been back I've delivered fresh rounds of misery to you. You have asked for precious little of me, and I have disappointed you at every turn."

"Not true! Daniel—" The finger he laid across her lips stifled her.

"If you had asked me to fetch you pebbles from the surface of the moon, I would not rest until I had found a way to make it happen. Instead, you've asked me to forgive Forsythe and Bane. It would be so easy to tell you that all is forgiven, but it would be a lie. To this hour I have rage festering inside me, and I want them both to suffer for what they've done."

He turned her wrist so that the bruise where Bane had driven the needle into her arm was exposed in the harsh light of day. Daniel bent his head, and the touch of his lips on her injured flesh was so gentle it was as though a butterfly had brushed against her skin. When he straightened, his face showed all the exhaustion of the last few days.

"But I *will* find a way to do as you ask," he said in a voice as soft as cashmere. He tucked a few strands of hair behind her ear before pulling her toward him to kiss her forehead. "I'm not sure how, but I'll find a way to do it. Clara, I will love you until my dying hour. I haven't done a very good job of making you happy yet, but I'm going to work harder at that."

He tilted her chin up so he could place a kiss on her lips. "I need to be on my own while I figure out how to accomplish this. Give me some time, Clara, and I promise I will find a way to do this."

Clara stood frozen on the sidewalk, watching Daniel's back as he strode down the street. With every fiber in her being she wanted to spring into a run and chase after him, offer him help or understanding, or even a shoulder to lean against.

But Daniel's instincts were right. She could not fix this for him. Seeking the Lord's peace and coming to terms with the bitter enmity that had been festering within him for decades was something only he could do.

❧

That evening, Clara was stunned to see Bane up and dressed when she brought him his dinner tray. He had obviously gone into her room, because he was wearing the boys' clothing she had discarded that morning.

"Get back into that bed," she gasped, worried that he would tear his stitches, if he had not done so already. She dumped the tray on the bedside table and scurried to prop him up and lead him back into bed.

"Take it easy with that tray," Bane said. "That looks like chicken soup you are being so careless with." Bane looked ravenous as he eyed the liquid still sloshing in the bowl.

"It is, and you're not getting any of it unless you sit down and start behaving like an invalid."

Bane sat on the edge of the mattress and picked up the bowl, wolfing down the soup before she could suggest that she wanted him *horizontal* in bed. "Sorry, no time to play invalid," he said between gulps of soup. "I want to be out of Baltimore before the sun rises tomorrow."

"So quickly?" The knowledge that in a few short hours she would never see Bane again was oddly painful. Somehow, now that she was safe at home it had been easier to minimize the danger that surrounded Bane, but he hadn't lost sight of it for a second.

"I certainly don't want anyone knowing I was ever under your roof," Bane said. "The sooner I'm out of town, the safer all of us will be. Manzetti said he would give me a ride to the railroad tracks. I'll hop a freight train out of town."

Bane went back to shoveling the soup down his throat. She drew a ragged breath when she realized this was likely to be the last hot meal Bane would enjoy for a very long time. Before she could dwell on it, her practical mind snapped into gear and she returned to the kitchen for another bowl of soup. She placed some cheese and a loaf of bread in a sack for him to take. She scanned the nearly bare pantry, wishing there was something else she could give to help ensure Bane's safety. The bread and cheese seemed so inadequate as she set the bag beside him on the bed.

"For your travels," she said. How would Bane even be able to walk, let alone hop on a passing freight train, with a fresh gunshot wound in his side?

"Thanks," he said as he polished off the remainder of the second bowl of soup. This was surely the last time she would ever see Bane, and a surge of regret filled her heart at the thought.

Bane must have caught the mournful look on her face, because he flashed her one of those reckless grins and reached up to remove one of the tiny diamond studs in his ear. Before she realized what he was doing, he pinned it through the collar of her dress. "That's to remember me by," he said. "If I survive the year, I'll send you the other one."

She did her best to smile in return. "I'll be waiting for that diamond."

CHAPTER 23

Daniel stared at the paper work before him on his immense walnut desk. Placing his signature at the bottom of that document would represent his complete and total surrender. It meant that Alfred Forsythe would be free to gorge himself on as many of Daniel's innovations as he could devour. Forsythe's company would grow fatter and richer. Daniel could feel the eyes of Lou Hammond, his lead attorney, on him, almost gloating as Daniel signed the last of the documents.

"I imagine Ian Carr will be delighted about this," Hammond said as he waved a document in the air to dry Daniel's freshly inked signature. At the mention of his partner's name, Daniel's face darkened. Ian would not be celebrating anything in the near future. In one of the most difficult conversations of his life, Daniel had told Ian of Jamie's machinations. When he finally comprehended the magnitude of what his only child had done, Ian had sobbed like a baby.

"Just file the paper work with the county attorney. I'll have my secretary draft an offer of licensure to be sent to Forsythe Industries on Monday."

Daniel was surprised at how easily the command had rolled from his tongue. He never thought he would live to see the day when his company offered their technology to Alfred Forsythe. Over the past years, each time Daniel learned that Forsythe had to replace his rails early or had his trains damaged due to the use of inferior equipment, Daniel could imagine his father reaching out from the grave to twist the knife in Forsythe's gut. That image had sustained Daniel for over a decade.

Now it was time to let his father rest in peace.

Daniel waited for his attorney to leave with the all-important documents, then pushed back from his desk and turned to watch the late afternoon sun from his office window. Clothing was strewn about the office, and a brand-new shaving case rested on a filing cabinet. He'd been living here in the three days since he had left Clara's house. Lorna was puzzled as to why he would not return to her home. His sister Katie had been there ever since the fire, and it was the logical place for him to go. *"After all, you did pay for the place,"* Lorna had told him.

How could he explain to his sisters that he needed solitude? They believed the sun rose and set on him, that he was some sort of invincible hero who could snap his fingers and all his problems would be magically solved. He would not bring his struggles before his sisters, who would try to cheer him up or dismiss the demons that were eating at him.

For what is a man profited, if he should gain the whole world, and lose his own soul?

The words came unbidden to his mind. Daniel was not much for scripture and verse, but he'd certainly heard the phrase enough in his life to know it applied directly to him. For years he had lavished wealth and attention on that house, and it had burned to the ground in less than an hour. Was the artwork and crystal worth yelling at Clara over? He had just signed papers that would bring him more wealth than he could possibly spend in a lifetime, and yet it brought him not an ounce of joy. Nothing. What he craved was to feel peace, and that could not be bought with riches or nurtured by living in a fine mansion. Neither could it be obtained by grinding Alfred Forsythe into the dust. Indulging his vengeance had brought him a sense of triumph, but never had it brought him peace. Now all he wanted was to find a way to quench the thirst in his soul.

His gaze was caught by the church on the corner of the street two blocks down. For years Daniel had been looking out this window, yet never once had he been tempted to set a foot inside. To do so would force him to confront raw, open wounds that were easier to ignore. It would have been the height of hypocrisy to sit in a church pew while his heart was roiling with vengeance. But he was surrendering his quest for revenge. He still felt polluted with the stain of bitterness, but the battle was over. He had let Forsythe win. Now that he was no longer plotting acts of aggression, would the bitterness fade and heal with time?

He had always demanded his sisters attend church. He wanted them to know the solace and grounding so many people found through abiding by the principles of Jesus. Daniel had always known his thirst for vengeance disqualified him for a godly life. He hardly needed to step inside a church to find that out.

Memories crowded to the forefront of his mind. It was hard to even remember who his mother had been before she became the hollow-eyed shadow of a woman, but once she had been a vibrant Christian who had taken joy in her family and her faith. Who had failed whom during those final years? It was his mother's horrific choice to put a rope around her neck and choke the life from her own body while her daughters were in the next room . . . and yet, Daniel could not stop believing that God had failed his mother. Wasn't the love of Jesus supposed to have saved her? Held her in the palm of His hand through the terrors of the night?

Coming to terms with these awful memories was the price Clara wanted him to pay in order to start a family with her. The outward motions of granting Forsythe access to his inventions had been done—now came the hard part.

The walls of the office were closing in on him. Impulsively Daniel grabbed his jacket and headed outside. He felt drawn to the church, as though the answer to his questions could be found inside the building.

The heavily paneled doors of the church creaked open, and Daniel slipped inside. As he sat in the back pew, a torrent of thoughts crashed through his mind. He would do or say *anything* for Clara, but how could he persuade his soul to accept something he instinctively rejected? He signed the papers that relinquished his vendetta against Forsythe, but the bitterness still smoldered. He had allowed Bane to be treated and walk out of Clara's house a free man. How much more would Clara need from him? He was sitting in the pew for several minutes before a minister walked down the center aisle toward him.

"Sir? I don't believe I know you. I'm Reverend Lewis."

"I don't attend here," Daniel said. "I was just passing by and had the impulse to step inside."

"You are more than welcome for as long as you wish. Or if I can answer any questions for you . . ."

The minister's offer dangled in the air. He clearly did not recognize Daniel, which is how Daniel wanted it. This minister was a stranger whom he need never see again, so perhaps he could speak frankly. "There is a woman I wish to marry," he began. He had never spoken of his intentions toward Clara to anyone, and the words echoed in the cavernous church. He drew a ragged breath and began again. "She is a devout woman, one who will insist on a commitment to the church before any kind of marriage would be considered."

The minister smiled knowingly. "Is there something preventing you from moving forward with your faith?"

His mother's image floated in his mind, and his hands clenched into fists. "My mother committed suicide," he said weakly. Even saying the word sounded foul, a repulsive word in this sanctuary of peace.

"I'm very sorry for that."

Daniel looked at the minister and voiced the thought he had never been able to say to another human being. "She believed in Jesus her entire life, but if I accept the Christian doctrine, it means I will have to believe my mother is burning in hell."

The minister's eyes widened, then dimmed in sorrow. "I'm sorry you have been led to believe that," he said. "I can't pretend to say I understand the grief that led your mother to reject the gift of life, but Jesus died on the cross for our sins, and that includes the sin of suicide. And nothing, not even your mother's own destructive actions, can separate her from God's eternal love. Do not let thoughts of this cause you to turn away from the gift of the Lord's light."

And as the minister spoke, sunlight broke through the clouds that had been blanketing the city all day and streamed through the stained-glass windows of the church, bathing the sanctuary in warm amber light. It could have been a freakish coincidence or the Lord sending a message—or it could be that the sunlight was a gift sent from his mother, letting him know that she was home.

Daniel gazed at the light, shades of gold and saffron blazing, and just as quickly as it appeared, it faded away into the twilight of the evening. The glimmering light had lasted no more than a few seconds, but it was enough. It had purified the memories of his mother that had always been stained with despair. He knew his mother now lived in a glow of sunlight. Relief washed through

Daniel. If the love of Jesus extended even after those awful final minutes of her life, then his mother was living within the shelter of the Lord at this very moment.

Reverend Lewis did not notice Daniel's distraction. "The signs of the Lord's love may not always be obvious," the minister said, "but throughout your life, the Lord will seed your path with many blessings. If you can learn to spot them, perhaps it will not be so difficult to sit beside your fiancée in good faith when you come into the church on Sundays."

The minister's words sparked a chord in Daniel. The Lord *had* blessed him. He had been blessed by being born into a loving family and possessing a sound mind and body. In his gritty world of steel mills and tenements, a sudden burst of inspiration had guided Daniel to Clara Endicott's doorstep, where he was given the immeasurable gift of her friendship. Throughout all the years and the ocean that had separated him from Clara, the Lord continued to nurture the bond that had woven them together. And surely, even when Clara had been temporarily besotted with a man who was not worthy of her, the Lord had sent her the warning signals which Clara had heeded.

He remembered the sight of Clara racing down the pier, hand in hand with Bane as the docking exploded behind them. Perhaps the Lord had even dropped that horrible, nasty boy into their midst as a lesson to him. If a hardened criminal like Bane had the insight and ability to make a change in his life, surely Daniel should have the fortitude to do the same.

The corner of his mouth turned up in a reluctant grin. Reverend

Lewis was sitting in the pew beside him, his face riddled with concern, and it would be horribly inappropriate to laugh. Under no circumstances should he give in to the hilarity that was welling up inside him, but the idea of Bane being a gift from God was too amusing to suppress. He knew he was grinning like an idiot and the minister likely thought he had lost his mind, but Daniel found that he just didn't care.

❧

Clara's father returned from New York with successful legislation in his pocket. Lloyd had listened with a combination of horror and pride as Clara recounted what had happened over the past week. There was no point in attempting to keep the incident quiet, as Jamie Carr's arrest was major news and she had spent an entire morning providing statements to the police.

About Bane, she had said as little as possible, and omitted the episode on *The Albatross* entirely. She had taken Bane's warning to heart about the danger she and her family would be in should the extent of her involvement with the destroyed opium ever be discovered.

"I think this would make for an interesting story," her father said as they relaxed in his study. "The downfall of Jamie Carr is a classic example of the dangers that a sense of entitlement can bring to our youth. It could prove to be a most instructive story, should you choose to write about it, Clara."

Clara sat curled up on the window seat in her father's study and looked at Lloyd in mild horror. The tragedy of what had befallen

Ian Carr was not something she would ever race into print, no matter how instructive it might be. "I couldn't do that to Daniel," she said. "He looked physically ill when he realized what this would do to his partner."

Clara nearly bit her tongue when she saw her father's sour reaction to Daniel's name, and she turned away to watch the wrens building their winter nest outside the window. It was true that Daniel had been less than gentlemanly over the last few weeks, and lately he seemed to have disappeared off the face of the earth. It had been almost five days since he had said good-bye to her on the sidewalk, and the only thing they heard from him came in the form of a single letter from his lawyer, noting that Daniel's lawsuit against them had been rescinded. Other than that, there had been nothing. That her father still harbored doubts about Daniel was obvious, but he was too cautious of treading on their fragile reconciliation to bring it up.

"This isn't about Daniel, this is about your career as a writer. Clara, you have a talent for communicating to an audience that is astounding. You must not shove this gift away."

"I'm not shoving it away. I just don't want to exploit this situation for my own gain. Daniel would not want his friend's personal tragedy splashed around in public any more than is necessary. I won't invade that family's privacy by taking advantage of my connections. I won't ever write *anything* that will exploit my connections with Daniel again. I learned my lesson the last time I tried to meddle in his business."

Her father raised one eyebrow, a single action that could always quell her into obedience when she was a child. "Clara, the true romance of your life is your *writing*, not Daniel Tremain. Your flair for communicating to the people and influencing public opinion must not be squandered."

Clara stared at her father. All her life she had sat at his feet and absorbed the words he spoke as though they were from on high. What an enormous force for good her father was, and what an odd sensation to realize that sometimes he could be wrong.

"Father, I admire you and I respect you for all the tireless work you have done, but I am not a lump of clay you can mold into one of your masterpieces. I'll write when the spirit moves me." She turned back to the wrens working a piece of ryegrass into the lining of their nest, and smiled at the simple domestic task that was a universal trait among all living creatures. "And you are wrong about the love of my life. Writing is important to me, and I don't think I'll ever give it up . . . but I met the love of my life when I was eleven years old. It might be nice to have international acclaim like Aunt Helen, or be as valiant as Clyde . . . but if I strip all the trappings away, what I truly want is to be Daniel Tremain's wife. I feel as though we have been called to be together. No other yearning in my life has been as strong or as sustained as that."

Skepticism was written across her father's face. "If this man is your destiny, then where is he?"

Good question! Clara straightened her shoulders. "Daniel has a few issues he needs to work through. His house burned down . . . issues with Ian . . ." Her voice trailed off. Daniel ought to be here beside her, and his continued absence was making her want to tear

Baltimore apart in search of him. She had already been to Lorna's house, where she had been told that Daniel had moved out last week. She had tried his office, where the employees told her he had stayed a few nights, but they'd seen precious little of him since. She was tempted to camp out in his office and wait for his return, but somehow that seemed a tad desperate. Daniel knew where she lived and was perfectly capable of finding his way to her door when he was ready.

In one hand she held the still-wriggling fish, and with the other Clara tried for the third time to extract the barbed hook from its mouth. Such a tiny little hook, but getting a grasp on the thin piece of metal as she pulled it through the rubbery fish was beyond her. She winced and turned her face away as she tugged one final time, but it was useless. She was a pathetic failure at fishing.

Clyde would be visiting for another week before returning to the Southwest, but lately he had been complaining of feeling hemmed in by town life. He had dragged her to this park for what was supposed to be a relaxing day outdoors, but Clara had forgotten that Clyde's boundless aptitude for country living was not a transferable skill.

She met Clyde's gaze in desperation. "I give up. Mercy. I'm waving a white flag."

Clyde took the fish with an exaggerated roll of his eyes. "Since the dawn of time, mankind has been snatching fish from the waters and managing to get them into the cooking pot. Our entire civilization would have ground to a miserable death through starvation were it up to you." Clara watched in amazement as Clyde removed the hook, flashed a tiny paring knife across the side and belly of the fish, and quickly filleted the trout before he had even completed his annoying little speech. "Think of that, Clara. All of mankind . . . dead, just because you're a squeamish girl."

Clara dried her hands on her skirt. "I'm a girl who knows where the nearest fish market is and how to purchase exactly what I need to put food on the table. Far more efficient than this venture into the wilderness."

Clyde eyed the park benches, the manicured pathways, and the low brick wall that rimmed the park. "*Wilderness*, is it?"

Clara had to hold back a smile. Perhaps a walled park on the outskirts of Baltimore was not such a terrible wilderness compared to the jungles and deserts that Clyde had mastered, but it was the limit of what Clara was capable of handling today.

Clara let Clyde bait her hook with a minnow before she cast it back into the stream. She had come with him today to get her mind off Daniel, whose continued absence was no longer worrying; it was infuriating. It had been a week since he had left her on that sidewalk. Reading the newspaper brought a fresh torrent of thoughts about Daniel. The stock price of Forsythe Industries had almost doubled when it was announced they would begin replacing their rails with the steel manufactured with Daniel's technology.

Not that she could share her concerns with anyone. Her father was convinced Daniel would only prove a distraction from her true calling in life, and Clyde was suspicious of any man who showed a romantic interest in her. Even though Clyde and Daniel had formed a truce during the horrific few days while she had been kidnapped, Clyde still had the irrational belief that no man was good enough for his baby sister.

Clara felt the distinctive tugging at the end of her line and sighed. "I had hoped it would be at least another ten minutes before I would have to go through this ordeal again." She pulled up the fish and watched it flop on the grass.

Clyde knelt beside her and guided her actions. "Get a good grasp on the fish," he said. "That's half your problem, which is causing . . . Well, here, why don't you let me do it."

"That's okay; I want to learn," she protested. All morning she had been trying to foist it off on Clyde, and now when she was finally ready, he took the fish from her hands.

Not that Clyde was making much progress, either. He squatted down beside her on the bank but seemed unusually distracted as he fumbled with the fish. Twice he started to remove the hook, but then hesitated and kept glancing behind her. Finally Clara turned around. It was hard to see because she was looking directly into the late afternoon sun, but it looked like a man on horseback was headed straight for them.

And the man on horseback looked like *Daniel.*

Clara stood, her heart surging in relief.

"Your father said you would be here," Daniel said as he dismounted. Clara's gaze swept across his broad shoulders and his skin flushed with health. Daniel was smiling broadly and his eyes were brimming with mirth as he glanced at the pile of fish at her feet. "Why, Clara, are you responsible for that massacre?"

She was absurdly relieved to find him among the living, but her ire quickly resurfaced and Clara tossed her rod on the ground. "Clyde slaughtered the fish," she said casually. "I've been sick with anxiety over you, but since it appears you are bright-eyed and the picture of health, I suppose I should stop worrying."

At least Daniel had the good grace to appear a bit embarrassed. He shifted on his feet and his gaze flicked to Clyde, then back to her. "I told you I needed to be on my own for a bit."

"Seven days," Clara muttered. "The entire earth was created in seven days, but I'm glad it was sufficient time for you to accomplish what you needed."

Daniel's grin broadened. "Thank you, it was!" He moved closer to her, and Clara felt a little of the strength go out of her knees. His face was radiating optimism, and that reckless smile made it so hard to resist him. "Let's go for a ride, Clara. Your brother's knife is making me nervous."

"Clyde's little paring knife has you spooked?"

"Not really, but courting the woman I love in front of her brother tends to put a damper on things. I thought we could ride over to the old Music Conservatory. You heard they are tearing it down today, right?"

She had seen the preparations for demolition all week as a work crew had lined up equipment and began stripping the old building of its valuables. A pang of nostalgia tugged at her. "Yes," she said slowly. "The thought of watching it being torn down is rather sad for me. I don't think I can bear to actually watch."

"Are you telling me you would not go to the funeral of an old friend?" Daniel asked.

"Funeral, yes," Clara said. "Execution by wrecking ball, I'd rather pass."

And yet that enigmatic gleam was back on Daniel's face. The sheer joy that was radiating behind Daniel's eyes was curious . . . and Clara realized she had not seen him so unabashedly happy since before his father had died. "Clara, I'm trying to sweep you off your feet and carry you away somewhere we can be alone for a moment. You are being terribly uncooperative."

Clyde sighed in exasperation. "Just get on the horse and go with the man. If I thought for one second his intentions were not honorable, he would not live to see another sunset." Clara looked at the growing pile of fish along the side of the stream, then at Daniel's magnetic smile.

"I suppose it beats gutting fish," she muttered as she shrugged into her jacket, "*but just barely*." Especially since leaving with Daniel meant a ride on his enormous black horse.

"Excellent." Daniel mounted his horse and Clara tamped down her anxiety as he leaned down to pull her up behind him. She wrapped her arms around Daniel's lean waist as the horse's gait picked up into a trot. Somehow she always felt safer when she was snug against Daniel. There would be time later to rake him over the coals for the seven days of sheer anxiety he had caused her, but for now she let relief trickle through her knowing that he was safe. She leaned up to whisper in his ear. "I really did miss you, Daniel."

One of his warm hands covered hers. "I missed you, too. Lately I've been plagued with the strangest urge to do something really nice for you."

She tightened her arms around him. "That must have been a shock to your system."

"Yes, and it took a little time to arrange, so pardon my tardiness."

"Tell me about it."

"Clara, where would be the fun in spoiling your surprise?"

She nudged him in the back. "I'm surprised I'm sitting with you on this horse at all."

"Patience is a virtue, Clara."

The conversation continued in such a fruitless vein for several miles. As they traveled down the thoroughfare toward Bolton Hill, the wide swaths of grassy meadow that lined the road became dotted with shops and homes. Riding double on a horse was simply not proper, and a few matrons looked askance at Clara clinging to Daniel as they trotted down the street. Clara had been through too much over the last few weeks to care about the opinions of others, and she pressed her face closer against Daniel's back.

At last they were back in Bolton Hill, and Clara could see the Music Conservatory at the end of the street. Several empty wagons were already lined up in front, probably to begin carting the rubble away as the demolition progressed.

As soon as they both dismounted, Clara stared at the old building. Beneath the steeply pitched roof she had spent the best hours of her life, and she tried to etch every line and detail of its beloved image into her memory. There was pounding coming from inside the building. No doubt they were knocking down some of the interior supports before the major wrecking would commence.

"I don't think I want to watch this," she said.

Daniel clasped her hand in his. "Let's go inside." He gave her no chance to refuse as his long legs went striding toward the building, pulling her along behind him. Before they had gone even five steps she heard crashing sounds coming from within. She winced, wondering which of the cherished old walls or beams had just been torn from its moorings.

"Daniel . . . do you think it is safe?"

"Trust me" was all he said. There was no front door—it had already been taken off its hinges and removed, making it easier to cart rubble through the opening. "I loved that old door," she said. It had been a gorgeous door, with leaded windows set inside elegantly wrought iron scrollwork. The way the sun used to flash prisms of light off those beveled windowpanes each time she entered the building made her feel like the old building was welcoming her inside.

"I know you did; that was why I had them remove it so it would not get damaged. The workers will hang a temporary door by nightfall for the duration of the renovation."

They stepped into the foyer, and Clara's gaze was amazed at the activity inside the building. It was swarming with workers, like bees inside a hive. So distracted was she at the sight of a man pulling out a section of the hand-carved staircase that it took a moment for Daniel's words to penetrate. Her gaze flew to his face.

"Renovation? Don't you mean demolition?"

Daniel turned her to face him, both his hands resting on her shoulders and the softest, gentlest look gleaming in his eyes. "I meant renovation. I've bought the place." Her mouth fell open and she couldn't even draw a breath to speak, but her heart filled with relief knowing that Daniel cared enough about those golden memories of their youth to save the building.

"But I thought the new Opera House is where most of the town's music is going to be played."

"It is. I bought this as a place to *live*," he said. "My own house burned down, you know."

"But, Daniel, you *hate* old buildings. I thought you liked everything to be new and modern."

"I do, but I know you have a fondness for this place, so I'm willing to compromise. If you are willing to live here *with me*, that is." She froze. She stood within the circle of his arms as the sound of hammers banging and workmen's voices echoed throughout the bare rooms. Daniel cupped the side of her face in his hand. "Clara, I've come a long way in the past few days. I have you to thank for hounding me about getting my life in order. I was a foul-tempered bear every time you brought it up, because it was easier to keep charging forward without stopping to re-open old wounds. I know you would not have pushed if you hadn't cared enough about us to brave it, and I thank God that you did. I've been able to accept that God has been working in my life. He did not abandon my mother, either before or after her death. And He didn't abandon me, even though I spent more than a decade congratulating myself on my brilliance, never giving proper credit where it was due."

It seemed almost too much to believe, but here was Daniel, her wise-cracking, irreverent friend speaking about God with warmth and ease. "If we were married, you would come to church with me?"

"Of course."

"But would it be more than that?" she pressed. "I wouldn't feel right about raising children together if you were merely going through the motions. They need the example of two believers."

He smiled down into her face, his eyes meeting hers, and there was no subterfuge and no hesitation. "Clara, let me be very clear. I believe that God chose us for each other before we were even out of the cradle. He made it possible for two people of starkly different backgrounds and temperaments to share a bond of such strength that no span of ocean or length of years or even meddling relatives could tear us asunder. How else could I have found my way out of that steel mill and straight onto your doorstep? That was God's doing, not ours."

Clara folded her hands around his. This moment was so perfect she could barely dare to breathe. "I've always known that." But now Daniel did, too, and the pieces of her life were falling into perfect place.

"I want to be married to you so I can kiss you whenever I want. So I can pull all those ridiculous pins from your hair and watch it spill across a pillow. I want to be married to you so I can roll over in the middle of the night and watch you sleep. I want to have children with you, so we can spoil them with as many musical instruments as we can fit into this wonderful old building." He clasped her hands between his and pressed a kiss to her trembling fingers. "How about it, Clara? Are you game?"

Longing was carved onto every plane of his beloved face. There was the barest hint of a tremble in his hands, and the way he held his breath let Clara know that he was nervous. Her brash, over-confident Daniel was harboring just the tiniest fear that she might actually turn him down.

She smiled up into his eyes. "I'm game."

Before the words were even out of her mouth, she felt herself being lifted off the floor and twirled in a circle. In the middle of the construction, surrounded by a dozen workmen and with the clattering of hammers, Daniel kissed her full on the mouth as though there were no tomorrow.

EPILOGUE

The dissonance pouring from the piano was completely void of any semblance of rhythm, accuracy, or appreciation of style. Rather, it was a brash assault against the very concept of musical integrity. Clara glanced at the watch hanging from a chain at her waist and breathed a sigh of relief, thanking the heavens that her son's hour of piano practice had come to an end.

"Time is up for today, Matthew. Let's go find something else to do."

The banging stopped. "Can't I keep playing just a little longer?" Matthew's angelic seven-year-old voice pleaded with her for more time, just as he did every day at the end of his allotted use of the piano.

"Sweetheart, it is your sister's turn to use the music room.

How can Lilly learn to play the piano if you are using it all the time?" Lilly was five years old, but if possible, she showed even less aptitude for music than her brother. After a full year of piano lessons, Lilly seemed to have regressed in her skills. Both of Clara's children had a boundless love of music and had embraced every instrument she and Daniel had placed before them, but love of music did not automatically come packaged with any identifiable trace of talent. Clara was glad Daniel had insulated their home with sound-absorbing materials so the neighbors could not hear the atrocities that emanated from their music room.

Lilly seemed to know precisely when her turn in the music room arrived and she materialized beside Clara, gazing with sheer rapture at the piano. "My turn now?"

"Yes, sweetie pie, it is your turn now." Clara could not help but smile at the delight she could see rolling through Lilly's compact little body. The child's eyes grew round with anticipation as she raced to the piano, both hands outstretched.

Matthew clung to the bench. "Do I have to get off already?"

"Yes, you do," Daniel said from behind her. "Now head outside and fetch the mail like a good lad."

Clara turned to see Daniel standing in the doorway of the music room, his tall frame filling the space. Her heart skipped a beat at the sight of her husband, still dashingly handsome with his flashing eyes and enigmatic smile. She watched as Daniel lifted Lilly onto the piano bench. "What would you like to play for us today, Lilly-pad?" he asked her. He pulled down a few sheets of simple tunes he had written for her.

Lilly ignored the sheet music. "Play my own songs," she said with relish. Lilly commenced mashing the keys, heedless of accuracy or rhythm. Daniel tried to hide his wince, but he met Clara's eyes over the glossy dark curls of his daughter. After eight years of marriage, Clara knew exactly what Daniel was thinking, and no speech was necessary to translate the bewildered look on his face. *How could such a thing have happened to us? How could we have produced these ham-fisted, tone-deaf offspring?*

She leaned down to kiss Lilly's forehead. "Daddy and I will be back in an hour to listen to your new song," she said. It was a relief to close the door on the music room as she and Daniel took refuge in the oversized study where they retreated at the end of each day.

"Maybe it will just take a little more time," he said as he took a seat behind his desk. He pinched the skin on the bridge of his nose and massaged away the tension brought on by Lilly's thrashing at the piano, but Clara could detect the laugh lines beginning to form along the side of his mouth.

"It is hopeless," she said. "When I was Lilly's age, I was playing Schubert." Not that Clara minded her children's lack of musical abilities. They were healthy and delightful children who were oblivious to the horror they were visiting on the world each time either of them picked up a musical instrument. She had learned enough from her father to know that someday her children's true talents would emerge, and when they did, she would be ready to help.

Matthew bounded into the room. "Here is the mail," he said. "Can I go upstairs and practice my guitar?" Last month Clyde had sent the boy a guitar from Mexico, but Matthew was no more skilled on strings than on keys.

She looked pointedly at the mail in his hand. "Practice your reading first. Then you can play your guitar."

Matthew looked at the first envelope. "This one is for Mister Daniel Tremain," he said as he carefully read the address line.

"And read the person it is from," Clara prompted. The return addresses were always more difficult, and Matthew finally sounded out the name of a bank where Daniel did business. Whenever the letter hailed from any place outside of Baltimore, Daniel took Matthew to the oversized globe in the corner and helped him locate the city. The next envelope was from the Patent Office in Washington, D.C., which Matthew was quite accustomed to seeing in the mail. The boy easily twirled the globe to the appropriate spot and showed Daniel how he could locate the city.

When Matthew reached the last piece of mail, he looked up at her. "This one is for you, but there is no return name on the outside."

Clara glanced at the letter. "That's odd. What is the city written in the left corner?"

Matthew struggled over the unfamiliar letters, until Daniel helped him sound it out. "London," Matthew finally said. Daniel took Matthew to the globe to show their son where London was, while Clara opened the letter with curiosity. It had been over eight years since she had lived in London, but she still corresponded with Mr. Benjamin, her former editor at *The Times*.

Inside the envelope was nothing but a newspaper article. No

letter, no personal message. It was an article printed in *The Times* about an incident involving the U.S. Marine Corps in Bombay.

Clara's brow wrinkled. The United States didn't have any sort of military presence in India, but she knew that the Marines guarded American embassies all over the world. She continued reading the story, and when she finally understood what the story was about, she gasped and her eyes grew round in astonishment.

"What was in the letter?" Daniel asked.

Clara glanced at her son, still standing beside the globe. "Matthew, go upstairs and practice your guitar." The boy needed no prodding as he raced out of the room. She waited until she heard the clatter of his footsteps tracking up the stairs and the closing of his bedroom door. Clara looked back to Daniel.

"I'm not exactly sure who sent it . . . probably Mr. Benjamin, my editor at *The Times*. He knew I was intensely interested in the story of a young girl who was sold into prostitution in India. It was a terrible incident in which the girl's mother was addicted to opium. The girl was thought lost forever, but apparently she has been rescued after all these years." Clara held up the story. "It seems that a contingent of U.S. Marines went looking for her, and she was finally discovered in Bombay. Poor child."

She passed the article to Daniel, and was about to discard the envelope when something rolled from the open flap and bounced on the floor near her feet. Clara looked down to see a tiny diamond earring winking up at her from the oriental rug.

A shiver raced down her spine.

Clara's heart pounded as she stared at that diamond, and when she was finally able to draw a breath, she grabbed the article back from Daniel's hands, reading it again with far more attention. Her gaze raced over the lines until she found the passage she was looking for. In a trembling voice, she summarized the passage for Daniel.

"It says here that the Marines were under the command of Second Lieutenant Alexander Christian. He led a team of six soldiers through the rural villages of eastern Maharashtra following rumors of a white child who had been sold into slavery. It says that Lieutenant Christian personally escorted the child to the British embassy, where she was reunited with members of her paternal family."

Her gaze flew to Daniel, who was looking at her with a quizzical expression on his face. "It is *Bane*," she said breathlessly. "Alexander Banebridge. He had warned me that half the world would be looking for him, so clearly he has changed his name." She reached down and retrieved the tiny diamond stud from where it had rolled at her feet. Its mate, which Bane had given her just hours before he had left her so many years ago, lay in her jewel box upstairs where she saw it every day. In all these years she had never heard a single word from Bane, but the sight of that diamond in her jewel box served as a daily reminder to keep him in her prayers. She had not known whether he was alive or long dead, but each night she prayed for Bane's safety.

"Well, Bane, it looks like you really can do anything." Sunlight flashed off the diamond between her fingers, and she remembered the night when she had stood at the side of a ship and watched his face as he turned his back on his old life forever.

"I suppose the fact that he isn't dead or in jail is cause for astonishment," Daniel said. His tone was dry, but Clara knew there was no rancor in Daniel's attitude toward Bane. Bane had earned Daniel's reluctant admiration long ago. "You've got that longing look on your face," Daniel said. "Like a mother hen missing one of her chicks. I'll track Bane down for you, if you have a hankering to see him again."

Clara strolled to the window, still reeling with the knowledge that Bane was alive and flourishing. "I don't think he wants to be found," she said. "The article is dated from almost two years ago. He probably wanted time to cover his tracks before sending us this letter. I suppose he could be anywhere in the world by now."

Daniel snorted. "I don't care if he is at the South Pole. If you want to see Bane, I'll find him for you."

She rolled the diamond stud between her fingers and stared at the shadows that lengthened across the lawn. "I think I'd like to see him again," she finally said. "I've always wanted to know what happened to Bane. He is like a great, unsolved mystery in my life."

Daniel reached for her hand and tugged her down onto his lap. He buried his face against the side of her neck and she squealed when she felt his teeth nip her earlobe. "If Bane is the great mystery in your life, then what am I?"

She smiled. "You are my rock, Daniel. You are the beginning and end of every dream I ever had."

And as she settled into his lap, Clara was bathed once again in the feeling that she was exactly where she belonged. A smile tugged at the corners of her mouth, and she gave thanks for the simple joys that blessed her life.

Discussion Questions

1. Daniel and Clara forge an intense bond, sparked by their shared love of music, when they are merely adolescents. Have you ever bonded with another person over a shared love of a musician, artist, or literary genre? Is there something about the adolescent years that makes it easier to forge intense friendships?

2. Do you think Reverend Endicott is a good father? Why or why not?

3. By the end of the book, Daniel has surrendered his quest for vengeance. Has there ever been a time in your life when you needed to let go of a grievance, knowing you will never receive justice? Did the decision bring you peace or is it still a struggle for you?

4. Bane tests Clara by offering her the freedom to walk away from him. It was Clara's willingness to accept Bane's challenge

that helps fuel Bane's conversion. Has there ever been anyone in your life who has helped inspire your faith?

5. Daniel and Clara's initial relationship was platonic, but it grew into something else as they grew older. What are the chances that a platonic friendship can blossom into a lasting romantic relationship? Is it possible that such relationships have *more* chance for success since they are founded upon something other than initial physical attraction?

6. Mrs. Garfield, the Professor's housekeeper, is fully aware of the criminal activities that are occurring in the Vermont mansion, but she does little to protest. What is the responsibility of a Christian when they are living in the midst of evil they have little or no chance of stopping?

7. Just as Daniel and Clara fantasized about becoming great composers, most children dream about becoming famous football players, rock stars, movie stars, etc. Very few will succeed in realizing these dazzling childhood ambitions, but does that mean their aspirations are wasted? What do we bring with us into adulthood from those childhood dreams?

8. Clara's father aggressively intervenes in her life to shape her destiny, first pushing her toward music, then separating her from Daniel. Although this had bad consequences in the novel, is it ever appropriate for a parent to intervene in their child's life when it appears the child is on the wrong path? What is the best way for a parent to influence a headstrong child?

About the Author

Elizabeth Camden received a master's in History from the University of Virginia and a master's in Library Science from Indiana University. She is a research librarian by day and scribbles away on her next novel by night. Elizabeth lives with her husband in central Florida.